D0630742

# THE PEOPLE IN THE CASTLE

## SELECTED STRANGE STORIES

Short Story Collections by Joan Aiken

*All You've Ever Wanted*
*More Than You Bargained For*
*A Necklace of Raindrops*
*A Small Pinch of Weather*
*The Windscreen Weepers*
*Smoke from Cromwell's Time*
*The Green Flash*
*A Harp of Fishbones*
*Not What You Expected*
*A Bundle of Nerves*
*The Faithless Lollybird*
*The Far Forests*
*A Touch of Chill*
*A Whisper in the Night*
*Up the Chimney Down*
*A Goose on Your Grave*
*A Foot in the Grave*
*Give Yourself a Fright*
*Shadows and Moonshine*
*A Fit of Shivers*
*The Winter Sleepwalker*
*A Creepy Company*
*A Handful of Gold*
*Moon Cake*
*Ghostly Beasts*
*The Snow Horse*
*The Serial Garden: The Complete Armitage Family Stories*
*The Monkey's Wedding*

The people in the castle
: selected strange
stories
33305236319012
5assi 05/02/16
WITHDRAWN

# THE PEOPLE IN THE CASTLE

## SELECTED STRANGE STORIES

JOAN AIKEN

Small Beer Press
Easthampton, MA

This is a work of fiction. All characters and events portrayed in this book are either fictitious or used fictitiously.

*The People in the Castle: Selected Strange Stories* copyright © 2016 by Elizabeth Delano Charlaff (joanaiken.com). All rights reserved. Page 254 is an extension of the copyright page.

Small Beer Press
150 Pleasant Street #306
Easthampton, MA 01027
smallbeerpress.com
weightlessbooks.com
info@smallbeerpress.com

Distributed to the trade by Consortium.

Library of Congress Cataloging-in-Publication Data

Names: Aiken, Joan, 1924-2004, author. | Aiken, Lizza, writer of introduction. | Link, Kelly, writer of introduction.
Title: The people in the castle : selected strange stories / Joan Aiken ; introduction by Lizza Aiken and Kelly Link.
Description: First edition. | Easthampton, MA : Small Beer Press, [2016]
Identifiers: LCCN 2015050134 (print) | LCCN 2016007991 (ebook) | ISBN 9781618731128 (hardback) | ISBN 9781618731135
Subjects: | BISAC: FICTION / Short Stories (single author). | FICTION / Fantasy / Short Stories. | FICTION / Literary. | FICTION / Fairy Tales, Folk Tales, Legends & Mythology.
Classification: LCC PR6051.I35 A6 2016 (print) | LCC PR6051.I35 (ebook) | DDC 823/.914--dc23
LC record available at http://lccn.loc.gov/2015050134

First edition 1 2 3 4 5 6 7 8 9

Set in Centaur 12 pt.
Cover art "The Castle in the Air" by Joan Aikman, 1939. © Blue Lantern Studio/Corbis.

Printed on 50# Natures Natural 30% PCR recycled paper by the Maple Press in York, PA.

# Table of Contents

# Introduction by Kelly Link

In 1924, Joan Aiken was born in a haunted house on Mermaid Street in Rye, England. Her father was the poet Conrad Aiken, perhaps most famous now for his short story "Silent Snow, Secret Snow" and her mother was Jessie MacDonald, who home-schooled Joan and filled her earliest years with *Pinocchio,* the Brontës, and the stories of Walter de la Mare, and much more. (Her stepfather Martin Armstrong was, as well, a poet; Joan Aiken's sister and brother, Jane Aiken Hodge and John Aiken, like Joan, became writers.) Aiken wrote her first novel at the age of sixteen (more about that later) and sold her first story to the BBC around the same time. In the fifties and sixties, she worked on the short story magazine *Argosy* and from 1964 on, she wrote two books a year or more, roughly one hundred in all. She wrote gothics, mysteries, children's novels, Jane Austen pastiches, and an excellent book for would-be authors, *The Way to Write for Children.* Her first book was the collection *All You've Ever Wanted and Other Stories,* followed by a second book of short stories *More Than You Bargained For*—stories from these collections were published in a kind of omnibus in the U.S., *Not What You Expected,* which was the first book by Aiken that I ever read. Her series of alternate history novels for children, a Dickensian sequence that starts with *The Wolves of Willoughby Chase,* has stayed in print, I believe, almost continuously since she began writing it, although I still remember being told by her agent, Charles Schlessiger, that when he delivered *The*

*Wolves of Willoughby Chase* to her publisher, her editor asked if Aiken would consider sending them another collection instead. (Well: the world is a different place now.) The "Wolves" sequence is bursting to the seams with exiled royalty, sinister governesses, spies, a goose boy, and plucky orphans—and, of course, the eponymous wolves. *The Telegraph* said of Aiken that "her prose style drew heavily on fairy tales and oral traditions in which plots are fast-moving and horror is matter-of-fact but never grotesque."

Many many years ago, I had a part-time job at a children's bookstore, which mostly—and happily—entailed reading the stock that we carried so we could make recommendations to adults who came in looking to buy books for their children. (Our customers were almost never children.) I reread the still ongoing "Wolves" novels and then began to track down the Aiken collections that I had checked out of the Coral Gables library to read as a child—collections whose titles still enticed: *The Far Forests, The Faithless Lollybird, A Harp of Fishbones.* When, eventually, I moved to Boston, I got a job at another bookstore, this one a secondhand shop on Newbury Street—in part so that I had a firsthand shot at hunting down out-of-print books for myself. I can still remember the moment at which, standing at the top of a platform ladder on wheels to reach the uppermost shelf to find something for a customer, I found Joan Aiken's first novel *The Kingdom and the Cave* as if it had only just appeared there (which it probably had. The Avenue Victor Hugo Bookshop's owner, Vincent McCaffrey, bought dozens of books each day).

And now, of course, it's quite possible to find almost any book that you might want online. (The world is a different place now.)

I recently spent a long weekend in Key West at a literary festival where the organizing theme was short stories. How delightful for me! There was much discussion on panels of the challenges that short stories present to their readers. The general feeling was that short stories could be difficult because their subject matter was so often grim; tragic. A novel you had time to settle into—novels wanted you to like them, it was agreed, whereas short stories were like Tuesday's child, full of woe, and required a certain kind of moral fortitude to properly digest. And yet it has always seemed to me that short stories have a kind of wild delight to them even when their subject is grim. They come at you in a rush and spin you about in an unsettling way and then go rushing off again. There is a kind of joy in the speed and compression necessary to make something very large happen in a small space. In contemporary short fiction, sometimes it's the language of the story that transmits the live-wire shock. Sometimes the structure of the story itself—the container—the way it unfolds—is the thing that startles or energizes or joyfully dislodges the reader. But: it does sometimes seem to me that for maybe the last quarter of the previous century, the subject matter of literary short fiction was somewhat sedate: marriage, affairs, the loss of love, personal tragedies, moments of self-realization. The weird and the gothic and the fanciful mostly existed in pockets of genre (science fiction, fantasy, horror, mystery, children's literature) as if literature were a series of walled gardens and not all the same forest. We had almost nothing in the vein of Joan Aiken's short stories, which practically spill over with mythological creatures and strange incident and mordant humor. And yet at the time when she began to write them, in the 1950s, when Aiken was an editor at *Argosy* as well as a featured author, there were any number of popular fiction magazines publishing writers like John Collier, O'Henry, Elizabeth Bowen, Sylvia Townsend Warner, Ray Bradbury, Roald Dahl. Magazines have smaller circulations now; there are fewer magazines with circulations quite so broad; and yet there are, once again, many established and critically acclaimed—as well as new and startlingly brilliant—writers working in the fantastic mode. The jolt that this kind of writing gives its reader is the pleasure of the unreal in the real; the joyful, collaborative effort that imagining an impossible thing requires of such a story's reader as well as its writer. It seems the right moment to introduce the stories of Joan Aiken to a new audience.

✲ ✲ ✲

The particular joys of a Joan Aiken story have always been her capacity for this kind of brisk invention; her ear for dialect; her characters and their idiosyncrasies. Among the stories collected in this omnibus, are some of the very first Joan Aiken stories that I ever fell in love with, starting with the title story "The People in the Castle," which is a variation on the classic tales of fairy wives. "The Cold Flame" is a ghost story as is, I suppose, "Humblepuppy," but one involves a volcano, a poet, and a magic-wielding, rather Freudian mother—while the other is likely to make some readers cry. In order to put together this omnibus, we went through every single one of Aiken's collections, talked over our choices with her daughter Lizza, reworked the table of contents, and then I sat down and over the course of six months, typed out every single one. I'm sorry that we couldn't include more—for example, two childhood favorites, "More Than You Bargained For" and "A Harp of Fishbones," but there was a great pleasure in reading and then rereading and then transcribing stories like "Hope" in which a harp teacher goes down the wrong alley and encounters the devil. And "A Leg Full of Rubies" may be, in its wealth of invention, the quintessential Joan Aiken short story: a man named Theseus O'Brien comes into a small town with an owl on his shoulder, and unwillingly inherits a veterinary practice, a collection of caged birds including a malignant phoenix, and a prosthetic leg full of rubies which is being used to hold up the corner of a table. Joan Aiken is the heir of writers like Saki, Guy de Maupassant and all the masters of the ghost story—M. R. James, E. F. Benson, Marjorie Bowen—I can't help but imagine that some readers will encounter these stories and come away with the desire to write stories as wild and astonishing and fertile as these.

In 2002, the International Conference on the Fantastic in the Arts invited Joan Aiken to be its guest. I went in order to hear her speak. She was so small that when it was time for her to give her lecture, she could not be seen over the podium—and so finally someone went and found a phone book and she stood on that. She talked about how her stepfather, Martin Armstrong, had been impatient in the morning at the breakfast table when the children wanted to tell their dreams. Other people's dreams are, he said, boring. And then Joan Aiken proceeded, in her lecture, to tell the audience about a city that she visited in a series of recurring dreams. She said that it was not a city that existed in the real world, but that after walking its streets for so many years in dreams, she knew it as well as she knew London or New York. In this city, she said, was everyone she had ever loved, both the living and the dead. We all listened, riveted. Did she talk about anything else? I don't remember. All I recall is her dream and the telephone book.

# The Power of Storytelling: Joan Aiken's Strange Stories

Joan Aiken once described a moment during a talk she was giving at a conference, when to illustrate a point she began to tell a story. At that moment, she said, the quality of attention in the room subtly changed. The audience, as if hypnotised, seemed to fall under her control.

> "Everyone was listening, to hear what was going to happen next."

From her own experience, whether as an addictive reader from early childhood or as a storyteller herself, learning to amuse a younger brother growing up in a remote village, by the time she was writing for a living to support her family, she had learned a great respect for the power of stories.

Like a sorcerer addressing her apprentice, in her heartfelt guide, *The Way to Write for Children,* she advises careful use of the storyteller's power:

> "From the beginning of the human race stories have been used—by priests, by bards, by medicine men—as magic instruments of healing, of teaching, as a means of helping

people come to terms with the fact that they continually have to face insoluble problems and unbearable realities."

Clearly this informed her desire to bring to her own stories as much richness, as many layers of meaning, and as much of herself, her extensive reading, and her own experience of life as she possibly could. Stories, she said, give us a sense of our own inner existence and the archetypal links that connect us to the past . . . they show us patterns that extend beyond ordinary reality.

Although she repudiated the idea that her writing contained any overt moral, nevertheless many of Joan Aiken's stories do convey a powerful sense of the fine line between good and evil. She habitually made use of the traditional conventions of folk tales and myths, in which right is rewarded and any kind of inhumanity gets its just deserts. Her particular gift, though, was to transfer these myths into richly detailed everyday settings that we would recognise, and then add a dash of magic; a doctor holds his surgery in a haunted castle, and so a ghost comes to be healed.

What Aiken brings to her stories is her own voice—and the assurance that these stories are for you. By reading them, taking part in them, not unlike the beleaguered protagonists she portrays as her heroes—struggling doctors, impatient teachers or lonely children—you too can learn to take charge of your own experience. It is possible, she seems to say, that just around the corner is an alternative version of the day to day, and by choosing to unloose your imagination and share some of her leaps into fantasy you may find—as the titles of some of her early story collections put it—*More than You Bargained For* and almost certainly *Not What You Expected* . . .

One of the most poignant, *hopeful,* and uplifting stories in this collection—and hope, Aiken believed, was the most transforming force—is "Watkyn, Comma." Here she uses the idea of a comma—in itself almost a metaphor for a short story—to express a sudden opening up of experience: "a pause, a break between two thoughts, when you take breath, reconsider . . ." and can seize the opportunity to discover something hitherto unimaginable.

In the course of one short story our expectations are confounded by the surprising ability with which Aiken generously endows her central character—to see something we would not have expected. By gently offering the possibility of previously unknown forces—our ability to develop new capacities, the will for empathy between the many creatures of our universe, our real will to learn to communicate—she leaves us feeling like the characters in the story—"brought forward."

Aiken draws us into a moment of listening—gives an example of how a story works its magic—and invites us to join in the process of creative sharing, believing, asking:

"Could I do this?"

And hearing her answer:

"Oh, never doubt it."

Aiken is perfectly capable of showing the dark side of the coin, of sharing our dangerous propensity to give in to nightmares and conjure monsters from the deep, but at her best and most powerful she allows her protagonists to summon their deepest strengths to *confront* their devils. In the story of this name, born from one of her own nightmares, even Old Nick is frustrated by a feline familiar called *Hope.*

This collection of stories, taken from her entire writing career, some of which I have known and been told since I was born, form a magical medicine chest of remedies for all kinds of human trials, and every form of unhappiness. The remedies are hope, generosity, empathy, humour, imagination, love, memory, dreams . . . Yes, sometimes she shows that it takes courage to face down the more hair-raising fantasies, and conquer our unworthy instincts, but in the end the reward is in the possibility of transformation. The Fairy Godmother is within us all.

*Lizza Aiken 2015*

# A Leg Full of Rubies

Night, now. And a young man, Theseus O'Brien, coming down the main street of Killinch with an owl seated upon his shoulder—perhaps the strangest sight that small town ever witnessed. The high moors brooded around the town, all up the wide street came the sighing of the river, and the August night was as gentle and full as a bucket of new milk.

Theseus turned into Tom Mahone's snug, where the men of the town were gathered peaceably together, breathing smoke and drinking mountain dew. Wild, he seemed, coming into the lamplit circle, with a look of the night on him, and a smell of loneliness about him, and his eyes had an inward glimmer from looking into the dark. The owl on his shoulder sat quiet as a coffee-pot.

"Well, now, God be good to ye," said Tom Mahone. "What can we do for ye at all?"

And he poured a strong drop, to warm the four bones of him.

"Is there a veterinary surgeon in this town?" Theseus inquired.

Then they saw that the owl had a hurt wing, the ruffled feathers all at odds with one another. "Is there a man in this town can mend him?" he said.

"Ah, sure Dr. Kilvaney's the man for ye," said they all. "No less than a magician with the sick beasts, he is. "And can throw a boulder farther than any man in the land." "'Tis the same one has a wooden leg stuffed full of rubies." "And keeps a phoenix in a cage." "And has all the minutes of his life numbered to the final grain of sand—ah, he's the man to aid ye."

And all the while the owl staring at them from great round eyes.

No more than a step it was to the doctor's surgery, with half Tom Mahone's customers pointing the way. The doctor, sitting late to his supper by a small black fire, heard the knock and opened the door, candle in hand.

"Hoo?" said the owl at sight of him, "who, whoo?" And who indeed may this strange man be, thought Theseus, following him down the stone passageway, with his long white hair and his burning eyes of grief?

Not a word was said between them till the owl's wing was set, and then the doctor, seeing O'Brien was weary, made him sit and drink a glass of wine.

"Sit," said he, "there's words to be spoken between us. How long has the owl belonged to you?"

"To me?" said Theseus. "He's no owl of mine. I found him up on the high moor. Can you mend him?"

"He'll be well in three days," said Kilvaney. "I see you are a man after my heart, with a love of wild creatures. Are you not a doctor, too?"

"I am," answered Theseus. "Or I was," he added sadly, "until the troubles of my patients became too great a grief for me to bear, and I took to walking the roads to rid me of it."

"Come into my surgery," said the doctor, "for I've things to show you. You're the man I've been looking for."

They passed through the kitchen, where a girl was washing the dishes. Lake-blue eyes, she had, and black hair; she was small, and fierce, and beautiful, like a falcon.

"My daughter," the doctor said absently. "Go to bed, Maggie."

"When the birds are fed, not before," she snapped.

Cage after cage of birds, Theseus saw, all down one wall of the room, finches and thrushes, starlings and blackbirds, with sleepy stirring and twittering coming from them.

In the surgery there was only one cage, but that one big enough to house a man. And inside it was such a bird as Theseus had never seen before—every feather on it pure gold, and eyes like candle-flames.

"My phoenix," the doctor said, "but don't go too near him, for he's vicious."

The phoenix sidled near the end of the cage, with his eyes full of malice and his wicked beak sideways, ready to strike. Theseus stepped away from the cage and saw, at the other end of the room, a mighty hour-glass that held in its twin globes enough sand to boil all the eggs in Leghorn. But most of the sand had run through, and only a thin stream remained, silting down so swiftly on the pyramid below that every minute Theseus expected to see the last grain whirl through and vanish.

"You are only just in time," Dr. Kilvaney said. "My hour has come. I hereby appoint you my heir and successor. To you I bequeath my birds. Feed them well, treat them kindly, and they will sing to you. But never, never let the phoenix out of his cage, for his nature is evil."

"No, no! Dr. Kilvaney!" Theseus cried. "You are in the wrong of it! You are putting a terrible thing on me! I don't want your birds, not a feather of them. I can't abide creatures in cages!"

"You must have them," said the doctor coldly. "Who else can I trust? And to you I leave also my wooden leg full of rubies—look, I will show you how it unscrews."

"No!" cried Theseus. "I don't want to see!"

He shut his eyes, but he heard a creaking, like a wooden pump-handle.

"And I will give you, too," said the doctor presently, "this hour-glass. See, my last grain of sand has run through. Now it will be your turn." Calmly he reversed the hour-glass, and started the sand once more on its silent, hurrying journey. Then he said,

"Surgery hours are on the board outside. The medicines are in the cupboard yonder. Bridget Hanlon is the midwife. My daughter feeds the birds and attends to the cooking. You can sleep tonight on the bed in there. Never let the phoenix out of its cage. You must promise that."

"I promise," said Theseus, like a dazed man.

"Now I will say good-bye to you." The doctor took out his false teeth, put them on the table, glanced round the room to see that nothing was overlooked, and then went up the stairs as if he were late for an appointment.

All night Theseus, uneasy on the surgery couch, could hear the whisper of the sand running, and the phoenix rustling, and the whet of its beak on the bars; with the first light he could see its mad eye glaring at him.

In the morning Dr. Kilvaney was dead.

It was a grand funeral. All the town gathered to pay him respect, for he had dosed and drenched and bandaged them all, and brought most of them into the world, too.

"'Tis a sad loss," said Tom Mahone, "and he with the grandest collection of cage-birds this side of Dublin city. 'Twas in a happy hour for us the young doctor turned up to take his place."

But there was no happiness in the heart of Theseus O'Brien. Like a wild thing caged himself he felt, among the rustling birds, and with the hating eye of the phoenix fixing him from its corner, and, worst of all, the steady fall of sand from the hour-glass to drive him half mad with its whispering threat.

And, to add to his troubles, no sooner were they home from the funeral than Maggie packed up her clothes in a carpet-bag and moved to the other end of the town to live with her aunt Rose, who owned the hay and feed store.

"It wouldn't be decent," said she, "to keep house for you, and you a single man." And the more Thomas pleaded, the firmer and fiercer she grew. "Besides," she said, "I wouldn't live another day among all those poor birds behind bars. I can't stand the sight nor sound of them."

"I'll let them go, Maggie! I'll let every one of them go."

But then he remembered, with a falling heart, the doctor's last command. "That is, all except the phoenix."

Maggie turned away. All down the village street he watched her small, proud back, until she crossed the bridge and was out of sight. And it seemed as if his heart went with her.

The very next day he let loose all the doctor's birds—the finches and thrushes, the starlings and blackbirds, the woodpecker and the wild heron. He thought Maggie looked at him with a kinder eye when he walked up to the hay and feed store to tell her what he had done.

The people of the town grew fond of their new doctor, but they lamented his sad and downcast look. "What ails him at all?" they asked one another, and Tom Mahone said, "He's as mournful as old Dr. Kilvaney was before him. Sure there's something insalubrious about carrying on the profession of medicine in this town."

But indeed, it was not his calling that troubled the poor young man, for here his patients were as carefree a set of citizens as he could wish. It was the ceaseless running of the sand.

Although there was a whole roomful of sand to run through the glass, he couldn't stop thinking of the day when that roomful would be dwindled to a mere basketful, and then to nothing but a bowlful. And the thought dwelt on his mind like a blight, since it is not wholesome for a man to be advised when his latter end will come, no matter what the burial service may say.

Not only the sand haunted him, but also the phoenix, with its unrelenting stare of hate. No matter what delicacies he brought it, in the way of bird-seed and kibbled corn, dry mash and the very best granite grit (for his visits to the hay and feed store were the high spots of his days), the phoenix was waiting with its razor-sharp beak ready to lay him open to the bone should he venture too near. None of the food would it more than nibble at. And a thing he began to notice, as the days went past, was that its savage brooding eye was always focused on one part of his anatomy—on his left leg. It sometimes seemed to him as if the bird had a particular stake or claim to that leg, and meant to keep watch and see that its property was maintained in good condition.

One night Theseus had need of a splint for a patient. He reached up to a high shelf, where he kept the mastoid mallets, and the crutches, and surgical chisels. He was standing on a chair to do it, and suddenly his foot slipped and he fell, bringing down with him a mighty bone-saw that came to the ground beside him with a clang and a twang, missing his left knee-cap by something less than a feather's breadth. Pale and shaken, he got up, and turning, saw the phoenix watching him as usual, but with such an intent and disappointed look, like the housewife who sees the butcher's boy approaching with the wrong joint.

A cold fit of shivering came over Theseus, and he went hurriedly out of the room.

Next day when he was returning home over the bridge, carrying a bag full of bird-mash, with dried milk and antibiotics added, and his mind full of the blue eyes and black hair of Maggie, a runaway tractor hurtled past him and crashed into the parapet, only one centimeter beyond his left foot.

And again Thomas shuddered, and walked home white and silent, with the cold thought upon him. He found the phoenix hunched on its perch, feathers up and head sunk.

"Ah, Phoenix, Phoenix," he cried to it, "why will you be persecuting me so? Do you want to destroy me entirely?" The phoenix made no reply, but stared balefully at his left leg. Then he remembered the old doctor's wooden leg full of rubies. "But I'll not wear it!" he cried to the bird, "not if it was stuffed with rubies and diamonds too!"

Just the same, in his heart he believed that the phoenix would not rest satisfied while he had the use of both his legs. He took to walking softly, like a cat, looking this way and that for all possible hazards, watching for falling tiles, and boiling saucepans, and galloping cattle; and the people of the town began to shake their heads over him.

His only happy hours were with Maggie, when he could persuade her to leave the store and come out walking with him. Far out of town they'd go, forgetting the troubles that lay at home. For Maggie had found her aunt was a small mean-minded woman who put sand in with the hens' meal and shingle among the maize, and Maggie couldn't abide such dealings.

"As soon as I've a little saved," said she, "I'll be away from this town, and off into the world."

"Maggie!" cried Theseus, and it was the first time he'd plucked up courage to do so. "Marry me, and I'll make you happier than any girl in the length and breadth of this land."

"I can't marry you," she said. "I could never, never marry a man who kept a phoenix in a cage."

"We'll give it away," he said, "give it away and forget about it." But even as he spoke he knew they could not. They kissed despairingly, up on the moors in the twilight, and turned homewards.

"I always knew that phoenix was a trouble-bringer," said Maggie, "from the day when Father bought it off a travelling tinker to add to his collection. He said at the time it was a bargain, for the tinker threw in the wooden leg and the great hour-glass as well, but ever after that day Father was a changed man."

"What did he give for it?" Theseus asked.

"His peace of mind. That was all the tinker asked, but it was a deal too much, I'm thinking, for that hateful bird with his wicked look and his vengeful ways."

When he had seen Maggie home, Theseus went to the Public Library, for he couldn't abide the thought of the doctor's house, dark and cold and silent with only the noise of the phoenix shifting on its perch. He took down the volume OWL to POL of the encyclopedia and sat studying it until closing time.

Next day he was along to see Maggie.

"Sweetheart," he said, and his eyes were alive with hope, "I believe I've found the answer. Let me have a half-hundredweight sack of layers' pellets."

"Fourteen shillings," snapped Aunt Rose, who happened to be in the shop just then. Her hair was pinned up in a skinny bun and her little green eyes were like brad-awls.

"Discount for cash payment," snapped back Theseus, and he planked down thirteen shillings and ninepence, kissed Maggie, picked up the sack, and hurried away home. Just as he got there a flying slate from the church struck him; if he'd not been wearing heavy boots it would have sliced his foot off. He ran indoors and shook his fist at the phoenix.

"There!" he yelled at it, pouring a troughful of layers' pellets. "Now get that in your gizzard, you misbegotten fowl!"

The phoenix cocked its head. Then it pecked at a pellet, neck feathers puffed in scorn, and one satiric eye fixed all the while on Theseus, who stood eagerly watching. Then it pecked another pellet, hanging by one claw from its perch. Then it came down on to the floor entirely and bowed its golden head over the trough. Theseus tiptoed out of the room. He went outside and chopped up a few sticks of kindling—not many, but just a handful of nice, dry, thin twigs. He came back indoors—the phoenix had its head down, gobbling—and laid the sticks alongside the cage, not too close, an artful width away.

Next evening, surgery done, he fairly ran up to the hay and feed store. "Come with me," he said joyfully to Maggie, "come and see what it's doing."

Maggie came, her eyes blazing with curiosity. When they reached the surgery she could hear a crackling and a cracking: the phoenix was breaking up twigs into suitable lengths, and laying them side by side. Every now and then it would try them out in a heap; it had a great bundle in the bottom of the cage but it seemed dissatisfied, and every now and then pulled it all to pieces and began again. It had eaten the whole sackful of pellets and looked plump and sleek.

"Theseus," said Maggie, looking at it, "we must let it out. No bird can build inside of a cage. It is not dignified."

"But my promise?"

"I never promised," said Maggie, and she stepped up to the cage door.

Theseus lifted a hand, opened his mouth in warning. But then he stopped. For the phoenix, when it saw what Maggie was at, inclined its head to her in gracious acknowledgment, and then took no further notice of her, but, as soon as the door was opened, began shifting its heap of sticks out into the room. If ever a bird was busy and preoccupied and in a hurry, that phoenix was the one.

"But we can't let it build in the middle of the floor," said Theseus.

"Ah, sure, what's the harm?" said Maggie. "Look, the poor fowl is running short of sticks.

As soon as Theseus had gone for more, she stepped over to the hour-glass, for her quick eye had noticed what he, in his excitement, had failed to see—the sand was nearly all run through. Quietly, Maggie reversed the glass and started the sand on its journey again, a thing she had often done for her father, unbeknownst, until the day when it was plain he would rather die than stay alive.

When Theseus came back the phoenix was sitting proudly on the top of a breast-high heap of sticks.

"We mustn't watch it now," said Maggie, "it wouldn't be courteous." And she led Theseus outside. He, however, could not resist a slant-eyed glance through the window as they passed. It yielded him a flash of gold—the phoenix had laid an egg in a kidney-basin. Moreover, plumes of smoke were beginning to flow out of the window.

"Good-bye, Phoenix," Maggie called. But the phoenix, at the heart of a golden blaze, was much too busy to reply.

"Thank heaven!" exclaimed Theseus. "Now I shall never know when the last of my sand was due to run through." Maggie smiled, but made no comment, and he asked her, "Is it right, do you think, to let the house burn down?"

"What harm?" said Maggie again. "It belongs to us, doesn't it?"

"What will the people of the town do, if I'm not here to doctor them?"

"Go to Dr. Conlan of Drumanough."

"And what about your father's leg full of rubies?" he said, looking at the phoenix's roaring pyre.

"We'd never get it out now," said she. "Let it go on holding up the kitchen table till they both burn. We've better things to think of."

And hand in hand the happy pair of them ran out of the town, up the road to the high moors and the world, leaving behind a pocketful of rubies to glitter in the ashes, and a golden egg for anyone who was fool enough to pick it up.

# A Portable Elephant

"You want to go into the forest? Gotta have a passport for that," said the man who sat with a machine pistol beside the thick tangle of rusted barbed wire that blocked the path into the trees.

"A passport to go into the forest? But where can I get a passport?"

Miles Pots gazed miserably at the armed guard. Miles was thin and droopy, he looked as if the east wind had always blown on him. His no-colour hair was ruffled up in a crest, his face was pale, he wore big black-rimmed glasses, and his likeness to a bird was increased by his habit of standing on one leg when in doubt or dismay, which he often was. Once he had been a schoolteacher, till things got too much for him.

"Passport office thirty miles along the boundary road, big black and white sign, can't miss it," said the bored guard.

Miles got back on his motor scooter and chugged through the endless shanty village that bordered the edge of the forest: little flimsy houses made of paper and string, egg boxes, soap crates, bleach bottles—anything that could be stuck together to keep out the weather. Dusty ground between them was strewn with rubbish and spoiled words: *like, I mean to say, sort of, gigantic, pleasure, supersonic, bargain, cheap, aggro, peace-loving*—words of this kind, crumpled, faded, chewed and discarded, lay scattered all over the place. At first Miles had tried to dodge them with his front wheel—but by now he had realized there was no help for it, trying to dodge them was too dangerous. There were plenty of people about, men, women, even children, mooching around among the dismal shacks, looking as bored as the guard with the machine pistol; Miles had his work cut out to avoid them, never mind the words that littered the ground.

On he rode, always aware of the forest on his right hand, hardly more than a hundred paces beyond the miserable row of houses, but out of bounds, separated from them by that uncrossable barricade of rusty barbed wire. Some people said the wire was electrified, but Miles could see no use for that; the most agile worm would never be able to wriggle through before he was spotted by the forest guards who sat with their guns on high lookout towers fifteen metres apart all the way along.

Behind them the forest towered like a green and gold wall. The trees were *huge,* higher than twelve-story buildings. Their shape could hardly be seen for the curtain of creepers and vines that hung over them, making the side of the forest really like a wall covered with tapestry, thick, bright, and complicated. Birds flew in and out; nobody stopped the birds going into the forest when they chose. Up at the top, single branches could be seen, moving gracefully in the wind; down at the bottom, small gaps were visible here and there. Near the ground, of course, the leaves and stems were soiled with dust like the scattered words; soiled, dry, and greasy with exhaust fumes—but oh, those branches up in the sky, how beautiful and green they showed against the sky!

Sometimes Miles, stopping for a warm brackish drink from his water-bottle, could look through a gap into the wood itself, which was all piled, lined, and crammed with crowded lavish greenery, growing sideways in layers, growing downwards, growing every possible way, growth packed thick like feathers in a cushion. So much there, so little here! Beyond the close undergrowth near the edge, Miles caught glimpses of wonderful trees, unbelievable trees, amazing foliage, red or gold or tawny, violet or peacock blue; he had never imagined such trees, not even in dreams. They said that once you were in the forest you never wished to come back; but of course you had to swear a solemn promise at the entry-point, and leave your passport or a cash deposit; otherwise they wouldn't let you in.

At last Miles came to the passport office, a tin shack with a big faded sign. To his dismay he saw outside it a hundred-metre-long line of people, patiently waiting. Miles braked and dismounted from his scooter; he shackled it to a lamp post with a piece of iron chain, and added himself to the end of the line, which shuffled along at the speed of one metre every half hour.

"At this rate it will take all day!" Miles lamented to the woman in front of him.

"Twenty-four hours is the average wait, they say," she told him flatly.

"Twenty-four hours!"

Now he understood why skinny tattered boys and weather-beaten shifty-looking men lounged along beside the queue, selling pale soggy pies and bags of leathery crisps. Some of the boys offered to "take your place while you get a bit of kip, mate."

"You planning to go into the forest?" Miles asked the woman in front.

"Of course. Why else would I be here? I've got a better chance than most," she said. "Got a certificate from my Parish Council. We want a garland of words for the Mayor when he retires. That should be enough to get me a passport. The people they come down on are those who want just one or two words, something they've forgotten, or to fill a hole. They get turned back at the rate of one every two minutes." She cast a sharp glance at Miles and said, "What are *you* after?"

"I'm freelance," he said. "Got a commission for a carpet of words to welcome a Nobel prizewinner."

"Oh, you'll be all right then," the woman said sourly. "You oughtn't to have any trouble. Lucky to get something like that, weren't you? Been freelancing long?"

"Not long," he said, wishing she'd mind her own business; people were staring and it made him feel conspicuous.

"What were you before?"

"I used to be a schoolmaster."

"Fond of kiddies?" she said suspiciously.

"No, I can't stand them!" he would have liked to shout, remembering how the little monsters used to plague and tease him, pretending to be deaf, pretending to stammer, dropping plastic bags of water on him, shooting chocolate beans at him through test-tubes, writing rude messages on the board, till he couldn't stand it a day longer. *Stop Selim,* they used to shout at him, *Old Backward Selim,* he had never discovered why. There was one girl who had been the worst of all—H. P. Sauce, the others called her—the very worst of his tormentors, a fat, pink, pop-eyed mocking girl with a big mop of black hair . . .

Luckily the line shuffled forward at that moment, and the woman turned and shoved vigorously at a man who was trying to slide in ahead of her. "Got to watch it," she hissed over her shoulder at Miles. "They pinch your place as soon as look at you." After a moment she added, "I suppose you got your companion?"—at least the words sounded like that; but Miles had pulled a paperback Shakespeare out of his pocket and pretended to be absorbed in it so as not to have to answer.

By nightfall he was nearly at the head of the queue. But just as it reached his turn the tin shutter was slammed down over the counter and a sign put up: "Closed till 8 a.m."

"Shame, really," said the man behind Miles. "You'd think they could manage a twenty-four hour shift, wouldn't you? All right for *us* to sleep on our feet in the street, but not for them, oh no."

By eight next morning Miles was aching, weary, hollow with hunger, and stiff in all his joints.

Sleepily he answered the sharp official questions. Age, twenty-three; profession, freelance writer, previously schoolteacher. Official commission? He showed his certificate, granting him leave to go into the Forest of Words for a period of not longer than four weeks in order to construct a carpet of words to lay under the feet of Herr Professor Doktor —— at the city of —— on such-and-such a date.

"Yes, well, this seems to be all right," said the officer at the desk, and issued Miles with a stiff little blood-brown folded ticket, not much bigger than an ice-cream wafer, watermarked and ink-stamped with his name and the date. "Got your companion, I suppose?"

"Companion, what companion?"

That was the word the woman had used; Miles began to feel uneasy.

"Can't enter the forest without an animal; have to produce it at the barrier. Otherwise they take your passport away again."

"Any animal?"

"Got to be portable, ennit? One you can carry. No use showing up with a two-ton grizzly, or a twenty-metre boa, would there be?" snapped the officer. "Where have you been all this time not to know that? *Next!*"

Miles found himself shoved aside. He stared doubtfully at his tiny brown passport, then slid it with care inside his breast pocket. It was riskily small, dangerously easy to lose, by theft or accident. Indeed the pie-boys were also offering magnetic theft-proof passport cases at expensive prices.

Miles asked one of the boys where he could acquire an animal.

"Animal? You kidding? Why, people travel hundreds of miles to get hold of animals. None round here, I can tell you that. Even the rats have been snapped up."

Now Miles noticed that in the other lines of people queueing patiently at the forest entrances, each and every traveller was lugging a pet-basket or birdcage, or had some creature on a lead—dog, cat, ferret, rabbit, tortoise. Some carried moth-eaten parrots or scrawny cockatoos on wrist or shoulder. Others had invisible wriggling passengers buttoned inside their jackets.

"Why do you need an animal to get into the forest?" Miles asked another boy, who simply shrugged.

"Don't ask me, mate. I ain't the gu'ment. I don't make the rules."

"Aren't there any pet shops?"

"Used to be one at Foil Town, fifteen miles along the border. You could try there."

Dejectedly, Miles unshackled his scooter and set off again. All along the way, he asked people about animals. He heard the going price for a cat was £500; for a dog, £1,000; mice were even more expensive because they could be carried in pockets; poisonous snakes were a bit cheaper than harmless ones, but in either case there weren't any; frogs and toads were unobtainable; scorpions, black widow spiders, and gila monsters fetched three or four hundred pounds apiece.

"Scorpions?"

"Anything that weighs over thirty grammes counts as an animal. Butterflies are a no go."

"Are there any scorpions?" asked Miles, bracing himself. But his informant, a man who sold him a leathery liver-sausage sandwich, said, "Nah. Ent seen a scorpion in two years."

Penalties were severe for stealing animals: a prison sentence and deprivation of your passport for life. But still thefts were common.

The pet shop, when Miles reached it, was another disappointment: a tin chalet, like the passport office. It contained some bowls of goldfish, some cocoons, and a minute scorpion. Miles had already learned that fish would not do; they did not qualify their owners for admission into the forest.

"Is this all you have?" he asked despairingly.

"Sorry, chum; I was just going to shut up shop, as a matter o' fact."

"You can't tell me of any animals *anywhere*?"

"I did hear something about an ad for a portable elephant, down Plastic Hamlet way; you could go and ask there. Or you could send for it, mail order; I've got the address written down somewhere."

"I'm not ordering a mail-order elephant! Anyway, I don't see how an elephant could be portable."

"Must be a midget breed, I reckon," said the shop owner. "Or a baby."

"Where is Plastic Hamlet?"

"Carry on west; you can't miss. There's a big plastic tower. Made o' lemonade bottles."

Miles carried on, and came to Plastic Hamlet, which looked like all the other places he had passed through, apart from the lemonade-bottle tower. At the foot of the tower, on a rough open patch of ground, strewn with chocolate wrappers and trodden words, he found a notice-board on a post, and among the weather-tattered cards: "Scooter for sale, going cheap", "Wanted, cat, any price paid", "Machete and poison darts, offers?", he found one that read "Portable elephant, £1,000", with an address in Leaf Lane.

Miles had already observed the street sign for Leaf Lane, a squalid alley leading towards the forest. He turned back and soon found it again. Number Ten was a small shanty built from compressed cereal packets tied in bundles; surely this hovel could not house an elephant? But behind it there was a bigger shed, a kind of aircraft hangar; perhaps the elephant was in there.

"Mr. Moor?" Miles said to the wizened little man who answered his knock. "My name is Miles Pots. I've come about your advertisement for an elephant."

"Noel? You want Noel?"

"Is Noel the name of the elephant?"

"Sure it is, didn't think he was a camel, did you? Noel's a good boy, good elephant. He won't play you no tricks. Loving nature, Noel has. You got a thousand nicker?"

"I have a credit card from my District Council, expenses up to a thousand."

Miles showed his card, wrote a draft, Mr. Moor checked and rechecked until at last he was satisfied.

"Right, now, I daresay you want to get acquainted. Noel's quarters are back there."

He led Miles round the side of his flimsy dwelling, lifted a bar out of two staples, and pulled aside a large door made from bashed-out bus panels.

Inside the big curved corrugated structure it was pitch dark. A strong smell came out to meet them—a sweetish, fusty, musty dusty smell, like no other that Miles had ever smelt.

"There he is, the boy," said Mr. Moor fondly. "Noel enjoys company, that he does. Hear 'im croon? Haven't a banana in your pocket, I don't suppose?"

Miles had not.

"I think I've a gum drop somewhere," he said, rummaging.

Meanwhile his eyes had become used to the gloom and he began to see—with disbelieving horror—a very large shape towering over him.

"*Portable?* You said—the advertisement said—a *portable* elephant?" he exclaimed in outrage. "*That's* not portable—it's just the regular size of elephant!"

"The ad never said portable by who, did it?" replied Moor reasonably. "Anyone could port old Noel, if they had a crane, or a big enough boat, or a decent-sized truck, or a jumbo jet. O' course he's portable. It's all a matter of relativity, ennit?"

"I can't carry *that* into the forest! I want my money back."

"No. No. No," said Mr. Moor, very shortly, sharply, and crisply. "Signed and sealed is signed and sealed. You bought 'im in good faith, he's yours. I don't like, and won't have, argumentation and disagreeables. Tell you what, though, I'll throw in his fodder, what's left, and you can have this place, into the bargain; I'm planning to move to Paper Village, they say there's Quality Homes there. So you can stop here with Noel. Maybe if you bathed him in hot water, he'd shrink. He wants feeding twice a day; just fill that rack. And give him plenty to drink, he's a thirsty beggar, aren't you, Noel boy?"

After which Mr. Moor clapped Miles on the back and Noel on the trunk, hopped on a moped which he wheeled from the shadows of the elephant shed, and disappeared down the dusty lane at a surprising turn of speed for one so bent and wizened.

Miles Pots was left alone with his new belonging.

However Mr. Moor appeared again, having gone round the block, and shouted, "You could try feeding 'im on gin. They say that's reducing." Then he left for good.

Noel the elephant was battleship-grey in colour, dusty and hairy; his big ears hung down like shapeless curtains, his little eyes twinkled and short tusks, which turned out at quarter-angles, like a ballerina's feet, gave him a carefree expression.

"Where can I get hot water in this wildnerness?" Miles peevishly shouted after Mr. Moor, who was long out of earshot.

"You can buy water at the pump on the corner of Polythene Place and Melanine Mews," suggested a girl who had ridden past on a bicycle during Miles's conversation with Mr. Moor and, evidently becoming interested, had dismounted and stood listening.

"But how in the world shall I heat it up?" objected Miles helplessly.

"Light a fire, of course."

"What with? I can't go into the forest for sticks." He wished the wretched girl would go on her way, instead of hanging about making useless suggestions.

"There's plenty of rubbish," pointed out the girl rather impatiently, and kicked a few crumbled words from under the wheels of her bike.

"Burn *those?*"

"Why not? They're no use to anyone, nor ever will be."

To Miles, burning words seemed like burning pearls and rubies. He stared at the girl with dislike. She was thin, with an unkempt tangle of black hair down her back, her dress was faded, and her stockings were in holes. Miles had a faint idea that he had seen her somewhere before.

Having no better idea of his own, he at last followed her suggestion. He bought a pail of water for a penny from a pump outside the rest center, a cardboard shack where bandages and insect-bite powder were also to be had. Then he raked up a heap of words, *sparkling, tops, pits, fantastic, best, worst, magic, mystery, holocaust, whizz kid, unbeatable value,* and set fire to them. They burned briskly, he was able to heat the water, and to shampoo Noel, scrubbing him with handfuls of more scrumpled words. The bicycle girl gave Miles a hand; she said she didn't mind, it helped pass the time while she waited for her baby lizard to grow another few grammes.

Noel absolutely adored his hot bath. Even Miles was affected by his rapture. And so the bath became a daily event. As the steaming pail was borne towards him, Noel would stand trumpeting with ecstasy; he sounded like a fanfare for tubas, trombones, bombardons, and fugelhorns. When the pail was set down he would delicately suck a little hot water up his trunk, then squirt it over himself, while Miles and the thin girl (her name was Hannah Palindrome) rubbed and massaged him with handfuls of tender fresh gripping classic and flattering words. Then Noel would kneel on all fours while the whole pailful was sloshed over him, running down his ears, tail, and toenails.

Very soon, Noel was the cleanest elephant to be seen along the whole of the border. He shone bright as a grey polished pebble from the beach, he smelt clean and wholesome, like a ripe tomato. He was plainly as healthy and happy as an elephant can be.

The ceremony of his daily bath became a popular spectacle among the bored people waiting for forest permits. Hannah, the bicycle girl, had the idea of charging twopence for admission to watch the bathing; she persuaded Miles to build a ring of benches in tiers so that the spectators were able to sit, and the ones who had not paid twopence were unable to see; the seats were made of crumpled Cola cans, stamped down and stuck together with chewing gum. They were not comfortable, but they were firm enough. With the gate money, Miles was able to buy more fodder when the pile in Mr. Moor's shed had run out.

All this was very fine; there was only one snag. Noel did not shrink from the washing. In fact he grew; the daily baths gave him a grand appetite. People brought him all kinds of delicacies, doughnuts and candy floss and crisps, but Miles was very particular about his diet and forbade most of these.

Meanwhile Miles's catarrh and hayfever, from which he suffered every summer, became acute, because of all the dust in the shanty town; he sneezed eleven times a minute, he could not breathe, his nose grew red as a radish from the constant blowing.

"Mint tea is good for hayfever, poor old Selim," said Hannah, and she kindly picked large bundles of mint, which grew wild among the rubbish, and dried it and chopped it and made mint tea. This helped a little. Noel became very addicted to mint tea too, and always sucked up a cupful when Miles had his.

Not a bad life, Hannah used to think peacefully, sitting on a stool made from compressed ice-cream cartons, and sipping her own mint tea. She had developed a hobby, she wove belts and neckties out of words picked up off the ground, *know what I mean, ever such a nice person, fun for the whole family, labour-saving devices.* She also, sometimes, made jewelry out of smaller words, polished—*level, noon, civic, peep.* Or she would make a pendant out of a few words strung together into a sentence: *Stiff, O Dairyman, in a myriad of fits. Was it a cat I saw?*

Miles could not see the point of these activities. Still, he had to admit that she meant well and her mint tea was drinkable.

"But it's no good, you know," she remarked. "Old Leon's not shrinking." For some reason, she always referred to Noel by his pet name. Miles could never understand why.

"I'm the one who's shrinking," he muttered, wiping the sweat from his forehead. Indeed he was thin as a hoe from hard work and scanty meals. "Maybe I'll give up and turn the job in."

Hannah gave him an impatient glance, but sighed and swallowed whatever she had been about to say. Instead she asked with seeming irrelevance, "How far does the forest go each way?"

"Didn't you know?" He stared at her in disapproval. "Why, it goes all the way round. Don't you know that? Where in the world did you go to school?"

"Why—" She gaped at him. "*You* taught me, of course. At Concrete College. Didn't you recognize me? *I* knew, right away. We used to call you Selim. And I used to blow cake crumbs at you through a pipette."

Studying her carefully, a thing he had never troubled to do before, Miles began to recognize her. Saucy, she had been called in those days, because her initials were H. P., and she had been quite the worst of all his persecutors, a fat pop-eyed mocking girl; despite being one of the dumbest of his students, didn't know a dipthong from a doughnut, she always had a sharp answer ready when he bawled at her, something that would make the rest of the class fall about laughing. He had really detested her, she had been one of the reasons why he gave up teaching. Now he saw that she looked much the same, really, only she wasn't fat now, and her eyes didn't pop out, though they were still big and grey, like glass marbles, and she wore a sadder, more thoughtful expression.

"Funny you not recognizing me," she said. "I always thought you knew me. More tea?"

"If there is a cup," said Miles. "I thought you were a horrible girl."

"Now *I* thought you were rather a duck," said Hannah. "That's what made it fun to see you get all hot and bothered."

He had been like an owl, she thought fondly—a moulting, downy owl, blinking in unkind daylight.

"Er—I never asked—why do you want to go into the forest?" he inquired.

"Oh well. I always thought I'd like to make a kind of thing out of words. You know? Like a sort of—well—like a kind of sculpture."

For a moment Miles had a flash of what she meant—a big, shapely, intricate structure, that would shine and glow and sparkle, and give out dark as well.

Rather sourly he remarked, "I'd be *very* surprised if they let you in for *that* reason," blowing his swollen tender nose for the hundredth time that hour. And missed the glance of sympathy she gave him.

Next day her lizard, which had been getting a highly nourishing diet of all the crisps, nougat, and Danish pastries thought unsuitable for Noel, was found to have grown the necessary ten grammes.

"I suppose you'll be on your way now," grunted Miles, shoveling Noel's mash into the rack. And he added flatly, "Congratulations," as if his feet hurt him.

"Well," said Hannah, "I've been thinking: how would it be if I swopped my lizard for Noel? You're in a hurry. I don't mind waiting. You could take the lizard and go into the forest."

Miles was utterly astounded. For a moment he thought he must have misheard her. No one in his whole life had ever done such a thing for him.

"You really mean that? You'd give me your lizard in exchange for Noel?" He stared at her with open mouth. "Well—that's—um—I take that very kindly. It's—it's very—acceptable. And it makes sense; you know how to look after Noel, he's taken quite a fancy to you. But," Miles added with a twinge of guilt, "are you sure?"

"Oh yes. Yes, I'm sure," she said quietly.

Miles did not wait another second, or look at her again, in case she changed her mind. He threw a leg over his bike, tucked the lizard in his pocket, and sped off along the dusty road to the nearest forest entrance.

Noel and Hannah, though, stood gazing after Miles as long as he was in sight. And Noel threw up his trunk and let out a long, piercing, echoing wail of grief.

"Pipe down, Leon my duck," said Hannah. "We've just got to make the best of things."

But she, too, sighed deeply as she went off to buy a pennyworth of water.

When he reached the passport point, Miles found himself behind a woman dressed in black from head to foot. She wept all the way along in queue, sobbing and snuffling. Miles wished that she would stop. It was an unsettling noise.

When the woman showed a tortoise to the guard, he said,

"Here, who are you trying to fool? That tortoise has been dead for days," and he threw it away disgustedly. Nor would he allow her through, no matter how she cried and beseeched him. "It was for a wreath of words for my baby's tombstone—she died last week—she was only seven months—"

"Can't help that, missis. Got to have a live animal, between thirty grammes and twenty kilos. That's the law."

As the woman turned to go, Miles saw her face.

"Here," he mumbled, "you'd better have this lizard. I daresay I'll be able to get hold of another. Take it. Go on, take it."

The woman gulped a few inaudible words, took the lizard, showed it to the bored guard, who shrugged and stamped her pass; then she hurried off into the forest, which received her like a dark green book opening and closing.

Miles shambled away from the checkpoint. His mind felt a bit numb. He hardly knew what to do with himself. The only thing of which he was certain was that he could not go back and tell Hannah that he had given away her lizard to a stranger. And yet that was the only thing he wanted to do. He longed for the cup of mint tea he knew she would have made him, and for Noel's welcoming bellows of joy.

A river ran into the forest not far away. Miles went and sat on its bank, by the wire barricade that bridged it.

"Can't use the fish from there!" called the guard from the checkpoint. "Fish ain't legal tender."

Miles did not trouble to reply. He squatted, peering into the thick grey-green muddy water, as if he hoped to see his own reflection there.

Several weeks passed by.

Noel missed Miles dreadfully. He moaned, he keened and droned. He pined and lost weight. His ears drooped. He seemed to find less enjoyment from his bath. Hannah began to worry about him. She, too, missed Miles, but at least she was able to cheer herself by imagining him in the forest. And she had developed a new hobby: she picked up trampled words, straightening them or rinsing them in Noel's bath water, and stitched them together. *Attractive, best deal, sought after, monster, hopefuly, impractical* . . . her idea was to make a big quilted patchwork blanket for Noel, now that winter was on the way; gale-force winds blew, Noel shivered at night and whimpered in his sleep, drifts of words blew about and piled in corners. "That elephant's not in good shape," said a boundary inspector who passed by in a truck. "I may have to send the Prevention Officer to have him painlessly put to sleep. We can't have elephant sickness along the border."

Then Hannah had a better idea. But she knew that she would have to act speedily. She spun words into a line, made a net from it, and packed up Noel's fodder. Taking a sandwich and flask of mint tea for herself, she climbed on to Noel's back and rode to the edge of the forest. Here, as she had hoped, she was able to pick up branches blown down in gales, just a few of them sufficiently long and straight and sappy for her purpose. When she had found five or six of these, with the suspicious frontier guards training their guns on her, she retreated out of danger. Then, while Noel watched, she made a kite, splicing her word-patchwork across the frame she had constructed, and fastening it tight. The kite, when completed, was big and handsome, like a great multicoloured star.

"*Looks* all right, Leon my boy," she said to the watching elephant. "But the thing is, will it fly?"

At first it would not; until she had made a tail from a series of words linked together, *new appeal fashion trendy custom-made love tender true.* Then it shot up into the sky like a live thing, wheeling about in the last light of the sun, which was sinking into a nest of storm clouds, while the wind sang and thrummed past the long line of linked sentences. Noel, with cocked head and outspread ears, threw up his trunk joyfully and followed the flight of the word-bird as it swooped and danced overhead.

"The next thing is, Leon," said Hannah, "will it carry us? That's what we shan't know till we try. And we can't try till after dark, or those fellows on their lookout will fill us so full of bullets that we shall look like Eccles cakes."

While twilight fell, she played her kite in the black and green curdled sky, as a fisherman plays a fish, letting it out as far as the line would take it, then reeling in again till the kite bucked and shied and flounced just above their heads. The wind blew stronger and stronger, towards the forest; they could, even from where they were, hear the trees groan and shriek and thrash their branches.

"There'll be some shelter down below, I expect, Leon my duck," said Hannah. "And somewhere under those trees we'll meet Selim again. You'll be glad to see him, eh?"

Noel crooned with pleasure at the name.

"You missed your bath today, boy," Hannah said. "Better have a splash in the river before we take off."

So while she ate her sandwich, Noel rinsed himself enjoyably in the water which looked dark as tar in the fading light. All the time the night grew darker and the wind blew harder; then Hannah hooked the kite line on to a strap made from word-webbing which she had buckled round Noel's midriff. She passed the line under a similar belt around herself, and waited for a really strong gust. When that came, she pulled in hard on the line, and felt the force of the wind lift both Noel and herself clean off the ground. Noel hooted with alarm and startled delight as he found himself suddenly swaying three metres above ground level at the rope's end.

"Just keep calm, Leon my lad," said Hannah, clutching a fold of his ear with one hand while she paid out line with the other. "The way this wind is setting, it will lift us nicely over the wire."

They were following the course of the river. Below them, they could see its dim gleam as they skimmed along, three or four metres above the surface.

"Just a little higher, to lift us over the wire," muttered Hannah, hauling in on the line. Up above them in the sky, which was now almost totally dark, the kite could be seen giving out a faint glow, like a luminous light-switch, as it raced ahead of them.

Then suddenly Noel let out a strange cry—like that of a dog who sees his master being carried past him on a train.

"What is it, Leon, old love?" said Hannah. "Don't be nervous. The ride won't last much longer."

But Noel was pointing with his trunk at a huddled figure on the river bank who sat and gazed into the soupy depths—Noel was pointing and crying and tooting all at the same time with the same trunk.

"Good gracious, that's never *Selim*?" gasped Hannah. "Selim! Selim! Is that you? What the blazes are you doing there? Why aren't you in the forest?"

And then, as they swept over him, she called, "Here, quick! Grab this!" and dropped the end of the kite line.

By pure good luck, Miles caught it, and, by pure good luck, the only athletic sport he had ever fancied was rope-climbing. Hand over hand he hauled himself up the dangling line, so that when they passed the barbed wire barricade, he was just a hair's breadth above it and out of danger.

Then they were bumping and thrashing through the forest branches. The line broke with a shrill twang and the kite, set free, flew off and vanished in the night sky. Its passengers tumbled down, among bushes and boughs, scratched and bruised, but not seriously hurt. They huddled in a dark group, feeling and hugging one another.

"Just listen to the words," said Hannah. "Just smell them!"

Sure enough, a wonderful fresh, aromatic, rainy, spicy smell floated all around them in the forest darkness, and a soft continuous murmuring rustling, chirping twittering nutritious warbling came from all directions; so that, weak, amazed, sore and battered as they were, still they seemed to be understanding more, in the space of a couple of minutes, than they had ever done before in the whole of their lives.

"What does—?" began Miles, but Hannah laid a finger on his lips, and a hand on Noel's trunk.

"Hush! Just listen!"

Probably they are listening still.

# A Room Full of Leaves

Once there was a poor little boy who lived with a lot of his relatives in an enormous house called Troy. The relatives were rich, but they were so nasty that they might just as well have been poor, for all of the good their money did them. The worst of them all was Aunt Agatha, who was thin and sharp, and the next worst was Uncle Umbert, who was stout and prosperous. We shall return to them later. There was also a fierce old nurse called Squab, and a tutor, Mr. Buckle, who helped to make the little boy's life a burden. His name was Wilfred, which was a family name, but he was so tired of hearing them all say: "You must live up to your name, child," that in his own mind he called himself Wil. It had to be in his mind, for he had no playmates—other children were declared to be common, and probably dangerous and infectious too.

One rainy Saturday afternoon Wil sat in his schoolroom finishing some Latin parsing for Mr. Buckle before being taken for his walk, which was always in one of two directions. If Squabb took him they went downtown "to look at the shops" in a suburb of London which was sprawling out its claws towards the big house; but the shops were never the ones Wil would have chosen to look at. If he went with Mr. Buckle they crossed the Common diagonally (avoiding the pond where rude little boys sailed their boats) and came back along the white-railed bridle path while Mr. Buckle talked about plant life.

So Wil was not looking forward with great enthusiasm to his walk, and when Squabb came in and told him that it was too wet to go out and he must amuse himself quietly with his jigsaw puzzles, he was delighted. He sat gazing dreamily at the jigsaw puzzles for a while, not getting on with them, while Squabb did some ironing. It was nearly dark, although the time was only three. Squabb switched on the light and picked a fresh heap of ironing off the fender.

All of a sudden there was a blue flash and a report from the iron; a strong smell of burnt rubber filled the room and the lights went out.

"Now I suppose the perishing thing's blown the fuse for this whole floor," exclaimed Squabb and she hurried out of the room, muttering something under her breath about newfangled gadgets.

Wil did not waste a second. Before the door had closed after her he was tiptoeing across the room and out of the other door. In the darkness and confusion no one would miss him for quite a considerable time, and he would have a rare opportunity to be on his own for a bit.

The house in which he lived was very huge. Nobody knew exactly how many rooms there were—but there was one for each day of the year and plenty left over. Innumerable little courtyards, each with its own patch of green velvet grass, had passages leading away in all directions to different blocks and wings. Towards the back of the house there were fewer courtyards; it drew itself together into a solid mass which touched the forest behind. The most important rooms were open to the public on four days a week; Mr. Buckle and a skinny lady from the town showed visitors around, and all the relics and heirlooms were carefully locked up inside glass cases where they could be gazed at—the silver washbasin used by James II, a dirty old exercise book belonging to the poet Pope, the little pot of neat's foot ointment left by Henry VIII, and all the other tiny bits of history. Even in those days visitors were careless about leaving things behind.

Wil was indifferent to the public rooms, though his relatives were not. They spent their lives polishing and furbishing and when everything was polished they went on endless grubbing searches through the unused rooms looking for more relics which could be cleaned up and sold to the British Museum.

Wil stood outside the schoolroom door listening. Down below he could hear the murmur of voices. Saturday was cheap visiting day—only two and six instead of five schillings—so there were twice as many people, and both Mr. Buckle and the skinny lady were at work escorting their little groups. Wil nodded to himself and slipped away, softly as a mouse, towards the back of the house where the tourists were never taken. Here it became darker and dustier, the windows were small, heavily leaded, and never cleaned. Little passages, unexpected stairways and landings wound about past innumerable doors, many of which had not been opened since Anne Boleyn popped her head around to say good-bye to some bedridden old retainer before taking horse to London. Tapestries hung thick with velvet dust—had Wil touched them they would have crumbled to pieces, but he slid past them like a shadow.

He was already lost, but he meant to be; he stood listening to the old house creaking and rustling around him like a forest. He had a fancy that if he penetrated far enough he would find himself in the forest without having noticed the transition. He was following a particularly crooked and winding passage, leading to a kind of crossroads or cross-passages from which other alleys led away, mostly dark, some with a faint gleam from a rain-streaked window far away down their length, and all lined with doors.

He paused, wondering which to choose, and then heard something which might have been the faintest of whispers—but it was enough to decide him on taking the passage directly fronting him. He went slowly to a door some twelve feet along it, rather a low, small door on his right.

After pushing he discovered that it opened outwards towards him. He pulled it back, stepped around, and gazed in bewilderment at what he saw. It was like a curtain, of a silvery, faded brown, which hung across the doorway. Then looking closer he saw that it was really *leaves*—piled high and drifted one on another, lying so heaped up that the entrance was filled with them, and if the door had swung inwards he could never have pushed it open. Wil felt them with his hand; they were not brittle like dead beech leaves, but soft and supple, making only the faintest rustle when he touched them. He took one and looked at it in the palm of his hand. It was almost a skeleton, covered with faint silvery marks like letters. As he stood looking at it he heard a little voice whisper from inside the room:

"Well, boy, aren't you coming in?"

Much excited, he stared once more at the apparently impenetrable wall of leaves in front of him, and said softly:

"How do I get through?"

"Burrow, of course," whispered the voice impatiently.

He obeyed and, stooping a little, plunged his head and arms among the leaves and began working his way inside them like a mole. When he was entirely inside the doorway he wriggled around and pulled the door shut behind him. The leaves made hardly any noise as he inched through them. There was just enough air to breathe, and a dryish, aromatic scent. His progress was slow, and it seemed to take about ten minutes before the leaves began to thin out, and striking upwards like a diver he finally came to the surface.

He was in a room, or so he supposed, having come into it through an ordinary door in a corridor, but the walls could not be seen at all on account of the rampart of leaves piled up all around him. Towards the center there was a clear space on the ground, and in this grew a mighty trunk, as large around as a table, covered with roughish silver bark, all protrusions and knobs. The branches began above his head, thrusting out laterally like those of an oak or beech, but very little could be seen of them on account of the leaves which grew everywhere in thick clusters, and the upper reaches of the tree were not visible at all. The growing leaves were yellow—not the faded yellow of autumn but a brilliant gold which illuminated the room. At least there was no other source of light, and it was not dark.

There appeared to be no one else under the tree and Wil wondered who had spoken to him and where they could be.

As if in answer to his thoughts the voice spoke again:

"Can't you climb up?"

"Yes, of course I can," he said, annoyed with himself for not thinking of this, and he began setting his feet on the rough ledges of bark and pulling himself up. Soon he could not see the floor below, and was in a cage of leaves which fluttered all around him, dazzling his eyes. The scent in the tree was like thyme on the Downs on a hot summer's day.

"Where are you?" he asked in bewilderment.

He heard a giggle.

"I'm here," said the voice, and he saw an agitation among the leaves at the end of a branch, and worked his way out to it. He found a little girl with freckles and reddish hair hidden under some kind of cap. She wore a long green velvet dress and a ruff, and she was seated comfortably swinging herself up and down in a natural hammock of small branches.

"Really I thought you'd *never* find your way here," she said, giving him a derisive welcoming grin.

"I'm not used to climbing trees," he excused himself.

"I know, poor wretch. Never mind, this one's easy enough. What's your name? Mine's Em."

"Mine's Wil. Do you live here?"

"Of course. This isn't really my branch—some of them are very severe about staying on their own branches—look at *him*." She indicated a very Puritanical-looking gentleman in black knee-breeches who appeared for a moment and then vanished again as a cluster of leaves swayed. "*I* go where I like, though. My branch isn't respectable—we were on the wrong side in every war from Matilda and Stephen on. As soon as the colonies were invented they shipped a lot of us out there, but it was no use, they left a lot behind. They always hope that we'll die out, but of course we don't. Shall I show you some of the tree?"

"Yes, please."

"Come along then. Don't be frightened, you can hold my hand a lot of the time. It's almost as easy as stairs."

When she began leading him about he realized that the tree was much more enormous than he had supposed; in fact he did not understand how it could be growing in a room inside a house. The branches curved about making platforms, caves, spiral staircases, seats, cupboards, and cages. Em led him through the maze, which she seemed to know by heart, pushing past the clusters of yellow leaves. She showed him how to swing from one branch to another, how to slide down the slopes and wriggle through the crevices and how to lie back in a network of boughs and rest his head on a thick pillow of leaves.

They made quite a lot of noise and several disapproving old faces peered at them from the ends of branches, though one crusader smiled faintly and his dog wagged its tail.

"Have you anything to eat?" asked Em presently, mopping her brow with her kerchief.

"Yes, I've got some cookies I didn't eat for my mid-morning snack. I'm not allowed to keep them of course; they'd be cross if they knew."

"Of course," nodded Em, taking a cookie. "Thanks. Dryish, aren't they—but welcome. Wait a minute and I'll bring you a drink." She disappeared among the boughs and came back in a few moments with two little greenish crystal cups full of a golden liquid.

"It's sap," she said, passing one over. "It has a sort of forest taste, hasn't it; it makes you think of horns. Now I'll give you a present."

She took the cups away and he heard her rummaging somewhere down by the trunk of the tree.

"There's all sorts of odds and ends down there. This is the first thing I could find. Do you like it?"

She looked at it critically. "I think it's the shoehorn that Queen Elizabeth used (she always had trouble with wearing too tight shoes). She must have left it behind here some time. You can have it anyway—you might find a use for it. You'd better be going now or you'll be in trouble and then it won't be so easy for you to come here another time."

"How shall I ever find my way back here?"

"You must stand quite still and listen. You'll hear me whisper, and the leaves rustling. Good-bye." She suddenly put a skinny little arm around his neck and gave him a hug. "It's nice having someone to play with; I've been a bit bored sometimes."

Wil squirmed out through the leaves again and shut the door, turning to look at it as he did so. There was nothing in the least unusual about its appearance.

When he arrived back in the schoolroom (after some false turnings) he found his Aunt Agatha waiting for him. Squabb and Buckle were hovering on the threshold, but she dismissed them with a wave of her hand. The occasion was too serious for underlings.

"Wilfred," she said in a very awful tone.

"Yes, Aunt Agatha."

"Where have you been?"

"Playing in the back part of the house."

"*Playing!* A child of your standing and responsibilities playing? Instead of getting on with your puzzle? What is that?" She pounced on him and dragged out the shoehorn which was protruding from his pocket.

"Concealment! I suppose you found this and intended to creep out and sell it to some museum. You are an exceedingly wicked, disobedient boy, and as punishment for running away and hiding in this manner you will go to bed as soon as I have finished with you, you will have nothing to eat but toast-gruel, and you will have to take off your clothes *yourself*, and feed *yourself*, like a common child."

"Yes, Aunt."

"You know that you are the Heir to this noble house (when your great-uncle Winthrop dies)?"

"Yes, Aunt."

"Do you know anything about your parents?"

"No"

"It is as well. Look at this." She pulled out a little case, containing two miniatures of perfectly ordinary people. Wil studied them.

"That is your father—our brother. He disgraced the family—he sullied the scutcheon—by becoming—*a writer*—and worse—he married a *female writer,* your mother. Mercifully for the family reputation they were both drowned in the *Oranjeboot* disaster, before anything worse could happen. You were rescued, floating in a pickle barrel. *Now* do you see why we all take such pains with your education? It is to save you from the taint of your unfortunate heritage."

Wil was still digesting this when there came a knock at the door and Mr. Buckle put his head around.

"There is a Mr. Slockenheimer demanding to see you, Lady Agatha," he said. "Apparently he will not take No for an answer. Shall I continue with the reprimand?"

"No, Buckle—you presume," said Aunt Agatha coldly. "I have finished."

Wil put himself to bed, watched minutely by Buckle to see that he did not omit to brush his teeth with the silver brush or comb his eyebrows with King Alfred's comb in the manner befitting an heir of Troy. The toast and water was brought in a gold porringer. Wil ate it absently; it was very nasty, but he was so overcome by the luck of not having been found out, and wondering how he could get back to see Em another time, that he hardly noticed it.

Next morning at breakfast (which he had with his relatives) he expected to be in disgrace, but curiously enough they paid no attention to him. They were all talking about Mr. Slockenheimer.

"Such a piece of luck," said Cousin Cedric. "Just as the tourist season is ending."

"Who is this man?" creaked Great-Aunt Gertrude.

"He is a film director, from Hollywood," explained Aunt Agatha, loudly and patiently. "He is making a film about Robin Hood and he has asked permission to shoot some of the indoor scenes in Troy—for which we shall all be handsomely paid, naturally."

"Naturally, naturally," croaked the old ravens, all around the table.

Wil pricked up his ears, and then an anxious thought struck him. Suppose Mr. Slockenheimer's people discovered the room with the tree?

"They are coming today," Uncle Umbert was shrieking into Great-Uncle Ulric's ear trumpet.

Mr. Slockenheimer's outfit arrived after breakfast while Wil was doing his daily run—a hundred times around the triangle of grass in front of the house, while Mr. Buckle timed him with a stop-watch.

A lovely lady shot out of the huge green motor car, and shrieked:

"Oh, you cute darling! Now you must tell me the way to the nearest milk bar," and whisked him back into the car with her. Out of the corner of his eye he saw that Mr. Buckle had been commandeered to show somebody the spiral staircase.

Wil ate his raspberry sundae in a daze. He had never been in the milk bar before, never eaten ice cream, never ridden in a car. To have it all following on his discovery of the day before was almost too much for him.

"Gracious!" exclaimed his new friend, looking at her wristwatch. "I must be on the set! I'm Maid Marian you know. Tarzan, I mean Robin, has to rescue me from the wicked baron at eleven in the Great Hall."

"I'll show you where it is," said Wil.

He expected more trouble when he reached home, but the whole household was disorganized: Mr. Buckle was showing Robin Hood how to put on the Black Prince's helmet (which was too big) and Aunt Agatha was having a long business conversation with Mr. Slockenheimer, so his arrival passed unnoticed.

He was relieved to find that the film was only going to be shot in the main public rooms, so there did not seem to be much risk of the tree being discovered.

After lunch Mr. Buckle was called on again to demonstrate the firing of the 9th Earl's crossbow (he shot an extra) and Wil was able to escape once more and reach in safety the regions at the back.

He stood on a dark landing for what seemed like hours, listening to the patter of his own heart. Then, tickling his ear like a thread of cobweb, he heard Em's whisper:

"Wil! Here I am! This way!" and below it he heard the rustle of the tree, as if it too were whispering: "Here I am."

It did not take him long to find the room, but his progress through the leaves was slightly impeded by the things he was carrying. When he emerged at the foot of the tree he found Em waiting there. The hug she gave him nearly throttled him.

"I've been thinking of some more places to show you. And all sorts of games to play!"

"I've brought you a present," he said, emptying his pockets.

"Oh! What's in those little tubs?"

"Ice cream. The chief electrician gave them to me."

"What a strange confection," she said, tasting it. "It is smooth and sweet but it makes my teeth chatter."

"And here's your present." It was a gold Mickey Mouse with ruby eyes which Maid Marian had given him. Em handled it with respect and presently stored it away in one of her hidey-holes in the trunk. Then they played follow-my-leader until they were so tired that they had to lie back on thick beds of leaves and rest.

"I did not expect to see you so soon," said Em as they lay picking the aromatic leaves and chewing them, while a prim Jacobean lady shook her head at them.

Wil explained about the invasion of the film company and she listened with interest.

"A sort of strolling players," she commented. "My father was one—flat contrary to the family's commands, of course. I saw many pieces performed before I was rescued from the life by my respected grandmother to be brought up as befitted one of our name." She sighed.

For the next two months Wil found many opportunities to slip off and visit Em, for Mr. Buckle became greatly in demand as an advisor on matters of costume, and even Squabb was pressed into service ironing doublets and mending hose.

But one day Wil saw his relatives at breakfast with long faces, and he learned that the company had finished shooting the inside scenes and were about to move to Florida to take the Sherwood Forest sequences. The handsome additional income which the family had been making was about to cease, and Wil realized with dismay that the old life would begin again.

Later when he was starting off to visit Em he found a little group, consisting of Aunt Agatha, Uncle Umbert, Mr. Slockenheimer and his secretary, Mr. Jakes, on one of the back landings. Wil shrank into the shadows and listened to their conversation with alarm.

"One million," Mr. Slockenheimer was saying. "Yes, sir, one million's my last word. But I'll ship the house over to Hollywood myself, as carefully as if it were a new-laid egg. You may be sure of that, Ma'am. I appreciate your feelings, and you and your family may go on living in it for the rest of your days. Every brick will be numbered and every floorboard will be lettered so that they'll go back in their exact places. This house certainly will be a gold mine to me—it'll save its value twice over in a year as sets for different films. There's Tudor, Gothic, Norman, Saxon, Georgian, Decorated, all under one roof."

"But we shall have to have salaries too, mind," said Uncle Umbert greedily. "We can't be expected to uproot ourselves like this and move to Hollywood all for nothing."

Mr. Slockenheimer raised his eyebrows at this, but said agreeably:

"Okay, I'll sign you on as extras." He pulled out a fistful of forms, scribbled his signature on them and handed them to Aunt Agatha. "There you are, Ma'am, twenty-year contracts for the whole bunch."

"Dirt cheap at the price, even so," Wil heard him whisper to the secretary.

"Now as we're finished shooting I'll have the masons in tomorrow and start chipping the old place to bits. Hangings and furniture will be crated separately. It'll take quite a time, of course; shouldn't think we'll get it done in less than three weeks." He looked with respect over his shoulders at a vista of dark corridor which stretched away for half a mile.

Wil stole away with his heart thudding. Were they actually proposing to pull down the house, *this* house, and ship it to Hollywood for film sets? What about the tree? Would they hack it down, or dig it up and transport it, leaves and all?

"What's the matter, boy?" asked Em, her cheek bulging with the giant sucker he had brought her.

"The film company's moving away, and they're going to take Troy with them for using as backgrounds for films."

"The whole house?"

"Yes."

"Oh," said Em, and became very thoughtful.

"Em."

"Yes?"

"What—I mean, what would happen to you if they found this room and cut the tree down, or dug it up?"

"I'm not sure," she said, pondering. "I shouldn't go *on* after that—none of us would in here—but as to exactly *what* would happen—; I don't expect it would be bad. Perhaps we should just go out like lamps."

"Well then it must be stopped," said Wil so firmly that he surprised himself.

"Can you forbid it? You're the Heir, aren't you?"

"Not till old Uncle Winthrop dies. We'll have to think of some other plan."

"I have an idea," said Em, wrinkling her brow with effort. "In my days, producers would do much for a well-written play, one that had never been seen before. Is it still like that nowadays?"

"Yes I think so, but we don't know anyone who writes plays," Wil pointed out.

"I have a play laid by somewhere," she explained. "The writer was a friend of my father—he asked my father to take it up to London to have it printed. My father bade me take care of it and I put it in my bundle of clothes. It was on the journey, as we were passing through Oxford, that I was seen and carried off by my respected grandmother, and I never saw my father or Mr. Shakespeere again, so the poor man lost his play."

"Mr. Shakespeare, did you say?" asked Wil, stuttering slightly. "What was the name of the play, do you remember?"

"I forget. I have it here somewhere." She began delving about in a cranny between two branches and presently drew out a dirty old manuscript. Wil stared at it with popping eyes.

*The Tragicall Historie of Robin Hoode*
A play by Wm. Shakespeere
Act I, Scene I. Sherwood Forest. Enter John
Lackland, De Bracy, Sheriff of Nottingham,
Knights, Lackeys and attendants.

JOHN L. Good sirs, the occasion of our coming hither
Is, since our worthy brother Coeur de Lion
Far from our isle now wars on Paynim soil,
The apprehension of that recreant knave
Most caitiff outlaw who is known by some
As Robin Locksley; by others Robin Hood;
More, since our coffers gape with idle locks
The forfeiture of his ill-gotten gains.
Thus Locksley's stocks will stock our locks enow
While he treads air beneath the forest bough.

"Golly," said Wil. "Shakespeare's *Robin Hood.* I wonder what Mr. Slockenheimer would say to this?"

"Well don't wait. *Go and ask him.* It's yours—I'll make you a present of it."

He wriggled back through the leaves with frantic speed, slammed the door, and raced down the passage towards the Great Hall. Mr. Slockenheimer was there superintending the packing of some expensive and elaborate apparatus.

"Hello, Junior. Haven't seen you in days. Well, how d'you like the thought of moving to Hollywood, eh?"

"Not very much," Wil said frankly. "You see, I'm used to it here, and—and the house is too; I don't think the move would be good for it."

"Think the dry air would crumble it, mebbe? Well, there's something to what you say. I'll put in air-conditioning apparatus at the other end. I'm sorry you don't take to the idea, though. Hollywood's a swell place."

"Mr. Slockenheimer," said Wil, "I've got something here which is rather valuable. It's mine—somebody gave it to me. And it's genuine. I was wondering if I could do a sort of swap—exchange it for the house, you know."

"It would have to be mighty valuable," replied Mr. Slockenheimer cautiously. "Think it's worth a million, son? What is it?"

"It's a play by Mr. Shakespeare—a new play that no one's seen before."

"Eh?"

"I'll show you," said Wil confidently, pulling out the MS.

"*The Tragicall Historie of Robin Hoode,*" read Mr. Slockenheimer slowly. "By Wm. Shakespeere. Well I'll be goshdarned. Just when I'd finished the indoor scenes. Isn't that just my luck? Hey, Junior—are you sure this is genuine?—Well, Jakes will know, he knows everything. Hey," he called to his secretary, "come and take a look at this."

The dry Mr. Jakes let out a whistle when he saw the signature.

"That's genuine, all right," he said. "It's quite something you've got there. First production of the original Shakespeare play by W. P. Slockenheimer."

"Well, will you swap?" asked Wil once more.

"I'll say I will," exclaimed Mr. Slockenheimer, slapping him thunderously on the back. "You can keep your mouldering old barracks. I'll send you twenty seats for the premiere. *Robin Hoode by Wm. Shakespeere.* Well, what do you know?"

"There's just one thing," said Wil, pausing.

"Yes, Bud?"

"These contracts you gave my uncle and aunt and the others. Are they still binding?"

"Not if you don't want."

"Oh, but I do—I'd much rather they went to Hollywood."

Mr. Slockenheimer burst out laughing. "Oh, I get the drift. Okay, Junior, I daresay they won't bother me as much as they do you. I'll hold them to those contracts as tight as glue. Twenty years, eh? You'll be of age by then, I guess? Your Uncle Umbert can be the Sheriff of Nottingham, he's about the build for the part. And we'll fit your Aunt Aggie in somewhere."

"And Buckle and Squab?"

"Yes, yes," said Mr. Slockenheimer, much tickled. "Though what you'll do here all on your own—however, that's your affair. Right, boys, pack up those cameras next."

Three days later the whole outfit was gone, and with them, swept away among the flash bulbs, cameras, extras, crates, props and costumes, went Squabb, Buckle, Aunt Agatha, Uncle Umbert, Cousin Cedric, and all the rest.

Empty and peaceful the old house dreamed, with sunlight shifting from room to room and no sound to break the silence, save in one place, where the voices of children could be heard faintly above the rustling of a tree.

# Furry Night

The deserted aisles of the National Museum of Dramatic Art lay very, very still in the blue autumn twilight. Not a whisper of wind stirred the folds of Irving's purple cloak; Ellen Terry's ostrich fan was smooth and unruffled; the blue-black gleaming breastplate that Sir Murdoch Meredith, founder of the museum, had worn as Macbeth held its reflection as quietly as a cottage kettle.

And yet, despite this hush, there was an air of strain, of expectancy, along the narrow coconut-matted galleries between the glass cases: a tension suggesting that some crisis had taken or was about to take place.

In the total stillness a listener might have imagined that he heard, ever so faintly, the patter of stealthy feet far away among the exhibits.

Two men, standing in the shadow of the Garrick showcase, were talking in low voices.

"This is where it happened," said the elder, white-haired man.

He picked up a splinter of broken glass, frowned at it, and dropped it into a litter bin. The glass had been removed from the front of the case, and some black tights and gilt medals hung exposed to the evening air.

"We managed to hush it up. The hospital and ambulance men will be discreet, of course. Nobody else was there, luckily. Only the Bishop was worried."

"I should think so," the younger man said. "It's enough to make anybody anxious."

"No, I mean he was *worried.* Hush," the white-haired man whispered, "here comes Sir Murdoch."

The distant susurration had intensified into soft, pacing footsteps. The two men, without a word, stepped farther back in the shadow until they were out of sight. A figure appeared at the end of the aisle and moved forward until it stood beneath the portrait of Edmund Keane as Shylock. The picture, in its deep frame, was nothing but a square of dark against the wall.

Although they were expecting it, both men jumped when the haunted voice began to speak.

> *"You may as well use question with the wolf*
> *Why he hath made the ewe bleat for the lamb. . . ."*

A sleeve of one of the watchers brushed against the wall, the lightest possible touch, but Sir Murdoch swung round sharply, his head outthrust, teeth bared. They held their breath, and after a moment he turned back to the picture.

> *"Thy currish spirit*
> *Govern'd a wolf, who, hang'd for human slaughter*
> *Even from the gallows did his fell soul fleet. . . ."*

He paused, with a hand pressed to his forehead, and then leaned forward and hissed,

> *"Thy desires*
> *Are wolvish, bloody, starv'd, and ravenous!"*

His head sank on his chest. His voice ceased. He brooded for a moment, and then resumed his pacing and soon passed out of sight. They heard the steps go lightly down the stairs, and presently the whine of the revolving door.

After a prudent interval the two others emerged from their hiding place, left the gallery, and went out to a car that was waiting for them in Great Smith Street.

"I wanted you to see that, Peachtree," said the elder man, "to give you some idea of what you are taking on. Candidly, as far as experience goes, I hardly feel you are qualified for the job, but you are young and tough and have presence of mind; most important of all, Sir Murdoch seems to have taken a fancy to you. You will have to keep an unobtrusive eye on him every minute of the day; your job is a combination of secretary, companion, and resident psychiatrist. I have written to Dr. Defoe, the local GP at Polgrue. He is old, but you will find him full of practical sense. Take his advice . . . I think you said you were brought up in Australia?"

"Yes," Ian Peachtree said. "I only came to this country six months ago."

"Ah, so you missed seeing Sir Murdoch act."

"Was he so very wonderful?"

"He made the comedies too macabre," said Lord Hawick, considering, "but in the tragedies there was no one to touch him. His Macbeth was something to make you shudder. When he said,

> *'Alarum'd by his sentinel, the wolf,*
> *Whose howl's his watch, thus with his stealthy pace,*
> *With Tarquin's ravishing strides, towards his design*
> *Moves like a ghost,'*

He used to take two or three stealthy steps across the stage, and you could literally see the grey fur rise on his hackles, the lips draw back from the fangs, the yellow eyes begin to gleam. It made a cold chill run down your spine. As Shylock and Caesar and Timon he was unrivalled. Othello and Antony he never touched, but his Iago was a masterpiece of villainy."

"Why did he give it up? He can't be much over fifty."

"As with other sufferers from lycanthropy," said Lord Hawick, "Sir Murdoch has an ungovernable temper. Whenever he flew into a rage it brought on an attack. They grew more and more frequent. A clumsy stagehand, a missed cue might set him off; he'd begin to shake with rage and the terrifying change would take place.

"On stage it wasn't so bad; he had his audiences completely hypnotized and they easily accepted a grey-furred Iago padding across the stage with the handkerchief in his mouth. But off stage it was less easy; the claims for mauling and worrying were beginning to mount up; Equity objected. So he retired, and, for some time, founding the museum absorbed him. But now it's finished; his temper is becoming uncertain again. This afternoon, as you know, he pounced on the Bishop for innocently remarking that Garrick's Hamlet was the world's greatest piece of acting."

"How do you deal with the attacks? What's the treatment?"

"Wolfsbane. Two or three drops given in a powerful sedative will restore him for the time. Of course, administering it is the problem, as you can imagine. I only hope the surroundings in Cornwall will be sufficiently peaceful so that he is not provoked. It's a pity he never married; a woman's influence would be beneficial."

"Why didn't he?"

"Jilted when he was thirty. Never looked at another woman. Some girl down at Polgrue, near his home. It was a real slap in the face; she wrote two days before the wedding saying she couldn't stand his temper. That began it all. This will be the first time he's been back there. Well, here we are," said Lord Hawick, glancing out at his Harley Street doorstep. "Come in and I'll give you the wolfsbane prescription."

The eminent consultant courteously held the door for his young colleague.

The journey to Cornwall was uneventful. Dr. Peachtree drove his distinguished patient, glancing at him from time to time with mingled awe and affection. Would the harassing crawl down the A30, the jam in Exeter, the flat tyre on Dartmoor, bring on an attack? Would he be able to cope if they did? But the handsome profile remained unchanged, the golden eyes in their deep sockets stayed the eyes of a man, not those of a wolf, and Sir Murdoch talked entertainingly, not at all discomposed by the delays. Ian was fascinated by his tales of the theatre.

There was only one anxious moment, when they reached the borders of Polgrue Chase. Sir Murdoch glanced angrily at his neglected coverts, where the brambles grew long and wild.

"Wait till I see that agent," he muttered, and then, half to himself, "'Oh, thou wilt be a wilderness again,/Peopled with wolves.'"

Ian devoutly hoped that the agent would have a good excuse.

But the Hall, hideous Victorian-Gothic barrack though it was, they found gay with lights and warm with welcome. The old housekeeper wept over Sir Murdoch, bottles were uncorked, the table shone with ancestral silver. Ian began to feel less apprehensive.

After dinner they moved outside with their nuts and wine to sit in the light that streamed over the terrace from the dining-room French windows. A great walnut tree hung shadowy above them; its golden, aromatic leaves littered the flagstones at their feet.

"This place has a healing air," Sir Murdoch said. "I should have come here sooner." Suddenly he stiffened. "Hudson! Who are those?"

Far across the park, almost out of sight in the dusk, figures were flitting among the trees.

"Eh," said the housekeeper comfortably, "they're none but the lads, Sir Murdoch, practicing for the Furry Race. Don't you worrit about them. They won't do no harm."

"On my land?" Sir Murdoch said. "Running across my land?"

Ian saw with a sinking heart that his eyes were turning to gleaming yellow slits, his hands were stiffening and curling. Would the housekeeper mind? Did she know her master was subject to these attacks? He felt in his pocket for the little ampoules of wolfsbane, the hypodermic syringe.

There came an interruption. A girl's clear voice was heard singing:

*"Now the hungry lion roars,*
*And the wolf behowls the moon—"*

"It's Miss Clarissa," said the housekeeper with relief.

A slender figure swung round the corner of the terrace and came towards them.

"Sir Murdoch? How do you do? I'm Clarissa Defoe. My father sent me up to pay his respects. He would have come himself, but he was called out on a case. Isn't it a gorgeous night?"

Sitting down beside them, she chatted amusingly and easily, while Ian observed with astonished delight that his employer's hands were unclenching and his eyes were becoming their normal shape again. If this girl was able to soothe Sir Murdoch without recourse to wolfsbane, they must see a lot of her.

But when Sir Murdoch remarked that the evening was becoming chilly and proposed that they go indoors, Ian's embryonic plan received a jolt. He was a tough and friendly young man who had never taken a great deal of interest in girls; the first sight, in lamplight, of Clarissa Defoe's wild beauty came on him with a shattering impact. Could he expose her to danger without warning her?

More and more enslaved, he sat gazing as Clarissa played and sang Ariel's songs. Sir Murdoch seemed completely charmed and relaxed. When Clarissa left, he let Ian persuade him to bed without the topic of the Furry Race coming up again.

Next morning, however, when Ian went down to the village for a consultation with cheerful, shrewd-eyed old Dr. Defoe, he asked about it.

"Heh," said the doctor. "The Furry Race? My daughter revived it five years ago. There's two villages, ye see, Polgrue, and Lostmid, and there's this ball, what they call the Furry Ball. It's not furry; it's made of applewood with a silver band round the middle, and on the band is written,

*Fro Lostmid Parish iff I goe*
*Heddes will be broke and bloode will flowe.*

"The ball is kept in Lostmid, and on the day of the race one of the Polgrue lads has to sneak in and take it and get it over the parish boundary before anybody stops him. Nobody's succeeded in doing it yet. But why do you ask?"

Ian explained about the scene the night before.

"Eh, I see; that's awkward. You're afraid it may bring on an attack if he sees them crossing his land? Trouble is, that's the quickest shortcut over the parish boundary."

"If your daughter withdrew her support, would the race be abandoned?"

"My dear feller, she'd never do that. She's mad about it. She's a bit of a tomboy, Clarissa, and the roughhousing amuses her—always is plenty of horseplay, even though they don't get the ball over the boundary. If her mother were still alive now . . . Bless my soul!" the old doctor burst out, looking troubled, "I wish Meredith had never come back to these parts, that I do. You can speak with Clarissa about it, but I doubt you'll not persuade her. She's out looking over the course now."

The two villages of Lostmid and Polgrue lay in deep adjacent glens, and Polgrue Chase ended on the stretch of high moorland that ran between them. There was a crossroads and a telephone box, used by both villages. A spinney of wind-bitten beeches stood in one angle of the cross, and Clarissa was thoughtfully surveying this terrain. Ian joined her, turning to look back towards the Hall and noticing with relief that Sir Murdoch was still, as he had been left, placidly knocking a ball around his private golf course.

It was a stormy, shining day. Ian saw that Clarissa's hair was exactly the colour of the sea-browned beech leaves and that the strange angles of her face were emphasized by the wild shafts of sunlight glancing through the trees.

He put his difficulties to her.

"Oh, dear," she said, wrinkling her brow. "How unfortunate. The boys are so keen on the race. I don't think they'd ever give it up."

"Couldn't they go some other way?"

"But this is the only possible way, don't you see? In the old days, of course, this all used to be common land."

"Do you know who the runner is going to be—the boy with the ball?" Ian asked, wondering if a sufficiently heavy bribe would persuade him to take a longer way round.

But Clarissa smiled, with innocent topaz eyes. "My dear, that's never decided until the very *last* minute. So that the Lostmidians don't know who's going to dash in and snatch the ball. But I'll tell you what we *can* do—we can arrange for the race to take place at night, so that Sir Murdoch won't be worried about the spectacle. Yes, that's an excellent idea; in fact, it will make it far more exciting. It's next Thursday, you know."

Ian was not at all sure that he approved of this idea, but just then he noticed Sir Murdoch having difficulties in a bunker. A good deal of sand was flying about, and his employer's face was becoming a dangerous dusky red. "'Here, in the sands,/Thee I'll rake up," he was muttering angrily, and something about murderous lechers.

Ian ran down to him and suggested that it was time for a glass of beer, waving to Clarissa as he did so. Sir Murdoch noticed her and was instantly mollified. He invited her to join them.

Ian, by now head over heels in love, was torn between his professional duty, which could not help pointing out to him how beneficial Clarissa's company was for his patient, and a strong personal feeling that the elderly wolfish baronet was not at all suitable company for Clarissa. Worse, he suspected that she guessed his anxiety and was laughing at it.

The week passed peacefully enough. Sir Murdoch summoned the chairmen of the two parish councils and told them that any trespass over his land on the day of the Furry Race would be punished with the utmost rigour. They listened with blank faces. He also ordered man traps and spring guns from the Dominion and Colonial Stores, but to Ian's relief it seemed highly unlikely that these would arrive in time.

Clarissa dropped in frequently. Her playing and singing seemed to have as soothing an effect on Sir Murdoch as the songs of the harpist David on touchy old Saul, but Ian had the persistent feeling that some peril threatened from her presence.

On Furry Day she did not appear. Sir Murdoch spent most of the day pacing—loping was really the word for it, Ian thought—distrustfully among his far spinneys, but no trespasser moved in the bracken and dying leaves. Towards evening a fidgety scuffling wind sprang up, and Ian persuaded his employer indoors.

"No one will come, Sir Murdoch, I'm sure. Your notices have scared them off. They'll have gone another way." He wished he really did feel sure of it. He found a performance of *Caesar and Cleopatra* on TV and switched it on, but Shaw seemed to make Sir Murdoch impatient. Presently he got up, began to pace about, and turned it off, muttering,

> *"And why should Caesar be a tyrant, then?*
> *Poor man! I know he would not be a wolf!"*

He swung round on Ian. "Did I do wrong to shut them off my land?"

"Well—" Ian was temporizing when there came an outburst of explosions from Lostmid, hidden in the valley, and a dozen rockets soared into the sky beyond the windows.

"That means someone's taken the Furry Ball," said Hudson, coming in with the decanter of sherry. "Been long enough about it, seemingly."

Sir Murdoch's expression changed completely. One stride took him to the French window. He opened it and went streaking across the park. Ian bolted after him.

"Stop! Sir Murdoch, stop!"

Sir Murdoch turned an almost unrecognizable face and hissed, "'Wake not a sleeping wolf!'" He kept on his way, with Ian stubbornly in pursuit. They came out by the crossroads and, looking down to Lostmid, saw that it was a circus of wandering lights, clustering, darting this way and that.

"They've lost him," Ian muttered. "No, there he goes!"

One of the lights broke off at a tangent and moved away down the valley, then turned and came straight for them diagonally across the hillside.

"I'll have to go and warn him off," Ian thought. "Can't let him run straight into trouble." He ran downhill towards the approaching light. Sir Murdoch stole back into the shade of the spinney. Nothing of him was visible but two golden, glowing eye points.

It was at this moment that Clarissa, having established her red-herring diversion by sending a boy with a torch across the hillside, ran swiftly and silently up the steep road towards the signpost. She wore trousers and a dark sweater and was clutching the Furry Ball in her hand.

Sir Murdoch heard the pit-pat of approaching footsteps, waited for his moment, and sprang.

It was the thick fisherman's-knit jersey with its roll collar that saved her. They rolled over and over, girl and wolf entangled, and then she caught him a blow on the jaw with the heavy applewood ball, dropped it, scrambled free, and was away. She did not dare look back. She had a remarkable turn of speed, but the wolf was overtaking her. She hurled herself into the telephone box and let the door clang to behind her.

The wolf arrived a second later; she heard the impact as the grey, sinewy body struck the door, saw the gleam of teeth through the glass. Methodically, though with shaking hands, she turned to dial.

Meanwhile Ian had met the red-herring boy just as his triumphant pursuers caught up with him.

"You mustn't go that way," Ian gasped. "Sir Murdoch's waiting up there and he's out for blood."

"Give over that thurr ball," yelled the Lostmidians.

"'Tisn't on me," the boy yelled back, regardless of the fact that he was being pulled limb from limb. "Caught ye properly, me fine fules. 'Tis Miss Clarissa's got it, and she'm gone backaway."

"*What?*"

Ian waited for no more. He left them to their battle, in which some Polgrue reinforcements were now joining, and bounded back up the murderous ascent to where he had left Sir Murdoch.

The scene at the telephone box was brilliantly lit by the overhead light. Clarissa had finished her call and was watching with detached interest as the infuriated wolf threw himself repeatedly against the door.

It is not easy to address your employer in such circumstances.

Ian chose a low, controlled, but vibrant tone.

"Down, Sir Murdoch," he said. "Down, sir! Heel!"

Sir Murdoch turned on him a look of golden, thunderous wrath. He was really a fine spectacle, with his eyes flashing, and great ruff raised in rage. He must have weighed all of a hundred and thirty pounds. Ian thought he might be a timber wolf, but was not certain. He pulled the ampoule from his pocket, charged the syringe, and made a cautious approach. Instantly Sir Murdoch flew at him. With a feint like a bullfighter's, Ian dodged round the call box.

"Olé," Clarissa shouted approvingly, opening the door a crack. Sir Murdoch instantly turned and battered it again.

"'Avaunt, thou damnéd door-keeper!'" shouted Ian. The result was electrifying. The wolf dropped to the ground as if stunned. Ian seized advantage of the moment to give him his injection, and immediately the wolf shape vanished, dropping off Sir Murdoch like a label off a wet bottle. He gasped, shivered, and shut his eyes.

"Where am I?" he said presently, opening them again. Ian took his arm, gently led him away from the door, and made him sit on a grassy bank.

"You'll feel better in a minute or two, sir," he said, and, since Shakespeare seemed so efficacious, added, "'The cure whereof, my lord,/'Tis time must do.'" Sir Murdoch weakly nodded.

Clarissa came out of her refuge. "Are you all right now, Sir Murdoch?" she asked kindly. "Shall I sing you a song?"

"All right, thank you, my dear," he murmured. "What are you doing here?" And he added to himself, "I really must not fly into these rages. I feel quite dizzy."

Ian stepped aside and picked up something that glinted on the ground.

"What's that?" asked Sir Murdoch with awakening interest. "It reminds me— May I see it?"

"Oh, it's my medallion," said Clarissa at the same moment. "It must have come off. . . ." Her voice trailed away. They both watched Sir Murdoch. Deep, fearful shudders were running through him.

"Where did you get this?" he demanded, turning his cavernous eyes on Clarissa. His fingers were rigid, clenched on the tiny silver St. Francis.

"It was my mother's," she said faintly. For the first time she seemed frightened.

"Was her name Louisa?" She nodded. "Then, your father—?"

"Here comes my father now," said Clarissa with relief. The gnarled figure of the doctor was approaching them through the spinney. Sir Murdoch turned on him like a javelin.

"'O thou foul thief!'" he hissed. "My lost Louisa! 'Stol'n from me and corrupted/By spells and medicines.'"

"Oh, come, come, come," said the doctor equably, never slowing his approach, though he kept a wary eye on Sir Murdoch. "I wouldn't put it quite like that. She came to me. *I* was quite looking forward to bachelorhood."

"'For the which I may go the finer, I will live a bachelor,'" murmured Ian calmingly.

"And I'll tell ye this, Sir Murdoch," Dr. Defoe went on, tucking his arm through that of Sir Murdoch like an old friend, "you were well rid of her." He started strolling at a gentle but purposeful pace back towards the Hall, and the baronet went with him doubtfully.

"Why is that?" Already Sir Murdoch sounded half convinced, quiescent.

"Firstly, my dear sir, Temper. Out of this world! Secondly, Macaroni Cheese. Every night until one begged for mercy. Thirdly, Unpunctuality. Fourthly, long, horrifying Dreams, which she insisted on telling at breakfast . . ."

Pursuing this soothing, therapeutic vein, the doctor's voice moved farther away, and the two men were lost in the shadows.

"So that's all right," said Clarissa on a deep breath of relief. "Why, Ian!"

Pent-up agitation was too much for him. He had grabbed her in his arms like a drowning man. "I was sick with fright for you," he muttered, into her hair, her ear, the back of her neck. "I was afraid—oh well, never mind."

"Never mind," she agreed. "Are we going to get married?"

"Of course."

"I ought to find my Furry Ball," she said presently. "They seem to be having a pitched battle down below; there's a good chance of getting it over the boundary while everyone's busy."

"But Sir Murdoch—"

"Father will look after him."

She moved a few steps away and soon found the ball. "Come on; through the wood is quickest. We have to put it on the Polgrue churchyard wall."

No one accosted them as they ran through the wood. Fireworks and shouting in the valley suggested that Lostmid and Polgrue had sunk their differences in happy saturnalia.

"Full surgery tomorrow," remarked Clarissa, tucking the Furry Ball into its niche. "Won't someone be surprised to see this."

When Ian and Clarissa strolled up to the terrace, they found Sir Murdoch and the doctor amiably drinking port. Sir Murdoch looked like a man who had had a festering grief removed from his mind.

"Well," the doctor said cheerfully, "we've cleared up some misunderstandings."

But Sir Murdoch had stood up and gone to meet Clarissa.

"'As I am a man/,'" he said gravely, "'I do think this lady/To be my child.'"

The two pairs of golden eyes met and acknowledged each other.

"That'll be the end of his little trouble, I shouldn't wonder," murmured the doctor. "Specially if she'll live at the Hall and keep an eye on him."

"But she's going to marry me."

"All the better, my dear boy. All the better. And glad I shall be to get rid of her, bless her heart."

Ian looked doubtfully across the terrace at his future father-in-law, but he recalled that wolves are among the most devoted fathers of the animal kingdom. Sir Murdoch was stroking Clarissa's hair with an expression of complete peace and happiness.

Then a thought struck Ian. "If *he's* her father—"

But Dr. Defoe was yawning. "I'm off to bed. Busy day tomorrow." He vanished among the dark trees.

So they were married and lived happily at the Hall. Clarissa's slightest wish was law. She was cherished equally by both father and husband, and if they went out of their way not to cross her in any particular, this was due quite as much to the love they bore her as to their knowledge that they had dangerous material on their hands.

# Hope

It was on a clear, frosty November evening, not many years ago, that Dr. Jane Smith, having occasion to visit a patient in the part of London known as Rumbury Town, was suddenly overtaken by the impulse to call on an old teacher of hers, a Miss Lestrange, who had a bedsitting-room on the edge of that district, where she earned a meager living by giving lessons on the harp.

Rumbury Town is a curious region of London. Not far from the big stations, adjacent to Islington, beyond, or anyway defying the jurisdiction of smokeless-fuel legislation, it lies enfolded generally in an industrial dusk of its own. The factories of Rumbury Town are not large, and their products are eccentric—artificial grass for butchers' windows, metal bedwinches, false teeth for sheep, slimmers' biscuits made from wood-pulp, catnip mice, plastic Christmas-tree decorations—these are a random sample of its exports. But the small gaunt chimneys, leaning from the factories at various precarious angles, belch black smoke as vigorously as any modern electric power station, and so do those of the houses, like rows of organ-stops, along the ill-lit, dour little terraced streets that lead up in the direction of Rumbury Waste, the ragged strip of tree-grown land fringing Rumbury Town on its eastern edge.

Rumbury Waste is a savage place enough, on no account to be visited after dark, but many a police officer would agree that the centre of Rumbury Town itself is far more of a hostile wilderness, far more dangerous. Here lies an area of mixed factories, business premises, and wholesale markets, interspersed with a few lanes of private dwellings and some dingy little shopping precincts; seamed by narrow alleys and shortcuts; a real maze where, it is said, only those born in Rumbury Town or who have spent at least forty years within earshot of the bells of St Griswold's, Rumbury, can ever hope to find their way.

So cold and clear was this particular evening, however, that even the smoke from the Rumbury chimneys had dwindled to a slaty wisp against the sky's duck-egg green; so little wind was there that in the derelict corners of factory lots where goldenrod and willow-herb cloaked piles of rubble, the withered leaves and feathery seeds drifted straight and unswerving to the ground.

Engines and presses in the factories had ceased their clanging and thudding; workers had gone home; in the centre of Rumbury Town the only sound to be heard was the distant, muted roar of London; and a nearer surge of pop music, sizzle of fish frying, and shouts of children from the few inhabited streets. Dr. Smith parked her car in one of these, locked it carefully, and went in search of her friend, Miss January Lestrange.

Rumbury Town seemed a curious environment for a spinster who taught the harp. And Miss Lestrange was a real spinster of the old-fashioned kind; she walked very slowly, with small, precise steps; she wore tight, pointed button boots, very shiny, which ended halfway up her calf, and long serge skirts, trimmed with rows of braid, which hung down over the boots; it was pure chance that Miss Lestrange's style of dressing was now once more the height of fashion, and a circumstance that she would certainly not have noticed; had she done so she might have been mildly irritated. Her grey hair was smoothly drawn back into a bun, and she wore pince-nez; all the children of Rumbury Town wondered how she managed to make them balance on her nose. Miss Lestrange kept herself to herself and never troubled her neighbors; many of them, if they had thought about it, would not have been surprised to be told that she was a thin, grey old ghost, occasionally to be seen gliding out on her small shopping errands. And the children, though they were not exactly frightened of her, never chalked on her door, or threw ice-lolly sticks after her, or sang rude rhymes about her, as they did about most other adults in the neighbourhood. Miss Lestrange, however, was no ghost, and although she had lived within sound of St Griswold's bells for forty years, was not a born citizen of the district; she still did not venture into the twilit heart of Rumbury Town.

"Why *do* you live here?" Dr. Smith asked, when she had knocked on the faded blue door with its postcard, J. LESTRANGE, HARP TUITION, and had been admitted, passing a small frantic-looking boy on his way out with a music-case under his arm.

"It amazes me the way some of them keep on coming," murmured Miss Lestrange, zipping its case over the harp, which was as tall, gaunt, and worn-looking as she herself. "I've told them and told them that you don't get a first-rate harpist once in a generation, but they all think they have the seed of it in them."

"What about that boy? Is he any good?"

Miss Lestrange shrugged.

"He's the same as the rest. I don't hold out false hopes and sweet promises. I send him away at the end of the lessons utterly despondent, limp as rhubarb, but by next time he's always plucked up heart again and thinks he'll be a second David. Well, Jane, it is nice to see you. What brings you here?"

"Suppose I said that I wanted some more lessons?" Dr. Smith asked with a small, grim smile.

"I should tell you what I told your parents. It would be a waste of their money, my time, and yours, to teach you for another five minutes."

"And they at least believed you. So I went away and trained for a doctor."

"And have turned into a good one, from what I hear." Miss Lestrange nodded at her ex-pupil affectionately. "I hope you will stay and take your evening meal with me and tell me about your work."

But her glance strayed a little doubtfully to the screened corner of the room where she cooked over a methylated-spirit lamp; she had been about to brew herself a nourishing or at least vitamin-rich soup, made from hot water, parsley, grown in her window-box, and salt.

"No, no, I came to invite you out. I have to pay one call on a patient not far from here, and then I thought we'd go to the Chinese restaurant at the corner of Inkermann Street. Put on your coat and let's be off."

Miss Lestrange was always businesslike.

"Well, that would certainly be a more enjoyable meal than the one I could have offered you," she said, put on her coat, and a black hat which had the shape though not the festive air of a vol-au-vent, and ushered out her visitor, locking the door behind them.

The little grimy street was silent and watchful. Half a dozen children stared, to see Miss Lestrange setting out at such an unwonted time of day, in such an unwonted manner, in a car, with a friend.

Dr. Smith reverted to her first, unanswered question.

"Why *do* you live here?"

"The rents are very low," Miss Lestrange said mildly. "Five pounds a year for my room."

"But in a better part of town you might get more pupils—bright ones . . ."

"The world is not that full of gifted harpists," Miss Lestrange said drily. "And this neighbourhood suits me."

"You have friends here?"

"Once I did. One friend. We have not seen each other for some time. But as one grows older," Miss Lestrange said calmly, "one requires fewer friends."

Reflecting that it would be difficult to have fewer friends than one, Dr. Smith brought her car to a halt by a large, grim tenement with a dozen arched entrances. The road that passed it was an old, wide, cobbled one, and on the opposite side began the cluttered, dusky jumble of piled-up factory, warehouse, shed, storehouse, office, factory and lumber-yard that like a great human badger-warren covered the heart of Rumbury Town.

"My patient lives just through here; I shan't be long."

"Who is your patient?" inquired Miss Lestrange, as the doctor turned to lift her black case from the rear seat of the car.

"Well, as a matter of fact he's quite well-known—the writer Tom Rampisham. Why, like you, he chooses to live in this godforsaken spot I don't know, but here he's lived for goodness knows how many years. He has a ground-floor flat in that gloomy block."

"Tom Rampisham," Miss Lestrange said musingly. "It is some time since he did one of his broadcasts. What's his trouble?"

"Heart. Well, I probably shan't be more than a few minutes. But here's a spare car-key in case you want to stroll about."

It looked an unpromising area for a stroll. But when Dr. Smith's few minutes lengthened to ten, and then to fifteen, Miss Lestrange, who seemed restless and disinclined to sit still, even after a long day's work, got out of the car, locked it, and stood irresolutely on the pavement.

For a moment she stared at the large, forbidding block into which the doctor had vanished. Then, with decision, she turned her back on it and struck off briskly across the road. Almost immediately opposite the car was a little opening in the cliff-like façade of warehouses, one of those narrow lanes which the denizens of Rumbury Town call *hackets*, which led inwards, with many angles and windings and sudden changes of direction, towards the heart of the maze.

Along this alley Miss Lestrange rapidly walked. It seemed as if she walked *from* rather than *to* anything in particular; her head was bent, her eyes fixed on the greasy cobbles, she ignored the entrances with their mysterious signs: Wishaw, Flock Sprayers; Saloop, Ear Piercing Specialists; Ample Tops; The Cake Candle Co.; Madame Simkins, Feathers; Sugg, Ganister Maker and Refractory Materials Manufacturer; Toppling Seashell Merchants; Shawl, String, and Sheepskin Co.; Willow Specialists and Wood Wool Packers. One and all, she passed them without a glance, even the Shawl, String, and Sheepskin office, which was in fact the source of her new harp-strings when the old ones had snapped under the inexpert fingers of the youth of Rumbury Town.

Miss Lestrange walked fast, talking to herself, as elderly people do who lead solitary lives.

"If he were ill he might ask for me," she muttered, going past Gay Injectors and Ejectors without sparing a thought to wonder what obscure goods or services their name denoted. "He once said he might; I remember his saying that if he were taken ill he might get in touch with me; it's queer that I can hardly remember what we quarreled about, and yet I can remember that."

The alley took a turn, widened, and led her into a melancholy little area of street market: crockery stalls, cheap clothing stalls, vegetable stalls, second-hand book and junk stalls. The traders were just closing up for the night, piling their unsold wares—of which there seemed to be a great many—back into cartons; the way was impeded by boxes of rubbish, and slippery with squashed vegetables, but Miss Lestrange stepped briskly round and over these obstacles without appearing to notice them.

"What did we quarrel about, all that long time ago?" she mused, neatly by-passing a pram loaded with dusty tins of furniture polish and stepping over a crate labeled SUPERSHINE WHOLESALE: WE PROMISE DAZZLING RESULTS. "It was something to do with his poetry, wasn't it?"

The lane narrowed again and she went on between overhanging cliffs of blackened brick, frowning a little, over her pince-nez, as she tried to summon up a young, lively, impatient face. What had he looked like, exactly? At one time she had known his face by heart—better than her own, for Miss Lestrange had never been one to spend much time gazing at herself in mirrors. Noticeable cheekbones, a lock of hair that always fell forward; that was all she could remember.

We Promise Dazzling Results.

"I don't *know* anything about poetry, Tom. How can I say if it's good or bad?"

"You've got an *opinion*, haven't you, girl? You can say what you *think*?"

"You don't really want me to say what I think. You just want me to praise them."

"Damn it, that's not true, January. January!" he said bitterly. "There never was a more appropriate bit of classification. If ever anybody was ice-cold, frozen hard, ungenerous, utterly unwilling to give an inch, it's you!"

"That's not true!" she had wanted to cry. "It's just that I can't praise what I don't understand, I won't make pretty speeches just to encourage. How can I tell about your poetry? How can I say if I don't know? It wouldn't be right."

But he had already stuffed the disputed poems into an old black satchel and gone striding off; that was the last time she had seen him.

She passed a café with an inscription in what looked like white grease on its window-glass: Sausages, potatoes, onions, peas; frying now, always frying. Why not try our fry?

A staggeringly strong, hot waft of sausage and onion came from the open door; inside were boys with tiny heads, tiny eyes, and huge feet in black boots; as she hurried by, Miss Lestrange felt their eyes investigating her and then deciding that she was not worth the trouble. The hot smell of food made her feel sick and reminded her that she was trembling with hunger; for her lunch at midday she had eaten half a hard-boiled egg, for her breakfast a cup of milkless tea.

"I suppose I shall have to put my fees up," she thought, frowning again.

A shrill whistle, with something familiar about it, disturbed her chain of thought, and she glanced ahead. It was the tune, not the whistle, that was familiar: in a moment she identified it as a tune she had written herself, an easy tune for beginners on the harp; she had called it *Snowdrops.*

And, rollerskating heedlessly in her direction, whistling it shrilly, but in tune, came the boy to whom she had just finished giving a lesson earlier that evening when Dr. Smith arrived.

Their surprise at meeting was equal. He had almost run into her; he skidded to a jerky stop, braking himself with a hand on the alley wall.

"Miss Lestrange! Coo, you're a long way from home, aren't you? You lost your way?"

"Good evening, David. No, I have not lost my way," Miss Lestrange replied briskly. "I am simply taking a walk." What is there surprising in that? her tone expressed.

David looked startled; then he gave her a teasing, disbelieving grin, which made his crooked eyebrows shoot off round the corners of his face. She had never noticed this trick before; but then of course in his lessons he never did grin; he was always sweatingly anxious and subdued.

"*I* don't believe you're just out for a walk; I think you're after that there buried treasure!"

"Buried treasure? What buried treasure, pray?"

"Why, the treasure they say's buried somewhere under the middle o' Rumbury Town. That's what *you're* after. But you won't find it! They say the old Devil's keeping an eye on it for himself. If I were you, Miss Lestrange, I'd turn back before you do get lost!"

"I shall do no such thing," Miss Lestrange said firmly, and she went on her way, and David went skating zigzag on his way, whistling again the little tune, *Snowdrops*—"Mi, re, doh, Snowdrops in the snow . . ."

But Miss Lestrange did turn and look once after David, slightly puzzled. He was so different, so much livelier and more sure of himself than during her lessons; he had quite surprised her.

But as for getting lost—what nonsense.

Nevertheless, in a couple of minutes, without being aware of it, Miss Lestrange did lose herself. She came to a point where five alleys met at an open space shaped like a star, chose one at random, walked a fair way along it, came to another similar intersection, and chose again. Rumbury Town folded itself round her. The green sky overhead was turning to navy-blue.

And all around her was dark, too; like the crater of an extinct volcano. An occasional orange streetlight dimly illuminated the alleyway. Not a sound to be heard. It was a dead world.

Suddenly Miss Lestrange felt uneasy. Her thoughts flew to the professional visit taking place behind her, from the vision of which she had so determinedly started away. Jane must have left him by now. Probably in the car, wondering where I've got to. I had better turn back.

She turned back. And came to the first of the star-shaped conjunctions of lanes.

"Which was mine?" She stood wondering. All four openings facing her looked blank, like shut drawers; she could find no recognizable feature in any of them. The names were just visible: Lambskin Alley, New Year Way, Peridot Lane, Hell Passage; none of them did she consciously remember seeing before.

"I'd surely have noticed New Year's Way," she thought, and so chose Hell Passage—not that it looked any more familiar than the rest. What may have caught her unwitting ear was the faint thrum and throb of music, somewhere far away in that direction; as she proceeded along the narrow passage the sound became steadily more identifiable as music, though Miss Lestrange could not put a name to the actual *tune*; but then the world of pop music was unfamiliar territory to her. At least, though, music meant people, and inhabited regions; just for a minute or two, back there, although she would not have admitted it to anybody, Miss Lestrange had felt a stirring of panic at the vacuum of silence all around her.

On she went; crossed another star-shaped conjunction of alleys and, by the light of one high-up orange sodium tube, hung where the youth of Rumbury Town were unlikely to be able to break it by throwing bottles, saw that Hell Passage still continued, bisecting the angle between Sky Peals Lane and Whalebone Way.

"Curious names they have hereabouts; it must be a very old quarter. I shall look up the names on the map if—when I get home. *Did* I come this way?" Miss Lestrange asked herself; another surge of anxiety and alarm swept over her as she passed the closed premises of the Prong, Thong, and Trident Company—surely she would have noticed *that* on the way along?

But the music was much louder now; at least, soon, she must encounter somebody whom she could ask.

Then, without any question, she knew she was lost. For Hell Passage came to a stop—or rather, it opened into a little cul-de-sac of a yard out of which there was no exit. Miss Lestrange could see quite plainly that there was no other exit because the yard was illuminated by a fierce, flicking, variable light which came from bundles of tarry rags stuffed into roadmenders' tripods and burning vigorously. These were set against the walls. There were about a dozen people in the yard, and Miss Lestrange's first reaction was one of relief.

"It's one of those pop groups," she thought. "I've heard it's hard for them, when they're starting, to find places to practice; I suppose if you can't afford to hire a studio, somewhere like this, far off and out of earshot, would be a godsend."

Somehow the phrase *out of earshot,* though she had used it herself, made her feel uncomfortable; the beat and howl of the music, failing to fight its way out of the narrow court, was so tremendous, that it gave her a slight chill to think what a long way she must be from any residential streets, for people not to have complained about it.

She glanced again at the group; decided not to ask them her way, and turned to go quickly and quietly back. But she was too late; she found somebody standing behind her: an enormously large, tall man, dressed in red velvet trousers and jacket, with a frilled shirt.

"Hey, now, you're not thinking of *leaving,* are you—when you just got here?" His voice was a genial roar, easily heard even above the boom of the music, but there was a jeering note under its geniality. "Surely not going to run off without hearing us, were you? Look, boys and girls," he went on, his voice becoming, without the slightest difficulty, even louder, "Look who's here! It's Miss Lestrange, Miss January Lestrange, come to give us her critical opinion!"

A wild shout of derisive laughter went up from the group in the court.

"Three cheers for Miss January Lestrange—the hippest harpist in the whole of toe-tapping Rumbury Town!"

They cheered her, on and on, and the tall man led her with grinning mock civility to a seat on an upturned Snowcem tin. The players began tuning their instruments, some of which, trumpets and basses, seemed conventional enough, but others were contrivances that Miss Lestrange had never laid eyes on before—zinc washtubs with strings stretched across, large twisted shells, stringed instruments that looked more like weapons—crossbows, perhaps—than zithers, strange prehistoric-looking wooden pipes at least six or seven feet long—and surely that was an actual *fire* burning under the kettle-drum?

"January!" the large man boomed, standing just behind the shoulder of Miss Lestrange. "Now, *there's* a chilly sort of name to give a spirited lady like yourself—a downright cold, miserable kind of dreary name, isn't it, boys and girls? The worst month of the year!"

"It is not!" snapped Miss Lestrange—but she did wish he would not stand so close, for his presence just out of sight gave her the cold grue—for some odd reason the phrase *Get thee behind me, Satan,* slipped into her mind—"January means hope, it means looking forward, because the whole year lies ahead."

But her retort was drowned in the shout from the group of players—"*We'll* soon warm her up!"

"Happy lot, ain't they?" confided the voice at her back. "Nick's Nightflowers, we call ourselves—from the location, see?" He pointed up and, by the light of the flaring rags, Miss Lestrange could just read the sign on the wall: OLD NICK S COURT, E.I. "And I'm Old Nick, naturally—happy to have you with us tonight, Miss Lestrange."

She flicked a glance sideways, to see if it would be possible to slip away once they began playing, but to her dismay most of the group were now between her and the entrance, blocking the way; from their grins, it was plain that they knew what she had in mind. And she had never seen such a unattractive crew—"Really, she thought, "if they had *tails* they could hardly look less human."

Old Nick, with his red velvet and ruffles, was about the most normal in appearance and dress, but she cared for him least of all, and unobtrusively edged her Snowcem tin cornerways until at least she had the wall at her back.

"Ready, all? Cool it now—real cool," called Nick, at which there was a howl of laughter. "One, two, three-*stomp!*"

The music broke out again. If music it could be called. The sound seemed to push Miss Lestrange's blood backward along her arteries, to flog on her eardrums, to slam in her lungs, to seize hold of her heart and dash it from side to side.

"I shan't be able to endure it for more than a minute or two," she thought quite calmly. "It's devilish, that's what it is—really devilish."

Just at the point when she had decided she could stand it no longer, half a dozen more figures lounged forward from a shadow at the side of the court, and began to dance. Boys or girls? It was hard to say. They seemed bald, and extraordinarily *thin*—they had white, hollow faces, deepset eyes under bulging foreheads, meaningless grins. "White satin!" thought Miss Lestrange scornfully. "And ruffles! What an extraordinarily dated kind of costume—like the pierrot troupes when I was young."

But at closer view the satin seemed transparent gauze, or chiffon. "I've never *seen* anyone so thin—they are like something out of Belsen," thought Miss Lestrange. "That one must have had rickets when young—his legs are no more than bones. They must all have had rickets," she decided.

"D'you like it?" boomed the leader in her ear. It seemed amazing that he could still make his voice heard above the row, but he could.

"Frankly, no," said Miss Lestrange. "I never laid eyes on such a spiritless ensemble. They all dance as if they wanted dosing with Parrish's Food and codliver oil."

"Hear that, gang?" he bawled to the troupe. "Hear that? The lady doesn't care for your dancing; she thinks you're a lily-livered lot."

The dancers paused; they turned their bloodless faces towards Miss Lestrange. For a moment she quailed, as tiny lights seemed to burn in the deep eye-sockets, all fixed on her. But then the leader shouted,

"And what's more, I think so too! Do it again—and this time, put some guts into it, or it'll be prong, thong, and trident, all right!"

The players redoubled their pace and volume, the dancers broke into a faster shuffle. And the leader, still making himself heard above the maniac noise, shouted,

"Hope! Where are you? Come along out, you mangy old tomcat, you!" And, to the group, "*He'll* soon tickle you up!"

A dismal and terrified wailing issued from the dancers at these words.

"Hope's a little pet of mine," confided the leader to Miss Lestrange. "Makes all the difference when they're a bit sluggish; *you* ought to like him too."

She distrusted his tone, which seemed to promise some highly unpleasant surprise, and looked round sharply.

A kind of ripple parted the musicians and dancers; at first Miss Lestrange could not see what had caused this, but, even through the music, she thought she could hear cries of pain or terror; then a wave of dancers eddied away from her and a gold-brown animal bounded through, snatching with sabre-teeth at a bony thigh as it passed.

"That's Hope," said the leader with satisfaction. "*That's* my little tiger-kitten. Isn't he a beauty? Isn't he a ducky-diddums? I powder his fur with pepper and ginger before we start, to put him in a lively mood—and *then* doesn't he chase them about if they're a bit mopish!"

Hope certainly had a galvanizing effect upon the dancers; as he slunk and bounded among them, their leaps and gyrations had the frenzy of a tarantella; sometimes he turned and made a sudden snarling foray among the musicians, which produced a wild flurry of extra discords and double drumbeats.

"Here, puss, puss! Nice pussy, then! There's a lady here who'd like to stroke you."

Hope turned, and silently sprang in their direction. Miss Lestrange had her first good look at him. He was bigger than a leopard, a brownish-ginger colour all over, with a long, angrily switching tail; his fangs glistened white-gold in the fiery light, his eyes blazed like carbuncles; he came towards Miss Lestrange slowly, stalking, with head lowered.

And she put out her right hand, confidently running it over his shoulder-blades and along the curving, knobbed spine; its bristles undulated under the light pressure. "There, then!" she said absently. Hope turned, and rubbed his harsh ruff against her hand; elevated his chin to be scratched; finally sat down beside her and swung the long tail neatly into place over formidable talons.

Miss Lestrange thoughtfully pulled his ears; she had always liked cats.

She turned to the leader again.

"I still don't think much of your dancers. And, to be honest, your music seems to me nothing but a diabolical row!"

Silence followed her words. She felt the dark cavities in their faces trained on her, and forced herself not to shrink.

"However, thank you for playing to me. And now I must be going," she ended politely.

"Dear me." The leader's tone was thoughtful. "That fairly puts us in our place, don't it, boys and girls? You certainly are a free-spoken one, Miss January Lestrange. Come now—I'm sure a nice lady, a dyed-in-the-wool lady like you, wouldn't want to be too hard on the lads, and *really* upset them. Just before you go—if—you *do* go—tell me, don't you think that, in time, if they practice hard enough, they might amount to something?'

"I am absolutely not prepared to make such a statement," Miss Lestrange said firmly. "Your kind of music is quite outside my province. And I have never believed in flattery." A kind of rustle ran through the group; they moved closer.

"Our kind of music ain't her province," the leader said. "That's true. Tell you what, Miss Lestrange. *You* shall give *us* a tune. Let's have some of *your* kind of music—eh? That'd be a treat for us, wouldn't it, gang?"

They guffawed, crowding closer and closer; she bit her lip.

"Fetch over the harp!" bawled Nick. "No one in our ensemble actually pays it," he explained to Miss Lestrange. "But we like to have one along always—you never know when someone may turn up who's a harp fancier. Like you. No strings, I'm afraid, but we can fix that easy."

A warped, battered, peeling old harp was dumped down before her; it had no strings, but one of the dancers dragged up a coil of what looked like telephone cable and began rapidly stringing it to and fro across the frame.

"Now," said Nick, "you shall delight us, Miss Lestrange! And if you *do*, then maybe we'll see about allowing you to leave. Really, you know, we'd hate to part from you."

An expectant pause had fallen: an unpleasant, mocking, triumphant silence.

"I haven't the least intention of playing that ridiculous instrument," Miss Lestrange said coldly. "And now, I'm afraid you'll have to excuse me; my friend will be wondering where I've got to. Come, Hope."

She turned and walked briskly to the entrance of the court; there was no need to push her way, they parted before her. Hope trotted at her side.

Far off, down Hell Passage, could be heard a faint, clear whistle, coming her way.

But, once out in the alley, Miss Lestrange tottered, and nearly fell; she was obliged to put a hand against the wall to support herself. Seized with a deep chill and trembling, she was afraid to trust her unsteady legs, and had to wait until the boy David reached her, whistling and zig-zagging along on his rollerskates.

"Coo, Miss Lestrange, I knew you'd get lost; and you did, didn't you? Thought I'd better come back and see where you'd got to. You all right?" he said, sharply scrutinizing her face.

"Yes, thank you, David. I'm quite all right now. I just went a bit farther than I intended. I'm a little tired, that's all."

She glanced back into Old Nick's Court. It was empty: empty and silent. The flares had gone out.

"Well, come on then, Miss Lestrange, just you follow me and I'll take you back to the other lady's car. You can hold on to my anorak if you like," he suggested.

"That's all right, thank you, David, I can manage now."

So he skated slowly ahead and she walked after him, and a little way in the rear Hope followed, trotting silently in the shadows.

When they came within view of the car—it took a very short time, really—David said, "I'll say goodnight then, Miss Lestrange. See you Thursday."

"Good night, David, and thank you." Then she called after him: "Practise hard, now!"

"Okay, Miss Lestrange."

There was an ambulance drawn up behind the car.

"Wait there!" she said to Hope. He sat down in the shadows of the alley-mouth.

As Miss Lestrange crossed the road, the ambulance rolled off. Dr. Smith stood looking after it.

"Sorry to be such a time," she said. "That poor man—I'm afraid he's not going to make it."

"You mean—Tom Rampisham?"

"I shouldn't be surprised if he dies on the way in. Oh—excuse me a moment—I'll have to lock up his flat and give the key to the porter."

Without thinking about it, Miss Lestrange followed her ex-pupil. She walked into the untidy room that she had last entered—how long? thirty years ago?—and looked at the table, covered with scrawled sheets of paper.

"I don't know who ought to take charge of this," Dr. Smith said, frowning. "I suppose he has a next-of-kin somewhere. Well—I'll worry about that tomorrow. Come along—*you* must be starving and exhausted—let's go."

Miss Lestrange was looking at the top sheet, at the heading HOPE, which was printed in large capitals. Halfway down the page a sentence began.

"*It was on a clear, frosty November evening, not many years ago . . .*"

The words trailed off into a blob of ink.

Dr. Smith led the way out. "It's terribly late. We can still get a meal at the Chinese place, though," she was saying. "And afterwards I'll phone up Rumbury Central and find out how—and find out. I really am sorry to have kept you so long. I hope you weren't frozen and bored."

"No . . . No. I—I went for a walk."

Miss Lestrange followed the doctor along the echoing concrete passage. And as she went—"I do hope," she was thinking, "oh, I do *hope* that Hope will still be there."

# Humblepuppy

Our house was furnished mainly from auction sales. When you buy furniture that way you get a lot of extra things besides the particular piece that you were after, since the stuff is sold in lots: Lot 13, two Persian rugs, a set of golf-clubs, a sewing-machine, a walnut radio-cabinet, and a plinth.

It was in this way that I acquired a tin deedbox, which came with two coal-scuttles and a broom cupboard. The deedbox is solid metal, painted black, big as a medium-sized suitcase. When I first brought it home I put it in my study, planning to use it as a kind of filing cabinet for old typescripts. I had gone into the kitchen, and was busy arranging the brooms in their new home, when I heard a loud thumping coming from the direction of the studio.

I went back, thinking that a bird must have flown through the window; no bird, but the banging seemed to be inside the deedbox. I had already opened it as soon as it was in my possession, to see if there were any diamonds or bearer bonds worth thousands of pounds inside (there weren't), but I opened it again. The key was attached to the handle by a thin chain. There was nothing inside. I shut it. The banging started again. I opened it.

Still nothing inside.

Well, this was broad daylight, two o'clock on a Thursday afternoon, people going past in the road outside and a radio schools programme chatting away to itself in the next room. It was not a ghostly kind of time, so I put my hand into the empty box and moved it about.

Something shrank away from my hand. I heard a faint, scared whimper. It could almost have been my own, but wasn't. Knowing that someone—something?—else was afraid too put heart into me. Exploring carefully and gently around the interior of the box I felt the contour of a small, bony, warm, trembling body with big awkward feet, and silky dangling ears, and a cold nose that, when I found it, nudged for a moment anxiously but trustingly into the palm of my hand. So I knelt down, put the other hand into the box as well, cupped them under a thin little ribby chest, and lifted out Humblepuppy.

He was quite light.

I couldn't see him, but I could hear his faint inquiring whimper, and I could hear his toenails scratch on the floorboards.

Just at that moment the cat, Taffy, came in.

Taffy has a lot of character. Every cat has a lot of character, but Taffy has more than most, all of it inconvenient. For instance, although he is very sociable, and longs for company, he just despises company in the form of dogs. The mere sound of a dog barking two streets away is enough to make his fur stand up like a porcupine's quills and his tail swell like a mushroom cloud.

Which it did the instant he saw Humblepuppy.

Now here is the interesting thing. I could feel and hear Humblepuppy, but couldn't see him; Taffy apparently, could see and smell him, but couldn't feel him. We soon discovered this. For Taffy, sinking into a low, gladiator's crouch, letting out all the time a fearsome throaty wauling like a bagpipe revving up its drone, inched his way along to where Humblepuppy huddled trembling by my left foot, and then dealt him what ought to have been a swinging right-handed clip on the ear. "Get out of my house, you filthy canine scum!" was what he was plainly intending to convey.

But the swipe failed to connect; instead it landed on my shin. I've never seen a cat so astonished. It was like watching a kitten meet itself for the first time in a looking-glass. Taffy ran round to the back of where Humblepuppy was sitting; felt; smelt; poked gingerly with a paw; leapt back nervously; crept forward again. All the time Humblepuppy just sat, trembling a little, giving out this faint beseeching sound that meant: "I'm only a poor little mongrel without a smidgeon of harm in me. *Please* don't do anything nasty! I don't even know how I came here."

It certainly was a puzzle how he had come. I rang the auctioneers (after shutting Taffy *out* and Humblepuppy *in* to the study with a bowl of water and a handful of Boniebisk, Taffy's favorite breakfast food).

The auctioneers told me that Lot 12, Deedbox, coal-scuttles and broom cupboard, had come from the Riverland Rectory, where Mr. Smythe, the old rector, had lately died aged ninety. Had he ever possessed a dog, or a puppy? They couldn't say; they had merely received instructions from a firm of lawyers to sell the furniture.

I never did discover how poor little Humblepuppy's ghost got into the deedbox. Maybe he was shut in by mistake, long ago, and suffocated; maybe some callous Victorian gardener dropped him, box and all, into a river, and the box was later found and fished out.

Anyway, and whatever had happened in the past, now that Humblepuppy had come out of his box, he was very pleased with the turn his affairs had taken, ready to be grateful and affectionate. As I sat typing I'd often hear a patter-patter, and feel his small chin fit itself comfortably over my foot, ears dangling. Goodness knew what kind of a mixture he was; something between a spaniel and a terrier, I'd guess. In the evening, watching television or sitting by the fire, one would suddenly find his warm weight leaning against one's leg. (He didn't put on a lot of weight while he was with us, but his bony little ribs filled out a bit.)

For the first few weeks we had a lot of trouble with Taffy, who was very surly over the whole business and blamed me bitterly for not getting rid of this low-class intruder. But Humblepuppy was extremely placating, got back in his deedbox whenever the atmosphere became too volcanic, and did his best not to be a nuisance.

By and by Taffy thawed. As I've said, he is really a very sociable cat. Although quite old, seventy cat years, he dearly likes cheerful company and generally has some young cat friend who comes to play with him, either in the house or the garden. In the last few years we've had Whisky, the black-and-white pub cat, who used to sit washing the smell of fish-and-chips off his fur under the dripping tap in our kitchen sink; Tetanus, the hairdresser's thick-set black, who took a fancy to sleep on top of our china-cupboard every night all one winter, and used to startle me very much by jumping down heavily on to my shoulder as I made the breakfast coffee; Sweet Charity, a little grey Persian who came to a sad end under the wheels of a police-car; Charity's grey-and-white stripey cousin Fred, whose owners presently moved from next door to another part of town.

It was soon after Fred's departure that Humblepuppy arrived, and from my point of view he couldn't have been more welcome. Taffy missed Fred badly, and expected *me* to play with him instead; it was very sad to see this large elderly tabby rushing hopefully up and down the stairs after breakfast, or hiding behind the armchair and jumping out on to nobody; or howling, howling, howling at me until I escorted him out into the garden, where he'd rush to the lavender-bush which had been the traditional hiding-place of Whisky, Tetanus, Charity, and Fred in succession. Cats have their habits and histories, just the same as humans.

So sometimes, on a working morning, I'd be at my wits' end, almost on the point of going across the town to our ex-neighbours, ringing their bell, and saying, "Please can Fred come and play?" Specially on a rainy, uninviting day when Taffy was pacing gloomily about the house with drooping head and switching tail, grumbling about the weather and the lack of company, and blaming me for both.

Humblepuppy's arrival changed all that.

At first Taffy considered it necessary to police him, and that kept him fully occupied for hours. He'd sit on guard by the deedbox till Humblepuppy woke up in the morning, and then he'd follow officiously all over the house, wherever the visitor went. Humblepuppy was slow and cautious in his explorations, but by degrees he picked up courage and found his way into every corner. He never once made a puddle; he learned to use Taffy's cat-flap and go out into the garden, though he was always more timid outside and would scamper for home at any loud noise. Planes and cars terrified him, he never became used to them; which made me still more certain that he had been in that deedbox for a long, long time, since before such things were invented.

Presently he learned, or Taffy taught him, to hide in the lavender-bush like Whisky, Charity, Tetanus, and Fred; and the two of them used to play their own ghostly version of touch-last for hours on end while I got on with my typing.

When visitors came, Humblepuppy always retired to his deedbox; he was decidedly scared of strangers; which made his behavior with Mr. Manningham, the new rector of Riverland, all the more surprising.

I was dying to learn anything I could of the old rectory's history, so I'd invited Mr. Manningham to tea.

He was a thin, gentle, quiet man, who had done missionary work in the Far East and fell ill and had to come back to England. He seemed a little sad and lonely; said he still missed his Far East friends and work. I liked him. He told me that for a large part of the nineteenth century the Riverland living had belonged to a parson called Swannett, the Reverend Timothy Swannett, who lived to a great age and had ten children.

"He was a great-uncle of mine, as a matter of fact. But why do you want to know all this?" Mr. Manningham asked. His long thin arm hung over the side of his chair; absently he moved his hand sideways and remarked, "I didn't notice that you had a puppy." Then he looked down and said, "Oh!"

"He's never come out for a stranger before," I said.

Taffy, who maintains a civil reserve with visitors, sat motionless on the nightstore heater, eyes slitted, sphinxlike.

Humblepuppy climbed invisibly on to Mr. Manningham's lap.

We agreed that the new rector probably carried a familiar smell of his rectory with him; or possibly he reminded Humblepuppy of his great-uncle, the Rev. Swannett.

Anyway, after that, Humblepuppy always came scampering joyfully out if Mr. Manningham had dropped in to tea, so of course I thought of the rector when summer holiday time came round.

During the summer holidays we lend our house and cat to a lady publisher and her mother who are devoted to cats and think it is a privilege to look after Taffy and spoil him. He is always amazingly overweight when we get back. But the old lady has an allergy to dogs, and is frightened of them too; it was plainly out of the question that she should be expected to share her summer holiday with the ghost of a puppy.

So I asked Mr. Manningham if he'd be prepared to take Humblepuppy as a boarder, since it didn't seem a case for the usual kind of boarding-kennels; he said he'd be delighted.

I drove Humblepuppy out to Riverland in his deedbox; he was rather miserable on the drive, but luckily it is not far. Mr. Manningham came out into the garden to meet us. We put the box down on the lawn and opened it.

I've never heard a puppy so wildly excited. Often I'd been sorry that I couldn't see Humblepuppy, but I was never sorrier than on that afternoon, as we heard him rushing from tree to familiar tree, barking joyously, dashing through the orchard grass—you could see it divide as he whizzed along—coming back to bounce up against us, all damp and earthy and smelling of leaves.

"He's going to be happy with you, all right," I said, and Mr. Manningham's grey, lined face crinkled into its thoughtful smile as he said, "It's the place more than me, I think."

Well, it was both of them, really.

After the holiday, I went to collect Humblepuppy, leaving Taffy haughty and standoffish, sniffing our cases. It always takes him a long time to forgive us for going away.

Mr. Manningham had a bit of a cold and was sitting by the fire in his study, wrapped in a shetland rug. Humblepuppy was on his knee. I could hear the little dog's tail thump against the arm of the chair when I walked in, but he didn't get down to greet me. He stayed in Mr. Manningham's lap.

"So you've come to take back my boarder," Mr. Manningham said.

There was nothing in the least strained about his voice or smile but—I just hadn't the heart to take back Humblepuppy. I put my hand down, found his soft wrinkly forehead, rumpled it a bit, and said,

"Well—I was sort of wondering: our old spoilt cat seems to have got used to being on his own again; I was wondering whether—by any chance—you'd feel like keeping him?"

Mr. Manningham's face lit up. He didn't speak for a minute; then he put a gentle hand down to find the small head, and rubbed a finger along Humblepuppy's chin.

"Well," he said. He cleared his throat. "Of course, if you're *quite* sure—"

"Quite sure." My throat needed clearing too.

"I hope you won't catch my cold," Mr. Manningham said. I shook my head and said, "I'll drop in to see if you're better in a day or two," and went off and left them together.

Poor Taffy was pretty glum over the loss of his playmate for several weeks; we had two hours' purgatory every morning after breakfast while he hunted for Humblepuppy high and low. But gradually the memory faded and, thank goodness, now he has found a new friend, Little Grey Furry, a nephew, cousin, or other relative of Charity and Fred. Little Grey Furry has learned to play hide-and-seek in the lavender-bush, and to use our cat-flap, and clean up whatever's in Taffy's food bowl, so all is well in that department.

But I still miss Humblepuppy. I miss his cold nose exploring the palm of my hand, as I sit thinking, in the middle of a page, and his warm weight leaning against my knee as he watches the commercials. And the scritch-scratch of his toenails on the dining-room floor and the flump, flump, as he comes downstairs, and the small hollow in a cushion as he settles down with a sigh.

Oh well. I'll get over it, just as Taffy has. But I was wondering about putting an ad into *Our Dogs* or *Pets' Monthly*: Wanted, ghost of a mongrel puppy. Warm, welcome, loving home. Any reasonable price paid.

It might be worth a try.

# Listening

He had been walking up Fifth Avenue for about ten minutes when the cat fell. He had been walking along, minding his own business, not looking about him—though it was a beautiful day, the first of spring, with a warm, keen wind ruffling the vapor trails in the sky and dislodging the pigeons from cornices where they sat sunning. He was preoccupied, to tell the truth, worrying over what he could ever find to say about Mrs. Schaber's lesson, which he was on his way to observe.

Listening, she taught. "What in God's name is *listening?*" he had asked Mark Calvert, who worked in the same department. "Oh, it's a form of musical appreciation—little Schaber's a bit of a nut, but she's quite a fine musician, too, in her way." He had not even met her, so far as he was aware—she was just another of the two-hundred-odd faceless names on the college faculty list. So now he had to give up his free day, this beautiful mild, melting, burgeoning day, to go and invigilate her class and decide whether or not she was able to teach kids to listen. Is there a craft about listening—an art that has to be learned?—he wondered. Don't we begin listening from the very moment we are born?

At that moment the cat hit. He was approaching the Twenty-eighth Street intersection when he heard the horribly distinctive sound—a loud, solid smack, accompanied by a faint, sharp cry; indeed he had *seen* it also, he must have seen about the last six inches of its fall, as he glanced up from his moody stride, and so was able to verify that cats do *not* always land on their feet—this poor beast, which must have come from about twenty floors up, landed flat on its side and then lay twitching. Its eyes were open but it must, please heaven, be on the point of death—ought he to *do* something about it? What *could* one do?

In no time a small crowd had collected.

"It fell from *way* up there," a woman kept saying hysterically. "I saw the whole thing—I was just crossing the street—"

"Do you think we should take it to a vet?" someone suggested.

"Oh, what's the use? The poor thing's dying anyway."

"Tell the super in the block? That looks like a valuable cat—"

"Lucky it didn't land on somebody—could probably kill a person—"

As they discussed it, the cat twitched again. Its eyes closed definitively.

"Oh, its poor owner. She'll wonder what *happened* to it—"

"Shouldn't have left her window open if you ask me—"

He left them and walked on. He was going to be late if he didn't hurry. It *had* looked like a valuable cat. Its fur was a rich mixture of browns and creams in which dark chocolate predominated, its eyes a wild fanatic blue. It seemed to belong to the luxury class, along with costly monogrammed luggage, gold accessories and jeweled watches: objects of conspicuous expenditure. And yet, poor thing, it had been alive, had its own nature—that faint piteous cry still hung in his ears, an expostulation against undeserved agony.

He *had* seen Mrs. Schaber before, it turned out; he recognized her as soon as he entered the classroom. She was the odd little woman whom he had passed one day in the main lobby while she was deep in conversation with a deaf and dumb student. He had been much struck by her at the time, two or three months back. She was quite short, only about five foot, with her dark hair coiled in a bun low on her neck. She wore jeans, a flannel shirt, a sweater tied by the arms around her waist, espadrilles; she looked like a student. But her face was that of a woman in her mid-forties—somewhat lined, especially around the mouth. Her eyes were large, brownish green, almond shaped, set wide apart; and her face was long and oval, with a particularly long jaw and upper lip, and a lower lip that extended, sometimes above the upper one, giving her a look of comical pugnacity. But what had attracted his attention on that occasion was the extreme vivacity of her face—dozens of expressions chased each other across it: sympathetic, hilarious, grave, intent, sorrowful, ecstatic, ferocious—while her hands, meanwhile, twinkled away with unbelievable speed, flicking their soundless deaf-and-dumb-language to the student she was addressing.

"Is *she* deaf and dumb too?" he had asked Charlie Whitney, with whom he had been walking on that occasion.

"Schaber? Lord, no! Talk the hind leg off a mule!"

She was doing so now, addressing her students in a flood of loquacity. But she broke off to greet him with a rather constricted smile.

"Oh—Professor Middlemass—good morning! Would you like to sit here? Or would you rather walk about? Please do just what you want—make yourself at home! I was—I was beginning to explain to the students that this morning I am going to play them tapes recorded on my trip to Europe and Africa last year. I shall analyze the background of each tape before I play it. Then, later in the lesson, I shall demonstrate the relation of the sounds they have heard to musical patterns and structures and explain how this in its turn demonstrates the relevance of music to language."

Nodding vaguely—she had rattled this out so fast that he hardly took in her meaning—he settled down to listen, observing that eighteen out of her nineteen students were present, and that they were watching her with expressions that ranged from indulgent amusement through skepticism and mild boredom to absorbed devotion. Only one boy looked wholly bored: he was stretched back in his seat with his blond hair stuck out in front, his head bowed forward. He appeared to be studying his shoelaces through the strands of his hair.

The tapes, when Mrs. Schaber began to play them, were a bit of a surprise: they were so extremely quiet. She had been allotted a soundproof music studio for her demonstration, and this was just as well, for some of the sounds were just barely audible. "Now, this is the Camargue: you can hear grasses rustling and, very far off, the noise of the sea. And after five minutes you will notice a faint drumming in the distance. That is the sound of hoofs: the wild horses. They never come very close; you will have to listen carefully.

"Now this recording was taken in Denmark, in the bog country: you can hear reeds and dry rushes; the sound is not dissimilar to the tape of the Camargue that I played you earlier, but this one was taken inland; there was a different quality to the air; it was less resonant. Also, after about three minutes of tape, you will hear a stork shifting about in its nest; I was standing close to a cottage that had a stork's nest on its roof."

Mrs. Schaber went on to describe in some detail what materials storks used in building their nests and then played her tape. As she listened to it herself, her face wore a recollecting, tranquil, amused expression.

Gradually, while the lesson proceeded, Middlemass observed how the students were becoming polarized by her exposition. The ones who had looked indulgent or bored at the start were now gazing drearily at the ceiling, picking their noses or their teeth, chewing gum, manifesting exasperation and tedium; others were watching Mrs. Schaber with fanatical attention. The blond boy still stared at his feet.

Toward the end of her batch of tapes came some that had been recorded in the Congo rain forest. Middlemass had always been fascinated by the thought of the jungle, ever since reading Duguid's *Green Hell;* he had not the least intention of ever walking into a jungle himself, but he occasionally liked to imagine doing so. Now he listened with careful interest to the rich silences, the ticking, cheeping, chirring, shrilling, buzzing, scraping sibilances that Mrs. Schaber had collected; for the first time he began to feel some groping acceptance of what she was proffering. He noticed, also, that the blond boy had taken his hands out of his pockets and had his head cocked in an attitude of acute attention.

During the second half of the lesson, Mrs. Schaber proceeded to play short snatches of music and demonstrate their resemblance to vocal patterns and to some of the natural sounds that she had presented earlier. This, Middlemass thought, was really interesting; the whole lesson began to cohere for him, and he changed his mind about what he would say in his report, which, half-phrased in his head already, had not been particularly enthusiastic. "Too divorced from reality—students did not seem very engaged—Mrs. Schaber has a gift, but it seems devoted to inessentials—" Now he resolved to say something more favorable.

At this point there came an interruption to the lesson. A secretary tapped at the door to say that Mrs. Schaber was wanted in the main office. "The police have just called up from your home, Mrs. Schaber; I'm afraid your apartment has been broken into, and they want you to go home and say what has been taken."

"Oh my god!" The poor little woman looked utterly stricken; her expressive face changed to a Greek mask of tragedy, mouth wide open, eyes dilated.

"Shall I go with you to the office?" Middlemass offered, touched by compassion because he had been filled with rather disparaging thoughts about her during the first half of her lesson and because she did seem as if she had sustained a mortal blow. The blond boy had already risen to his feet, moved compactly forward, and taken her arm. But Middlemass accompanied them anyway; he felt the need somehow to demonstrate his friendly feeling and sympathy.

While Mrs. Schaber talked on the phone in the secretary's room, it became plain that matters were even worse than she had feared.

"Oh no, not all my *tapes?*" she cried out. "What could they want those for? Smashed—wrecked—oh, *no!*"—pressing her clenched fist against her thin chest as if she were trying, forcibly, to push her anguished, expanded heart back into position. Wordlessly, the secretary went to fetch her a cup of coffee. The blond boy stood silent with his eyes fixed on her face. When she had laid the receiver back in its rest and was staring across the room, quite dazed, with fixed, sightless eyes, Middlemass asked her gently:

"Is it very bad?"

"They have taken a whole *lot* of stuff," she muttered, "and all the rest they have destroyed—smashed up. Everything—"

Inattentively, she gulped at the coffee the secretary had handed her.

"I keep wondering whether I forgot to lock the door—when I went out this morning—the super found it open, that was why he phoned the police—I was so nervous—in a hurry—*did* I forget to lock it?"

"Oh, no!" Middlemass exclaimed, horrified. "You don't mean to say that you were nervous because of *me*—because your lesson was going to be observed—that on account of *that* you might have forgotten to lock up—?"

"Of *course* I was nervous!" she said. "Naturally I was nervous! Excuse me—they want me right away—I must go back to the classroom and collect my things—"

"I am most sorry this has happened," he said, following her back along the corridor, wondering if his words were getting through to her at all. "I had been enjoying your lesson so much—it seemed to me one of the most interesting and original discourses that I have ever listened to—"

In his own ears, his voice sounded horribly forced and insincere. He wondered if *that* was one of the things he had learned from her lesson. How to detect the falsity in human utterance? And yet what he had said was the truth—*meant* to be the truth, he told himself. He noticed the blond boy's eyes on him, assessing, skeptical.

"I'm going to give you a very good report," he told poor Mrs. Schaber, as she began collecting her gear in the classroom. "If that helps to cheer you up at all—"

"Well—thank you—of course it does," she answered distractedly, shoveling tapes into a big worn woolen bag, filled already with a mass of untidy odds and ends. It was evident that she heard him only with a single thread of attention; the rest of her mind was elsewhere. "It's like having lost a whole continent, a whole *world*," she murmured. "Years and years of work."

"Well, you've still got the Congo forest, because you had it here," the blond boy reminded her, and at that she suddenly gave him her flashing urchin grin, thrusting forward the long lower jaw and lower lip, nodding her head up and down.

"That's true! One forest left—perhaps it will seed itself. But there's not all that amount of *time* left."

When Mrs. Schaber had gone, Middlemass walked out of the college. He felt too disturbed to want to eat in the cafeteria and talk to colleagues; he wanted a long period of time and solitude to settle his feelings. Poor little woman, so stricken and bereft—he thought of her returning to her wrecked apartment, like a bird to its robbed nest. And the worst of it was the anxiety as to whether it had been her own carelessness that had invited the thieves; he knew how such an idea would haunt *him*, if he had been the victim. He imagined her trying and trying again to resurrect the process of her departure in the morning, to discover whether she had in fact let the door unlocked—had she taken the key out of her purse, had she put it back—as if it could make any real difference to the disaster itself.

Walking along Fifty-seventh Street, Middlemass tried to calm his mind by wandering into a number of art galleries, at random, looking first at a show of nineteenth-century portrait photographs, then at some watercolor landscapes, then some classic Matisses, magically soothing, then some semiabstract sculpture, recognizable articles broken into fragments and reunited into strange disjointed forms—then a show of cartoons—a collection of Japanese prints—one of book illustrations from the 'nineties. He was moving westwards all the time; he thought he would presently buy a sandwich and eat it in the park. The day was still idyllically fine and warm.

In a small room adjoining the exhibition of book illustrations there was a show by a minor artist whose name was unknown to him; the title of the exhibition was simply "Collages." Through the open door he caught a glimpse of quiet, restful black and white forms. He stepped inside, meaning to give the show a quick two minutes and then go in search of his sandwich.

The collages, contained inside plain wood frames, were made up from all kinds of materials—fabrics, press cuttings, bits of wood, of metal, of oilcloth, tar cloth, wire netting, string, bent wire, gauze, clay, foam rubber—all dyed or stained either black or white. They had been assembled, molded, pressed, organized into shapes that were vaguely human, vaguely monstrous in outline: straining bodies were suggested, extended limbs, odd movements of exuberant dance, of cowering terror, of sad, limp resignation. The titles, on labels beside the frames, were all single words: Waiting; Fearing; Hoping; Expecting; Exulting.

Despite a general feeling of distaste for what he considered rather pretentious, facile stuff, without the merit of true creativity, Middlemass found himself oddly struck by these forms—they seemed to touch on some nerve in him that was not normally affected but had, perhaps, been bruised already that day. He walked slowly around the room, considering the occupant of each frame in turn—as if they had been creatures in cages, he told himself.

Returning, finally, toward the door, he looked at the last frame, which had the title "Begging." A crippled, bandaged creature crouched, huddled, in the middle of the frame; its head, composed of wire netting, seemed to be swathed in wrappings and gave the impression of blind, listening urgency. One of its limbs, a bent pipe wrapped in tarred rag, extended, pleadingly, right out of the frame, and was flattened at the extremity into the approximate form of a hand; to this hand a small white square of paper in the shape of a visiting card had been fastened by staples.

Moving closer, to discover whether the tiny characters on the card were real letters, real words, he received a shock. Neatly printed across the white, in black India ink, he read his own name: JOHN MIDDLEMASS, M.D.

He gasped and then laughed. Turning to the girl at the desk, in an attempt to cover the extraordinary agitation he felt at this strange, this outrageous portent, he said:

"What an amazing thing! The name—this name here, in the picture—on the card—it's *my* name, John Middlemass!—Only I'm not a doctor," he added.

"Is that so?" The girl—thin, dark, long-haired, wan—looked at him with a wholly uninterested, lackluster indifference which immediately seemed to reduce the coincidence to minimal proportions. After all, her look suggested, *somebody* in the whole of New York has to have that name—what's so peculiar about *your* having it? Why are you making such a to do? "Perhaps the artist got it out of the phone book," she suggested, yawning. "But you're not a doctor, you say?" she added kindly, as if to humor him.

"No, no, I'm a teacher—" Feeling foolish, as if he had made a fuss about nothing at all, he left the gallery and went to buy his sandwich. Bacon, lettuce, and tomato. Then he walked up Madison Avenue, feeling the sun warm on his shoulder blades, and turned left, toward the park. He could hear sparrows chirping and one shrill bird cry, far in the distance, that took him back in memory to a spring holiday on Cape Cod.

The day was so warm that all the park benches were filled. Finally, unable to find a seat on one, he settled on a slope of warm rock near the pond, looking south toward the Plaza Hotel. The water in the pond was low, and patches of reeds stood out on small mud islands; as he ate his sandwich, he noticed how neatly gulls landed on the surface of the water to swim and drink and preen themselves and how clumsily pigeons, unable to land on the water, thumped down on an island of rock and then waddled to the edge in order to drink. Planes droned overhead, and helicopters stuttered; an ambulance siren wailed and gibbered not far off on its way across town.

Presently Middlemass began to be aware of the couple who sat on the end of the bench nearest him, a girl and a boy, intent on their conversation with each other. It was not so much the human pair he noticed as their animals. The boy had a dog, which he allowed to roam loose: a kind of black mongrel with traces of retriever. A loose-jointed, floppy, active dog that went on forays, dashing off splashily round the verge of the pond, and returned every now and then, damp, smiling, panting, to lavish affection on its master.

But the girl had a cat; making the second cat I've seen today, thought Middlemass with a sudden shiver, remembering his earlier horrible experience. What a strange day it had been! But that was how life piled up in the city, one event splashing on top of another like lava from a volcanic eruption, hardly time to assimilate an experience before the next one came tumbling about you.

This cat, though, the cat in the park, was a very different creature from that poor, dead, expensive, elegant piece of fur that had no doubt long since been shoveled off the sidewalk and into some garbage can. This cat in the park was half white, half ginger in color. It was an old cat; its fur was patchy, molting, dusty, its ears were tattered, its nose was scarred, its tail looked moth-eaten. The girl had it on a leash, but she was paying no attention to it, and while she talked to her boyfriend the cat sulked, squatting behind the bench on which the pair sat, with its head thrust forward, as if it found the whole park, the dusty ground, the beaten-up grass, the muddy pond, the dingy sparrows, hopelessly distasteful, as if it were fed up with the world and its own ancient disheveled body.

Every now and then the black dog, returning from one of its excursions, would suddenly, with a kind of delighted surprise, rediscover the sulky cat and would then roll it over and over, tousling and biting it, rubbing its fur in the dust. The cat retaliated with what seemed a kind of resigned rage, spitting and kicking, tail bushed out, ears flattened.

"*Don't* do that, Buster," the boy would call absently, and the girl would say, "Oh, it's all right, never mind, Ginger quite enjoys it really," a statement which Middlemass, watching, considered to be quite patently untrue; it seemed to him that the cat disliked the dog's teasing roughness to the whole of its capacity for feeling.

Presently the couple rose to walk away. The dog instantly darted off ahead, delighted to be on the move again; but the cat, as if obstinately determined not to cooperate in any way during this disagreeable outing, now refused to budge. Before, it had sat sulkily ignoring its surroundings; now it wished to delay and sniff round the legs of the bench. The girl, impatient to be gone, jerked crossly at its lead, and, when it still would not follow, dragged it up bodily by the leash so that it hung in its collar, choking and scowling.

"*Don't* do that to the cat," Middlemass wanted to call out. "Pick it up properly!" But rage choked him, quite as much as its collar was choking the cat. When the girl put it down it did slowly begin to follow, trotting a few steps, then stopping to sniff things at the side of the path; its pace was not nearly fast enough to satisfy its mistress, who several times either dragged it along bodily, sliding on its feet, or again hoisted it up on the end of the leash. Middlemass felt an intense relief when the couple had passed out of view. He hated that girl; he really loathed her—But the cat was an old one, he told himself; it must have become used to such treatment years ago—No, it was no use; how *could* the horrible girl be so insensitive to the feelings of the creature she lived with?

His hands were clenched so tightly that the knuckles, when he finally relaxed them, felt swollen and quite painful. He looked down at his hands, thinking ruefully, not so elastic as they used to be. I am growing old. I should have interfered. Why didn't I? Because if I had, the girl would only have thought that I was a meddlesome old busybody. "Mind your own business, Mister," she would have said. "This cat belongs to me and I can do what I like with it."

Interfering gets you nowhere. And where does noninterfering get you?

The day had clouded and cooled. He walked over to Fifth Avenue to catch a bus home, thinking about the various disagreeable tasks that awaited him: tax forms to be filled out, bills to be paid, household articles to be repaired, business letters to be written. However inconspicuously we endeavor to conduct our lives, creeping along, keeping our heads well down out of the line of fire, still in the end we fall prey to circumstances, he thought, and I suppose the final knockout is not one single blow, so much as a whole series of minor assaults, to which, in the end, we wearily succumb.

I'd just as soon be nibbled to death by ducks, he remembered somebody saying; where in the world could that extraordinary phrase have come from?

His bus drew to a stop, and he climbed on to it and walked along the aisle, hoping for a seat in the back row, so that he need not travel sitting sideways, which he disliked. My life, he thought, is assembled out of an endless procession of unimportant choices.

The back row was all occupied, so he took the last of the side seats, in hopes that presently somebody might get off, and then he could switch seats. The bus had a long way to go, all down Fifth Avenue. As it slowly jerked and clanked through the heavy afternoon traffic, his mind went back to Mrs. Schaber; poor woman, she would be at home now, examining her wrecked possessions, listening to the callous comments of the police, who,s as Middlemass knew from experience, never offered the slightest hope of getting back any of the lost property. They were not interested in that; the only thing that concerned them at all was the possibility of identifying the thieves.

"It's like losing a whole *world*," she had moaned.

But at least, thought Middlemass, she had a world to lose.

At Twenty-eighth Street he suddenly thought of the cat—the first cat. It must have happened just about here. You'd never guess it now. People were darting to and fro on the pavement at that point, with their usual manic speed. The patch of blood would have been sanded over and swept away. So we come; so we go. What had made him think of the cat? Before that his mind had been on Mrs. Schaber and her loss.

Then he heard the sound again: a faint, querulous grumbling mew; the sigh of meow let out by a cat who is shut up, bored, exasperated, wishing to remind its owner of the tedium of its plight: a kvetch in cat language.

For a moment Middlemass wondered if perhaps he might be going mad; haunted by the ghost of a cat; of two cats. But then, turning his head slightly, he saw the girl close beside him on his right, sitting at the window end of the row of back seats, had a covered basket on her lap. And as the quiet, complaining conversational mew came again, she bent her head close over the basket, opened the lid a crack, and murmured to the occupant: "Hush. Hush! We'll be home very soon."

Looking up she met the eyes of Middlemass. He smiled at her—she was a small, thin, dark girl, not unlike the one at the desk in the gallery. And, like the girl in the gallery, she did not return his smile, just gave him a steady, thoughtful look, as if it would take much more than a smile to make her trust him, or allow him to impinge on any of her concerns.

Rebuffed, he turned his head away and rose to his feet; the bus had reached his stop, anyway.

Returned home, he sat down at his desk, impatiently turning his back on the untidiness which, hurrying out into the sunny morning, he had promised himself that he would later set to rights.

He pulled an official college report form toward him, and, in the blank for Instructor's Name, printed MRS. MARCIA SCHRABER. In the blank for Subject, he wrote LISTENING. In the blank for Observer, he wrote his own name, Prof. John Middlemass, and the date. Then, in the section headed "Comments" he began to write:

"Mrs. Schraber has something very important to teach her students, but I am not sure what it is. . . ."

There he stopped, holding the pen, staring at the blank form and his own name printed across the Observer space, while his mind's eye went back to fix, again, on that melancholy, huddled, crippled figure, gagged, blindfold, beseeching, mutely extending his own name out of the wooden frame.

# Lob's Girl

Some people choose their dogs, and some dogs choose their people. The Pengelly family had no say in the choosing of Lob; he came to them in the second way, and very decisively.

It began on the beach, the summer when Sandy was five, Don, her older brother, twelve, and the twins were three. Sandy was really Alexandra, because her grandmother had a beautiful picture of a queen in a diamond tiara and high collar of pearls. It hung by Granny Pearce's kitchen sink and was as familiar as the doormat. When Sandy was born everyone agreed that she was the living spit of the picture, and so she was called Alexandra and Sandy for short.

On this summer day she was lying peacefully reading a comic and not keeping an eye on the twins, who didn't need it because they were occupied in seeing which of them could wrap the most seaweed around the other one's legs. Father—Bert Pengelley—and Don were up on the Hard painting the bottom boards of the boat in which Father went fishing for pilchards. And Mother—Jean Pengelly—was getting ahead with making the Christmas puddings because she never felt easy in her mind if they weren't made and safely put away by the end of August. As usual, each member of the family was happily getting on with his or her own affairs. Little did they guess how soon this state of affairs would be changed by the large new member who was going to erupt into their midst.

Sandy rolled onto her back to make sure that the twins were not climbing on slippery rocks or getting cut off by the tide. At the same moment a large body struck her forcibly in the midriff and she was covered by flying sand. Instinctively she shut her eyes and felt the sand being wiped off her face by something that seemed like a warm, rough, damp flannel. Its owner was a large and bouncy young Alsatian, or German shepherd, with topaz eyes, black-tipped prick ears, a thick, soft coat, and a bushy black-tipped tail.

"*Lob!*" shouted a man further up the beach. "Lob, come here!"

But Lob, as if trying to atone for the surprise he had given her, went on licking the sand off Sandy's face, wagging his tail so hard all the while that he kept knocking up more clouds of sand. His owner, a gray-haired man with a limp, walked over as quickly as he could and seized him by the collar.

"I hope he didn't give you a fright?" the man said to Sandy. "He meant it in play—he's only young."

"Oh, no, I think he's *beautiful*," said Sandy truly. She picked up a bit of driftwood and threw it. Lob, whisking easily out of his master's grip, was after it like a sand-colored bullet. He came back with the stick, beaming, and gave it to Sandy. At the same time he gave himself, though no one else was aware of this at the time. But with Sandy, too, it was love at first sight, and when, after a lot more stick-throwing, she and the twins joined Father and Don to go home for tea, they cast many a backward glance at Lob being led firmly away by his master.

"I wish we could play with him every day," Tess sighed.

"Why can't we?" said Tim.

Sandy explained, "Because Mr. Dodsworth, who owns him, is from Liverpool, and he is only staying at the Fisherman's Arms till Saturday."

"Is Liverpool a long way off?"

"Right at the other end of England from Cornwall, I'm afraid."

It was a Cornish fishing village where the Pengelly family lived, with rocks and cliffs and a strip of beach and a little round harbor, and palm trees growing in the gardens of the little whitewashed stone houses. The village was approached by a narrow, steep, twisting hill-road, and guarded by a notice that said LOW GEAR FOR 1 ½ MILES, DANGEROUS TO CYCLISTS.

The Pengelly children went home to scones with Cornish cream and jam, thinking they had seen the last of Lob. But they were much mistaken. The whole family was playing cards by the fire in the front room after supper when there was a loud thump and a crash of china in the kitchen.

"My Christmas puddings!" exclaimed Jean, and ran out.

"Did you put TNT in them, then?" her husband said.

But it was Lob, who, finding the front door shut, had gone around to the back and bounced in through the open kitchen window, where the puddings were cooling on the sill. Luckily only the smallest was knocked down and broken.

Lob stood on his hind legs and plastered Sandy's face with licks. Then he did the same for the twins, who shrieked with joy.

"Where does this friend of yours come from?" inquired Mr. Pengelly.

"He's staying at the Fisherman's Arms—I mean the owner is."

"Then he must go back there. Find a bit of string, Sandy, to tie to his collar."

"I wonder how he found his way here," Mrs. Pengelly said, when the reluctant Lob had been led whining away and Sandy had explained about their afternoon's game on the beach. "Fisherman's Arms is right round the other side of the harbor."

"Lob's owner scolded him and thanked Mr. Pengelly for bringing him back. Jean Pengelly warned the children that they had better not encourage Lob any more if they met him on the beach, or it would only lead to more trouble. So they dutifully took no notice of him the next day until he spoiled their good resolutions by dashing up to them with joyful barks, wagging his tail so hard that he winded Tess and knocked Tim's legs from under him.

They had a happy day, playing on the sand.

The next day was Saturday. Sandy had found out that Mr. Dodsworth was to catch the half-past-nine train. She went out secretly, down to the station, nodded to Mr. Hoskins, the stationmaster, who wouldn't dream of charging any local for a platform ticket, and climbed up on the footbridge that led over the tracks. She didn't want to be seen, but she did want to see. She saw Mr. Dodsworth get on the train, accompanied by an unhappy-looking Lob with drooping ears and tail. Then she saw the train slide away out of sight around the next headland, with a melancholy wail that sounded like Lob's last good-bye.

Sandy wished she hadn't had the idea of coming to the station. She walked home miserably, with her shoulders hunched and her hands in her pockets. For the rest of the day she was so cross and unlike herself that Tess and Tim were quite surprised, and her mother gave her a dose of senna.

A week passed. Then, one evening, Mrs. Pengelly and the younger children were in the front room playing snakes and ladders. Mr. Pengelly and Don had gone fishing on the evening tide. If your father is a fisherman, he will never be home at the same time from one week to the next.

Suddenly, history repeating itself, there was a crash from the kitchen. Jean Pengelly leaped up, crying, "My blackberry jelly!" She and the children had spent the morning picking and the afternoon boiling fruit.

But Sandy was ahead of her mother. With flushed cheeks and eyes like stars she had darted into the kitchen, where she and Lob were hugging one another in a frenzy of joy. About a yard of his tongue was out, and he was licking every part of her that he could reach.

"Good heavens!" exclaimed Jean. "How in the world did *he* get here?"

"He must have walked," said Sandy. "Look at his feet."

They were worn, dusty, and tarry. One had a cut on the pad.

"They ought to be bathed," said Jean Pengelly. "Sandy, run a bowl of warm water while I get the disinfectant."

"What'll we do about him, Mother?" said Sandy anxiously.

Mrs. Pengelly looked at her daughter's pleading eyes and sighed.

"He must go back to his owner, of course," she said, making her voice firm. "Your dad can get the address from the Fisherman's tomorrow, and phone him or send a telegram. In the meantime he'd better have a long drink and a good meal."

Lob was very grateful for the drink and the meal, and made no objection to having his feet washed. Then he flopped down on the hearthrug and slept in front of the fire they had lit because it was a cold, wet evening, with his head on Sandy's feet. He was a very tired dog. He had walked all he way from Liverpool to Cornwall, which is more than four hundred miles.

The next day Mr. Pengelly phoned Lob's owner, and the following morning Mr. Dodsworth arrived off the night train, decidedly put out, to take his pet home. That parting was worse than the first. Lob whined, Don walked out of the house, the twins burst out crying, and Sandy crept up to her bedroom afterward and lay with her face pressed into the quilt, feeling as if she were bruised all over.

Jean Pengelly took them all into Plymouth to see the circus on the next day and the twins cheered up a little, but even the hour's ride in the train each way and the Liberty horses and performing seals could not cure Sandy's sore heart.

She need not have bothered, though. In ten days' time Lob was back—limping, this time, with a torn ear and a patch missing out of his furry coat, as if he had met and tangled with an enemy or two in the course of his four-hundred-mile walk.

Bert Pengelly rang up Liverpool again. Mr. Dodsworth, when he answered, sounded weary. He said, "That dog has already cost me two days that I can't spare away from my work—plus endless time in police stations and drafting newspaper advertisements. I'm too old for these ups and downs. I think we'd better face the fact, Mr. Pengelly, that it's your family he wants to stay with—that is, if you'd be willing to have him."

Bert Pengelly gulped. He was not a rich man, and Lob was a pedigree dog. He said cautiously, "How much would you be asking for him?"

"Good heavens, man, I'm not suggesting I'd sell him to you. You must have him as a gift. Think of the train fares I'll be saving. You'll be doing me a good turn."

"Is he a big eater?" Bert asked doubtfully.

By this time the children, breathless in the background listening to one side of this conversation, had realized what was in the wind and were dancing up and own with their hands clasped beseechingly.

"Oh, not for his size," Lob's owner assured Bert. "Two or three pounds of meat a day and some vegetables and gravy and biscuits—he does very well on that."

Alexandra's father looked over the telephone at his daughter's swimming eyes and trembling lips. He reached a decision. "Well, then, Mr. Dodsworth," he said briskly, "we'll accept your offer and thank you very much. The children will be overjoyed and you can be sure Lob has come to a good home. They'll look after him and see he gets enough exercise. But I can tell you," he ended firmly," if he wants to settle in with us he'll have to learn to eat a lot of fish."

So that was how Lob came to live with the Pengelly family. Everybody loved him and he loved them all. But there was never any question who came first with him. He was Sandy's dog. He slept by her bed and followed her everywhere he was allowed.

Nine years went by, and each summer Mr. Dodsworth came back to stay at the Fisherman's Arms and call on his erstwhile dog. Lob always met him with recognition and dignified pleasure, accompanied him for a walk or two—but showed no signs of wishing to return to Liverpool. His place, he intimated, was definitely with the Pengellys.

In the course of nine years Lob changed less than Sandy. As she went into her teens he became a little slower, a little stiffer, there was a touch of gray on his nose, but he was still a handsome dog. He and Sandy still loved one another devotedly.

One evening in October all the summer visitors had left, and the little fishing town looked empty and secretive. It was a wet, windy dusk. When the children came home from school—even the twins were at high school now, and Don was a full-fledged fisherman—Jean

Pengelly said, "Sandy, your Aunt Rebecca says she's lonesome because Uncle Will Hoskins has gone out trawling, and she wants one of you to go and spend the evening with her. You go, dear; you can take your homework with you."

Sandy looked far from enthusiastic.

"Can I take Lob with me?"

"You know Aunt Becky doesn't really like dogs—Oh, very well." Mrs. Pengelly sighed. "I suppose she'll have to put up with him as well as you."

Reluctantly Sandy tidied herself, took her schoolbag, put on the damp raincoat she had just taken off, fastened Lob's lead to his collar, and set off to walk through the dusk to Aunt Becky's cottage, which was five minutes' climb up the steep hill.

The wind was howling through the shroud of boats drawn up on the Hard.

"Put some cheerful music on, do," said Jean Pengelly to the nearest twin. "Anything to drown that wretched sound while I make your dad's supper." So Don, who had just come in, put on some rock music, loud. Which was why the Pengellys did not hear the truck hurtle down the hill and crash against the post office wall a few minutes later.

Dr. Travers was driving through Cornwall with his wife, taking a late holiday before patients began coming down with winter colds and flu. He saw the sign that said STEEP HILL. LOW GEAR FOR 1 ½ MILES. Dutifully he changed into second gear.

"We must be nearly there," said his wife, looking out of her window. "I noticed a sign on the coast road that said the Fisherman's Arms was two miles. What a narrow, dangerous hill! But the cottages are very pretty. Oh, Frank, stop, *stop!* There's a child, I'm sure it's a child—by the wall over there!"

Dr. Travers jammed on his brakes and brought the car to a stop. A little stream ran down by the road in a shallow stone culvert, and half in the water lay something that looked, in the dusk, like a pile of clothes—or was it the body of a child? Mrs. Travers was out of the car in a flash, but her husband was quicker.

"Don't touch her, Emily!" he said sharply. "She's been hit. Can't be more than a few minutes. Remember that truck that overtook us half a mile back, speeding like the devil? Here, quick, go into that cottage and phone for an ambulance. The girl's in a bad way. I'll stay here and do what I can to stop the bleeding. Don't waste a minute."

Doctors are expert at stopping dangerous bleeding, for they know the right places to press. This Dr. Travers was able to do, but he didn't dare do more; the girl was lying in a queerly crumpled heap, and he guessed she had a number of bones broken and that it would be highly dangerous to move her. He watched her with great concentration, wondering where the truck had got to and what other damage it had done.

Mrs. Travers was very quick. She had seen plenty of accident cases and knew the importance of speed. The first cottage she tried had a phone; in four minutes she was back, and in six an ambulance was wailing down the hill.

Its attendant lifted the child onto a stretcher as carefully as if she were made of fine thistledown. The ambulance sped off to Plymouth—for the local cottage hospital did not take serious accident cases—and Dr. Travers went down to the police station to report what he had done.

He found that the police already knew about the speeding truck—which had suffered from loss of brakes and ended up with its radiator halfway through the post-office wall. The driver was concussed and shocked, but the police thought he was the only person injured—until Dr. Travers told his tale.

At half-past nine that night Aunt Rebecca Hoskins was sitting by her fire thinking aggrieved thoughts about the inconsiderateness of nieces who were asked to supper and never turned up, when she was startled by a neighbor, who burst in, exclaiming, "Have you heard about Sandy Pengelly, then, Mrs. Hoskins? Terrible thing, poor little soul, and they don't know if she's likely to live. Police have got the truck driver that hit her—ah, it didn't ought to be allowed, speeding through the place like that at umpty miles an hour, they ought to jail him for life—not that that'd be any consolation to poor Bert and Jean."

Horrified, Aunt Rebecca put on a coat and went down to her brother's house. She found the family with white shocked faces; Bert and Jean were about to drive off to the hospital where Sandy had been taken, and the twins were crying bitterly. Lob was nowhere to be seen. But Aunt Rebecca was not interested in dogs; she did not inquire about him.

"Thank the Lord you've come, Beck," said her brother. "Will you stay the night with Don and the twins? Don's out looking for Lob and heaven knows when we'll be back; we may get a bed with Jean's mother in Plymouth."

"Oh, if only I'd never invited the poor child," wailed Mrs. Hoskins. But Bert and Jean hardly heard her.

That night seemed to last forever. The twins cried themselves to sleep. Don came home very late and grim-faced. Bert and Jean sat in a waiting room of the Western Counties Hospital, but Sandy was unconscious, they were told, and she remained so. All that could be done for her was done. She was given transfusions to replace all the blood she had lost. The broken bones were set and put in slings and cradles.

"Is she a healthy girl? Has she a good constitution?" the emergency doctor asked.

"Aye, doctor, she is that," Bert said hoarsely. The lump in Jean's throat prevented her from answering; she merely nodded.

"Then she ought to have a chance. But I won't conceal from you that her condition is very serious, unless she shows signs of coming out of this coma."

But as hour succeeded hour, Sandy showed no signs of recovering consciousness. Her parents sat in the waiting room with haggard faces; sometimes one of them would go to telephone the family at home or to try to get a little sleep at the home of Granny Pearce, not far away.

At noon next day Dr. and Mrs. Travers went to the Pengelly cottage to inquire how Sandy was doing, but the report was gloomy:

"Still in a very serious condition." The twins were miserably unhappy. They forgot that they had sometimes called their elder sister bossy and only remembered how often she had shared her pocket money with them, how she read to them and took them for picnics and helped with their homework. Now there was no Sandy, no Mother and Dad, Don went around with a gray, shuttered face, and worse still, there was no Lob.

The Western Counties Hospital is a large one, with dozens of different departments and five or six connected buildings, each with three or four entrances. By that afternoon it became noticeable that a dog seemed to have taken up position outside the hospital, with the fixed intention of getting in. Patiently he would try first one entrance and then another, all the way around, and then begin again. Sometimes he would get a little way inside, following a visitor, but animals were, of course, forbidden, and he was always kindly but firmly turned out again. Sometimes the guard at the main entrance gave him a pat or offered him a bit of sandwich—he looked so wet and beseeching and desperate. But he never ate the sandwich. No one seemed to own him or to know where he came from; Plymouth is a large city and he might have belonged to anybody.

At tea time Granny Pearce came through the pouring rain to bring a flask of hot tea with brandy in it to her daughter and son-in-law. Just as she reached the main entrance the guard was gently but forcibly shoving out a large, agitated, soaking wet Alsation dog.

"No, old fellow, you can *not* come in. Hospitals are for people not for dogs."

"Why, bless me," exclaimed old Mrs. Pearce. "That's Lob! Here, Lob, Lobby boy!"

Lob ran to her, whining. Mrs. Pearce walked up to the gate.

"I'm sorry, madam, you can't bring that dog in here," the guard said.

Mrs. Pearce was a very determined old lady. She looked the porter in the eye.

"Now, see here, young man. That dog has walked twenty miles from St. Killan to get to my granddaughter. Heaven knows how he knew she was here, but it's plain he knows. And he ought to have his rights! He ought to get to see her! Do you know," she went on bristling, "that dog has walked the length of England—*twice*—to be with that girl? And you think you can keep him out with your fiddling rules and regulations?"

"I'll have to ask the medical officer," the guard said weakly.

"You do that, young man." Granny Pearce sat down in a determined manner, shutting her umbrella, and Lob sat patiently dripping at her feet. Every now and then he shook his head, as if to dislodge something heavy that was tied around his neck.

Presently a tired, thin, intelligent-looking man in a white coat came downstairs, with an impressive, silver-haired man in a dark suit, and there was a low-voiced discussion. Granny Pearce eyed them, biding her time.

"Frankly . . . not much to lose," said the older man. The man in the white coat approached Granny Pearce.

"It's strictly against every rule, but as it's such a serious case we are making an exception," he said to her quietly. "But only *outside* her bedroom door—and only for a minute or two."

Without a word, Granny Pearce rose and stumped upstairs. Lob followed close to her skirts, as if he knew his hope lay with her.

They waited in the green-floored corridor outside Sandy's room. The door was half shut. Bert and Jean were inside. Everything was terribly quiet. A nurse came out. The white-coated man asked her something and she shook her head She had left the door ajar and through it could now be seen a high, narrow bed with a lot of gadgets around it. Sandy lay there, very flat under the covers, very still. Her head was turned away. All Lob's attention was riveted on the bed. He strained toward it, but Granny Pearce clasped his collar firmly.

"I've done a lot for you, my boy, now you behave yourself," she whispered grimly. Lob let out a faint whine, anxious and pleading.

At the sound of that whine Sandy stirred just a little. She sighed and moved her head the least fraction. Lob whined again. And then

Sandy turned her head right over. Her eyes opened, looking at the door.

"Lob?" she murmured—no more than a breath of sound. "Lobby, boy?"

The doctor by Granny Pearce drew a quick, sharp breath. Sandy moved her left arm—the one that was not broken—from below the covers and let her hand dangle down, feeling, as she did in the mornings, for Lob's furry head. The doctor nodded slowly.

"All right," he whispered. "Let him go to the bedside. But keep a hold of him."

Granny Pearce and Lob moved to the bedside. Now she could see Bert and Jean, white-faced and shocked, on the far side of the bed. But she didn't look at them. She looked at the smile on her granddaughter's face as the groping fingers found Lob's wet ears and gently pulled them. "Good boy," whispered Sandy, and fell asleep again.

Granny Pearce led Lob out into the passage again. There she let go of him and he ran off swiftly down the stairs. She would have followed him, but Bert and Jean had come out into the passage, and she spoke to Bert fiercely.

"*I* don't know why you were so foolish as not to bring the dog before! Leaving him to find the way here himself—"

"But, Mother!" said Jean Pengelly. "That can't have been Lob. What a chance to take! Suppose Sandy hadn't—" She stopped, with her handkerchief pressed to her mouth.

"Not Lob? I've known that dog nine years! I suppose I ought to know my own granddaughter's dog?"

"Listen, Mother," said Bert. "Lob was killed by the same truck that hit Sandy. Don found him—when he went to look for Sandy's schoolbag. He was—he was dead. Ribs all smashed. No question of that. Don told me on the phone—he and Will Hoskins rowed a half mile out to sea and sank the dog with a lump of concrete tied to his collar. Poor old boy. Still—he was getting on. Couldn't have lasted forever."

"*Sank him at sea?* Then what—?"

Slowly old Mrs. Pearce, and then the other two, turned to look at the trail of dripping-wet footprints that led down the hospital stairs.

In the Pengelly's garden they have a stone, under the palm tree. It says: "Lob. Sandy's dog. Buried at sea."

# Old Fillikin

Miss Evans, the math teacher, had thick white skin, pocked like a nutmeg grater; her lips were pale and thick, often puffed out in annoyance; her thick hair was the drab color of old straw that has gone musty; and her eyes, behind thick glass lenses, stared angrily at Timothy.

"Timothy, how often have I *told* you?" she said. "You have got to show your working. Even if these were the right answers—which they are not—I should give you no marks for them, because no working is shown. How, may I ask, did you arrive at this answer?"

Her felt-tip made two angry red circles on the page. All Timothy's neat layout—and the problems were tidily and beautifully set out, at least—all that neat arrangement had been spoiled by a forest of furious red *X*'s, underlinings, and crossings-out that went from top to bottom of the page, with a big *W* for Wrong beside each answer. The page was horrible now—like a scarred face, like a wrecked garden. Timothy could hardly bear to look at it.

"Well? How did you get that answer? Do you *understand* what I'm asking you?"

The trouble was that when she asked him a sharp question like that, in her flat, loud voice, with its aggressive north-country vowels—*answer, ask,* with a short *a* as in grab or bash—he felt as if she were hammering little sharp nails into his brain. At once all his wits completely deserted him, the inside of his head was a blank numbness, empty and echoing like a hollow pot, as if his intelligence had escaped through the holes she had hammered.

"I don't know," he faltered.

"You *don't know?* How can you not *know?* You must have got those answers *some*how! Or do you just put down any figures that come into your head? If you'd gotten them *right,* I'd assume you'd copied the answers from somebody else's book—but it's quite plain you didn't do that."

She stared at him in frustrated annoyance, her eyes pinpointed like screw-tips behind the thick glass.

Of course he would not be such a fool as to copy someone else's book. He hardly ever got a sum right If he had a whole series correct, it would be grounds for instant suspicion.

"Well, as you have this whole set wrong—plainly you haven't grasped the principle at all—I'll just have to set you a new lot. Here—you can start at the beginning of Chapter VIII, page 64, and go as far as page 70."

His heart sank horribly. They were all the same kind—the kind he particularly hated—pages and pages of them. It would take him the whole weekend—and now, late on Friday evening—for she had kept him after class—he was already losing precious time.

"Do you understand? Are you following me? I'd better explain the principle again"

And she was off, explaining; her gravelly voice went on and on, about brackets, bases, logarithms, sines, cosines, goodness knows what, but now, thank heaven, his mind was set free, she was not asking questions, and so he could let his thoughts sail off on a string, like a kite flying higher and higher. . . .

"Well?" she snapped. "Have you got it now?"

"Yes—I think so."

"What have I been saying?"

He looked at her dumbly.

But just then a merciful bell began to ring, for the boarders' supper.

"I've got to go," he gasped, "or I'll miss my bus."

Miss Evans unwillingly gave in.

"Oh, very well. Run along. But you'll *have* to learn this, you know—you'll never pass exams, never get *any*where, unless you do. Even farmers need math. Don't think *I* enjoy trying to force it into your thick head—it's no pleasure to *me* to have to spend time going over it all again and again."

He was gathering his books together—the fat, ink-stained gray textbook, the glossy blue new one, the rough notebook, the green exercise book filled with angry red corrections—horrible things, he loathed the very sight and feel of them. If only he could throw them down the well, burn them, never open them again, Some day he would be free of them.

He hurried out, ran down the steps, tore across the school courtyard. The bus was still waiting beyond the gate; with immense relief he bounded into it and flung himself down on the prickly moquette seat.

If only he could blot Miss Evans and the hateful math out of his mind for two days; if only he could sit out under the big walnut tree in the orchard and just draw and draw and let his mind fly like a kite, and think of nothing at all but what picture was going to take shape under his pencil, and in what colors, later, he could paint it; but now that plan was spoiled, he would have to work at those horrible problems for hours and hours, with his mind jammed among them, like a mouse caught in some diabolical machinery that it didn't invent and doesn't begin to understand.

The bus stopped at a corner by a bridge, and he got out, climbed a fence, and walked across fields to get to the farm where he lived. There was a way around by a cart track, the way the postman came, but it took longer. The fields smelled of warm hay, and the farmyard of dry earth, and cattle cake, and milk, and tractor oil; a rooster crowed in the orchard, and some ducks quacked close at hand; all these were homely, comforting, familiar things, but now they had no power to comfort him; they were like helpless friends holding out their hands to him as he was dragged away to prison.

"These are *rules,* can't you see?" Miss Evans had stormed at him. "You have to learn them."

"Why?" he wanted to ask. "Who made those rules? How can you be certain they were right? Why do you turn upside down and multiply? Why isn't there any square root of minus one?"

The next morning he went out and sat with his books in the orchard, under the big walnut, by the old well. It would have been easier to concentrate indoors, to work on the kitchen table, but the weather was so warm and still that he couldn't bear not to be out of doors. Soon the frosts would begin; already the walnut leaves, yellow as butter, were starting to drift down, and the squashy walnut rinds littered the dry grass and stained his bare feet brown. The nights were drawing in.

For some reason he remembered a hymn his granny used to say to him:

Every morning the red sun
Rises warm and bright,
But the evening soon comes on
And the dark cold night.

The words had frightened him, he could not say why.

He tried to buckle his mind to his work. "If $r \geq 4$, $r$ weighings can deal with $2r - 1$ loads—" but his thoughts trickled away like a river in sand. He had been dreaming about his grandmother, who had died two years ago. In his dream they had been here, in the orchard, but it was winter, thick gray frost all over the grass, a fur of frost on every branch and twig and grass-blade. Granny had come out of the house with her old zinc pail to get water from the well.

"Tap water's no good to you," she always used to say. "Never drink water that's passed through metal pipes. It'll line your innards with tin, you'll end up clinking like a moneybox. Besides, tap water's full of those floorides and kloorides and wrigglers they put in it—letting on as if it's for your good—hah! I'd not pay a penny for a hundred gallons of the stuff. Well water's served me all my life long, and it'll go on doing. Got some taste to it—not like that nasty flat stuff."

"I'll wind up the bucket for you, Granny," he said, and took hold of the heavy well handle.

"That's me boy! One hundred and eight turns."

"A hundred and eight is nine twelves. Nine tens are ninety, nine elevens are ninety-nine, nine twelves are a hundred and eight."

"Only in your book, lovie. In mine it's different. We have different ones!"

An ironic smile curved her mouth, she stood with arms folded over her clean blue-and-white print apron while he wound and counted. Eighty-nine, ninety, ninety-one, ninety-two . . .

When he had the dripping, double-cone-shaped well bucket at the top and was going to tilt it, so as to fill her small pail, she had exclaimed, "Well, look who's come up with it! Old Fillikin!"

And that, for some reason, had frightened him so much that he had not dared look into the bucket but dropped it, so that it went clattering back into the well and he woke up.

This seemed odd, remembering the dream in daylight, for he had loved his grandmother dearly. His own mother had died when he was two, and Granny had always looked after him. She had been kind, impatient, talkative, always ready with an apple, a hug, a slice of bread-and-dripping if he was hungry or hurt himself. She was full of unexpected ideas and odd information.

"Husterloo's the wood where Reynard the fox keeps his treasure. If we could find that, I could stop knitting, and *you* could stop thinking. You think too much, for a boy your age."

"The letter *N* is a wriggling eel. His name is No one, and his number is Nine."

"Kings always die standing up, and that's the way I mean to die."

She had, too, standing in the doorway, shouting after the postman, "If you don't bring me a letter tomorrow, I'll write your name on a leaf and shut it in a drawer!"

Some people had thought she was a witch because she talked to herself such a lot, but Timothy found nothing strange about her; he had never been in the least frightened of her.

"Who were you talking to, Granny?" he would say, if he came into the kitchen when she was rattling off one of her monologues.

"I was talking to Old Fillikin," she always answered, just as, when he asked, "What's for dinner, Granny?" she invariably said "Surprise pie with pickled questions."

"Who's Old Fillikin?" he asked once, and she said, "Old Fillikin's my friend. My familiar friend. Every man has a friend in his sleeve."

"Have I got one, Granny?"

"Of course you have, love. Draw his picture, call him by his name, and he'll come out."

Now, sitting by the well, in the warm, hazy sunshine, Timothy began to wonder what Old Fillikin, Granny's familiar friend, would have looked like if he had existed. The idea was, for some reason, not quite comfortable, and he tried to turn his mind back to his math problem.

"*R* weighings can deal with *2r* - I loads . . ." but somehow the image of Old Fillikin would keep sneaking back among his thoughts, and, almost without noticing that he did so, he began to doodle in his rough notebook.

Old Fillikin fairly leaped out of the page: every stroke, every touch of the point filled him in more swiftly and definitely. Old Fillikin was a kind of hairy frog; he looked soft and squashy to the touch—like a rotten pear, or a damp eiderdown—but he had claws too, and a mouthful of needle-sharp teeth. His eyes were very shrewd—they were a bit like Granny's eyes—but there was a sad, lost look about them too, as there had been about Granny's, as if she were used to being misunderstood. Old Fillikin was not a creature you would want to meet in a narrow high-banked lane with dusk falling. At first Timothy was not certain of his size. Was he as big as an apple, so that he could float, bobbing, in a bucket drawn up from a well, or was he, perhaps, about the size of Bella the Tamworth sow? The pencil answered that question, sketching in a gate behind Old Fillikin, which showed that he was at least two feet high.

"Ugh!" said Timothy, quite upset at his own creation, and he tore out the page from his notebook, crumpled it up, and dropped it down the well.

$$\begin{array}{ccc} dy = & \lim & f(x+dx) - f(x) \\ \hline dx = & dx \to 0 & x \end{array}$$

"*Numbers!*" he remembered Granny scoffing, year ago, when he was hopelessly bogged down in his seven times table. "Some people think they can manage everything by numbers. As if they were set in the ground like bricks!"

"How do you mean, Granny?"

"As if you daren't slip through between!"

"But how *can* you slip between them, Granny? There's nothing between one and two—except one and a half."

"You think there's only one lot of numbers?"

"Of course! One, two, three, four, five, six, seven, eight, nine, ten. Or in French," he said grandly, "it's *un, deux, trois*—"

"Hah!" she said. "Numbers are just a set of rules that some bonehead made up. They're just the fence he built to keep fools from falling over the edge."

"What edge?"

"Oh, go and fetch me a bunch of parsley from the garden!"

That was her way of shutting him up when she'd had enough. She liked long spells by herself, did Granny, though she was always pleased to see him again when he came back.

"The *arrow* $\rightarrow$ tends to a given value as a limit . . ."

"Timothy!" called his father. "Aunt Di says it's lunchtime."

"Okay! Coming!"

"Did I see you drop a bit of paper down the well just now?"

"Yes, I did," he admitted, rather ashamed.

"Well, don't! Just because we don't drink the water doesn't mean that the well can be used as a rubbish dump. After dinner you go and fish it out."

"Sorry, Dad."

During the meal his father and Aunt Di were talking about a local court case: a man who had encouraged, indeed trained, his dog to go next door and harass the neighbors, bite their children, and dig holes in their flowerbeds. The court had ordered the dog to be destroyed. Aunt Di, a dog lover, was indignant about this.

"It wasn't the dog's fault! It was the owner. They should have had *him* destroyed—or sent him to prison!"

If I had a dog, thought Timothy, I could train it to go and wake Miss Evans every night by barking under her window, so that she'd fall asleep in class. Or it could get in through her cat door and pull her out of bed . . .

"Wake up, boy, you're half asleep," said his father. "It's all that mooning over schoolbooks, if you ask me. You'd better come and help me cart feed this afternoon."

"I've got to finish my math first. There's still loads to do."

"They give them too much homework, if you ask *me,*" said Aunt Di. "Addles their minds."

"Well, you get that bit of paper out of the well, anyway," said his father.

He could see it, glimmering white down below; it had caught on top of the bucket, which still hung there, though nobody used it. He had quite a struggle to wind it up—the handle badly needed oiling and shrieked at every turn. At last, leaning down, he was able to grab the crumpled sheet; then he let go of the handle, which whirled around crazily as the bucket rattled down again.

But, strangely enough, the crumpled sheet was blank. Timothy felt half relieved, half disappointed; he had been curious to see if his drawing of Old Fillikin was as nasty as he had remembered. Could he have crumpled up the wrong sheet? But no other had a picture on it. At last he decided that the damp atmosphere in the well must have faded the pencil marks. The paper felt cold, soft, and pulpy—rather unpleasant. He carried it indoors and poked it into the kitchen coal stove.

Then he did another hour's work indoors, scrambling through the problems somehow, anyhow. Miss Evans would be angry again, they were certain to be wrong—but, for heaven's sake, he couldn't spend the whole of Saturday at the horrible task. He checked the results, where it was possible to do so, on his little pocket calculator; blessed, useful little thing, it came up with the results so humbly and willingly, flashing out solutions far faster than his mind could. Farmers need math too, he remembered Miss Evans saying; but when I'm a farmer, he resolved, I shall have a computer to do all those jobs, and I'll just keep to the practical work.

Then he was free, and his father let him drive the tractor, which of course was illegal, but he had been doing it since he was ten and drove better than Kenny the cowman. "You can't keep all the laws," his father said. "Some just have to be broken. All farmers' sons drive tractors. Law's simply a system invented to protect fools," as Granny had said about the numbers.

That night Timothy dreamed that Old Fillikin came up out of the well and went hopping and flopping across the fields in the direction of Markhurst Green, where Miss Evans lived. Timothy followed in his dream and saw the ungainly yet agile creature clamber in through the cat door. "*Don't!* Oh, please, *don't!*" he tried to call. "I didn't mean—I never meant *that*—"

He could hear the flip-flop as it went up the stairs, and he woke himself, screaming, in a tangle of sheet and blanket.

On Sunday night the dream was even worse. That night he took his little calculator to bed with him and made it work out the nine-times table until there were no more places on the screen.

Then he recited Granny's hymn: "Every morning the red sun/ Rises warm and bright,/But the evening soon comes on/And the dark cold night."

If only I could stop my mind working, he thought. He remembered Granny saying, "If we could find Reynard's treasure in Husterloo wood, *I* could stop knitting and *you* could stop thinking." He remembered her saying, "Kings die standing, that's the way I mean to die."

At last he fell into a light, troubled sleep.

On Mondays, math was the first period, an hour and a half. He had been dreading it, but in another way he was desperately anxious to see Miss Evans, to make sure that she was all right. In his second dream, Old Fillikin had pushed through her bedroom door, which stood ajar, and hopped across the floor. Then there had been a kind of silence filled with little fumbling sounds; then a most blood-curdling scream—like the well handle, as the bucket rattled down.

It was only a dream, Timothy kept telling himself as he rode to school on the bus; nothing but a dream.

But the math class was taken by Mr. Gillespie. Miss Evans, they heard, had not come in. And, later, the school grapevine passed along the news. Miss Evans had suffered a heart attack last night; died before she could be taken to the hospital.

When he got off the bus that evening and began to cross the dusk-filled fields toward home, Timothy walked faster than usual and looked warily about him.

Where—he could not help wondering—was Old Fillikin now?

# She Was Afraid of Upstairs

My cousin Tessie, that was. Bright as a button, she was, good as good, neat as ninepence. And clever, too. Read anything she would, time she were five. Papers, letters, library books, all manner of print. Delicate little thing, peaky, not pretty at all, but, even when she was a liddle un, she had a way of putting things into words that'd surprise you. "Look at the sun a-setting, Ma," she'd say. "He's wrapping his hair all over his face." Of the old postman, Jumper, on his red bike, she said he was bringing news from Otherwhere. And a bit of Demerara on a lettuce leaf—that was her favorite treat—a sugarleaf, she called it. "But I haven't been good enough for a sugarleaf today," she'd say. "Have I, Ma?"

Good she mainly was, though, like I said, not a bit of harm in her.

But upstairs she would not go.

Been like that from a tiny baby, she had, just as soon as she could notice anything. When my Aunt Sarah would try to carry her up, she'd shriek and carry on, the way you'd think she was being taken to the slaughterhouse. At first they thought it was on account she didn't want to go to bed, maybe afraid of the dark, but that weren't it at all. For she'd settle to bed anywhere they put her, in the back kitchen, the broom closet under the stairs, in the lean-to with the copper, even in the coal-shed, where my Uncle Fred once, in a temper, put her cradle. "Let her lie there," he said, "if she won't sleep up in the bedroom, let her lie there."

And lie there she did, calm and peaceable, all the livelong night, and not a chirp out of her.

My Aunt Sarah was fair put about with this awkward way of Tessie's, for they'd only the one downstairs room, and evenings, you want the kids out of the way. One that won't go upstairs at night is a fair old problem. But, when Tessie was three, Uncle Fred and Aunt Sarah moved to Birmingham, where they had a back kitchen and a little bit of garden, and in the garden my Uncle Fred built Tessie a tiny cabin, not much bigger than a packing-case it wasn't, by the back kitchen wall, and there she had her cot, and there she slept, come rain, come snow.

Would she go upstairs in the day?

Not if she could help it.

"Run up, Tessie, and fetch me my scissors—or a clean towel—or the hair brush—or the bottle of chamomile," Aunt Sarah might say, when Tessie was big enough to walk and to run errands. Right away, her lip would start to quiver and that frantic look would come in her eye. But my Aunt Sarah was not one to trifle with. She'd lost the big battle, over where Tessie was to sleep. She wasn't going to have any nonsense in small ways. Upstairs that child would have to go, whether she liked it or not. And upstairs she went, with Aunt Sarah's eye on her, but you could hear, by the sound of her feet, that she was having to drag them, one after the other, they were so unwilling it was like hauling rusty nails out of the wood. And when she was upstairs, the timid tiptoeing, it was like some wild creature, a squirrel or a bird that has got in by mistake. She'd find the thing, whatever it was, that Aunt Sarah wanted, and then, my word, wouldn't she come dashing down again as if the Militia were after her, push the thing, whatever it might be, into her mum's hands, and then out into the garden to take in big gulps of the fresh air. Outside was where she liked best to be, she'd spend whole days in the garden, if Aunt Sarah left her. She had a little patch, where she grew lettuce and cress, Uncle Fred got the seeds for her, and then people used to give her bits of slips and flower-seeds, she had a real gift for getting things to grow. That garden was a pretty place, you couldn't see the ground for the greenstuff and flowers. Narcissus, bluebells, sweetpeas, marigolds.

Of course the neighbors used to come and shove their oar in. Neighbors always will. "Have a child that won't go upstairs? I'd not allow it if she were mine," said Mrs. Oakley that lived over the way. "It's fair daft if you ask me. *I'd* soon leather her out of it." For in other people's houses Tessie was just the same—when she got old enough to be taken out to tea. Upstairs she would not go. Anything but that.

Of course they used to try and reason with her, when she was old enough to express herself.

"Why won't you go, Tessie? What's the matter with upstairs? There's nothing bad up there. Only the beds and the chests-of-drawers. What's wrong with that?"

And Aunt Sarah used to say, laughing, "You're nearer to heaven up there."

But no, Tessie'd say, "It's bad, it's bad! Something bad is up there." When she was very little she'd say, "Darkwoods. *Darkwoods.*" And, "Grandfather Moon! I'm frightened, I'm frightened!" Funny thing that, because, of the old moon itself, a-sailing in the sky, she wasn't scared a bit, loved it dearly, and used to catch the silvery light in her hands, if she were out at night, and say that it was like tinsel falling from the sky.

Aunt Sarah was worried what would happen when Tessie started school. Suppose the school had an upstairs classroom, then what? But Uncle Fred told her not to fuss herself, not to borrow trouble; very likely the child would have got over all her nonsense by the time she was of school age, as children mostly do.

A doctor got to hear of her notions, for Tessie had the diptheery, one time, quite bad, with a thing in her throat, and he had to come ever so many times.

"Tis isn't a proper place to have her," he says, for her bed was in the kitchen—it was winter then, they couldn't expect the doctor to go out to Tessie's little cubbyhole in the garden. So Aunt Sarah began to cry and carry on, and told him how it was.

"I'll soon make an end of that nonsense," says he, "for now she's ill she won't notice where she is. And then, when she's better, she'll wake up and find herself upstairs, and her phobia will be gone." That's what he called it, a phobia. So he took Tessie out of her cot and carried her upstairs. And, my word, didn't she create! Shruk! You'd a thought she was being skinned alive. Heads was poking out of windows all down the street. He had to bring her down fast. "Well, she's got a good strength in her, she's not going to die of the diptheery, at all events," says he, but he was very put out, you could see that. Doctors don't like to be crossed. "You've got a wilful one there, Missus," says he, and off he goes, in high dudgeon. But he must have told another doctor about Tessie's wilfulness, for a week or so later, along comes a Doctor Trossick, a mind doctor, one of them pussycologists, who wants to ask Tessie all manner of questions. Does she remember this, does she remember that, when she was a baby, and *why* won't she go upstairs, can't she tell him the reason, and what's all this about Grandfather Moon and Darkwoods? Also, what about when her Ma and Pa go upstairs, isn't she scared for them too?

"No, it's not dangerous for them," says Tessie. "Only for me."

"But *why* is it dangerous for you, child? What do you think is going to happen?"

"Something dreadful! The worst possible thing!"

Dr. Trossick made a whole lot of notes, asked Tessie to do all manner of tests on a paper he'd brought, and then he tried to make her go upstairs, persuading her to stand on the bottom step for a minute, and then on the next one, and the one after. But by the fourth step she'd come to trembling and shaking so bad, with the tears running down, that he hadn't the heart to force her any farther.

So things stood, when Tessie was six or thereabouts. And then one day the news came: the whole street where they lived was going to be pulled down. Redevelopment. Rehousing. All the little two-ups, two-downs were to go, and everybody was to be shifted to high-rise blocks. Aunt Sarah, Uncle Fred, and Tessie were offered a flat on the sixteenth floor of a block that was already built.

Aunt Sarah was that upset. She loved her little house. And as for Tessie—"It'll kill her for sure," Aunt Sarah said.

At that, Uncle Fred got riled. He was a slow man, but obstinate.

"We can't arrange our whole life to suit a child," he said. "We've been offered a Council flat—very good, we'll take it. The kid will have to learn she can't have her own way always. Besides," he said, "there's lifts in them blocks. Maybe when she finds she can go up in a lift, she won't take on as much as if it was only stairs. And maybe the sixteenth floor won't seem so bad as the first or second. After all, *we'll* all be on one level—there's no stairs in a flat."

Well, Aunt Sarah saw the sense in that. And the only thing she could think of was to take Tessie to one of the high-rise blocks and see what she made of it. Her cousin Ada, that's my Mum, had already moved into one of the tower blocks, so Aunt Sarah fetched Tessie over to see us one afternoon.

All was fine to start with, the kid was looking about her, interested and not too bothered, till they went into the lift and the doors closed.

"What's this?" says Tessie then.

"It's a lift," says Aunt Sarah, "and we're going to see your Auntie Ada and Winnie and Dorrie."

Well, when the lift started going up, Aunt Sarah told us, Tessie went white as a dishclout, and time it got up to the tenth, that was where we lived, she was flat on the floor. Fainted. A real bad faint it was, she didn't come out of it for ever so long, and Aunt Sarah was in a terrible way over it.

"What have I done, what have I done to her," she kept saying.

We all helped her get Tessie home again. But after that the kid was very poorly. Brain fever, they'd have called it in the old days, Mum said. Tossing and turning, hot as fire, and delirious with it, wailing and calling out about Darkwoods and Grandfather Moon. For a long time they was too worried about her to make any plans at all, but when she begun to mend, Aunt Sarah says to Uncle Fred, "*Now* what are we going to do?"

Well, he was very put out, natural, but he took his name off the Council list and began to look for another job, somewhere else, where they could live on ground level. And at last he found work in a little seaside town, Topness, about a hundred miles off. Got a house and all, so they was set to move.

They didn't want to shift before Tessie was middling better, but the Council was pushing and pestering them to get out of their house, because the whole street was coming down; the other side had gone already, there was just a big huge stretch of grey rubble, as far as you could see, and half the houses on this side was gone too.

"What's *happening?*" Tessie kept saying as she looked out of the window. "What's happening to our world?"

She was very pitiful about it.

"Are they going to do that with my garden too?" she'd say. "All my sweetpeas and marigolds?"

"Don't you worry, dearie," says Aunt Sarah. "You can have a pretty garden where we're going."

"And I won't have to sleep upstairs?"

"No, no, Dad'll fix you a cubbyhole, same as he has here."

So they packed up all their bits and sticks and they started off. Sam Whitelaw lent them his grocery van for the move, and he drove it too.

It was a long drive—over a hundred miles, and most of it through wild, bare country. Tessie liked it all right at first. She stared at the green fields and the sheep, she sat on Aunt Sarah's lap and looked out of the window, but after a few hours, when they were on the moor, she began to get very poorly, her head was as hot as fire, and her hands too. She didn't complain, but she began to whimper with pain and weakness, big tears rolled down, and Aunt Sarah was bothered to death about her.

"The child wasn't well enough to shift yet. She ought to be in a bed. What'll we do?"

"We're only halfway, if that," says Mr. Whitelaw. "D'you want to stop somewhere, Missus?"

The worst of it was, there weren't any houses round here—not a building to be seen for miles and miles.

On they went, and now Tessie was throwing herself from side to side, delirious again, and crying fit to break her mother's heart.

At last, ahead of them—it was glimmery by then, after sunset of a wintry day—they saw a light, and came to a little old house, all by itself, set a piece back off the road against a wooded scawp of hill.

"Should we stop here and see if the folk will help us?" suggested Mr. Whitelaw, and Aunt Sarah says, "Oh, yes. Yes! Maybe they have a phone and can send for a doctor. Oh I'm worried to death," she says. "It was wicked to move the child so soon."

The two men went and tapped at the door and somebody opened it. Uncle Fred explained about the sick child, and the owner of the house—an old, white-haired fellow, Aunt Sarah said he was—told them, "I don't have a phone, look'ee, I live here all on my own. But you're kindly welcome to come in and put the poor little mawther in my bed."

So they all carried Tessie in among them—by that time she was hardly sensible. My poor aunt gave a gasp when she stepped inside, for the floor was really naught but a barn or shippen, with a floor of beaten earth and some farm stuff, tumbrils and carts and piles of turnips.

"Up here," says the old man, and shows them a flight of stone steps by the wall.

Well, there was nothing for it; up they had to go.

Above was decent enough, though. The old fellow had two rooms, fitted up as bedroom and kitchen, with an iron cooking-stove, curtains at all the windows, and a bed covered with old blankets, all felted-up. Tessie was almost too ill to notice where she'd got to. They put her on the bed, and the old man went to put on a kettle—Aunt Sarah thought the child should have a hot drink.

Uncle Fred and Mr. Whitelaw said they'd drive on in the van and fetch a doctor, if the old man could tell them where to find one.

"Surely," says he, "there's a doctor in the village—Wootten-under-Edge, five miles along. Dr. Hastie—he's a real good un, he'll come fast enough."

"Where is this place?" says Uncle Fred. "Where should we tell him to come?"

"He'll know where it is," says the old man. "Tell him Darkwoods Farm."

Off they went, and the old man came back to where Aunt Sarah was trying to make poor Tessie comfortable. The child was tossing and fretting, whimpering and crying that she felt so ill, her head felt so bad!

"She'll take a cup of my tansy tea. That'll soothe her," said the old man, and he went to his kitchen and brewed up some green drink in an old blue-and-white jug.

"Here, Missus," said he, coming back. "Try her with a little of this."

A sip or two did seem to soothe poor Tessie, brung her to herself a bit, and for the first time she opened her eyes and took a look at the old man.

"Where is this place?" she asked. She was so weak, her voice was no more than a thread.

"Why, you're in my house," said the old man. "And very welcome you are, my dear!"

"And who are you?" she asked next.

"Why, lovey, I'm old Tom Moon the shepherd—old Grandfather Moon. I lay you never expected you'd be sleeping in the moon's house tonight!"

But at that, Tessie gave one screech, and fainted dead away.

Well, poor Aunt Sarah was that upset, with trying to bring Tessie round, but she tried to explain to Mr. Moon about Tessie's trouble, and all her fears, and the cause of her sickness.

He listened, quiet and thinking, taking it all in.

Then he went and sat down by Tessie's bed, gripping hold of her hand.

She was just coming round by then, she looked at him with big eyes full of fright, as Aunt Sarah kneeled down by her other side.

"Now, my dearie," said Mr. Moon. "You know I'm a shepherd, I never hurt a sheep or a lamb in my life. My job is to look after 'em, see? And I'm certainly not a-going to hurt you. So don't you be frit now—there's nothing to be frightened of. Not from old Grandfather Moon."

But he could see that she was trembling all over.

"You've been scared all your life, haven't you, child?" said he gently, and she nodded, Yes.

He studied her then, very close, looked into her eyes, felt her head, and held her hands.

And he said, "Now, my dearie, I'm not going to tell ye no lies. I've never told a lie yet—you can't be lying to sheep or lambs. Do ye believe that I'm your friend and wish you well?"

Again she gave a nod, even weaker.

He said, "Then, Tessie my dear, I have to tell you that you're a-going to die. And *that's* what's been scaring you all along. But you were wrong to be in such a fret over it, lovey, for there's *naught to be scared of*. There'll be no hurt, there'll be no pain, it be just like stepping through a door. And I should know," he said, "for I've seen a many, many sheep and lambs be taken off by weakness or the cold. It's no more than going to sleep in one life and waking up in another. Now do ye believe me, Tessie?"

Yes, she nodded, with just a hint of a smile, and she turned her eyes to Aunt Sarah, on the other side of the bed.

And with that, she took and died.

# Some Music for the Wicked Countess

Mr. Bond was a young man who had just arrived in a small village to take up the post of schoolmaster there. The village was called Castle Kerrig but the curious thing about it was that there was no castle and never had been one. There was a large wood around three-quarters of its circumference which came almost to the door of the schoolmaster's little house, and beyond that the wild hills and bog stretched for miles.

There were only ten children needing to be taught; it hardly seemed worth having a school there at all, but without it they would have had to travel forty miles by bus every day, and a schoolmaster was far cheaper than all that gasoline, so Mr. Bond was given the job. It suited him very well, as he did not have to waste too much time in teaching and had plenty left for his collections of birds' eggs, moths, butterflies, fossils, stones, bones, lizards and flowers, and his piano-playing.

There was a tinny old piano in the school, and when he and the children were bored by lessons he would play tunes and songs to them for hours at a time while they listened in a dream.

One day the eldest of the children, Norah, said:

"Faith, 'tis the way Your Honor should be playing to the Countess up at the Castle for the wonder and beauty of your melodies does be out of this world entirely."

"The Castle?" said Mr. Bond curiously. "What castle is that? There's no castle near here, is there?"

"Ah, sure, 'tis the Castle in the forest I mean. The Wicked Countess would weep the eyes out of her head to hear the tunes you do be playing."

"Castle in the forest?" The schoolmaster was more and more puzzled. "But there's no castle in the forest—at least it's not marked on the two and a half-inch map of the district."

"Begorrah, and doesn't Your Honor know that the whole forest is stiff with enchantment, and a leprechaun peeking out of every bush of it, the way you'd be thinking it was nesting time and them after the eggs?"

"What nonsense, my dear Norah. You really must learn not to come to me with these tales."

But all the children gathered around him exclaiming and persuading.

"Faith, and isn't it the strangest thing that Your Worship should not be believing in these enchantments, and you playing such beautiful music that the very ravens from the Castle, and the maidens out of the forest are all climbing and fluttering over each other outside the windows to get an earful of it?"

Mr. Bond shooed them all off rather crossly, saying that school was over for the day and he had no patience with such silliness.

Next day was the last day of term, and Norah was leaving. Mr. Bond asked her what she was going to do.

"Going into service up at the Castle. They're in need of a girl in the kitchen, I'm told, and Mother says 'twill be good experience for me."

"But there *isn't* any castle," said Mr. Bond furiously. Was the girl half-witted? She had always seemed bright enough in school.

"Ah, Your Honor will have your bit of fun. And what else could I do, will you be telling me that?"

Mr. Bond was forced to agree that there were no other jobs to be had. That afternoon he started out into the forest, determined to search for this mysterious castle and see if there really was some big house tucked away in the trees, but though he walked for miles and miles, and came home thirsty and exhausted long after dusk, not a thing did he see, neither castle, house nor hut, let alone leprechauns peeking out of every bush.

He ate some bread and cheese in a bad temper and sat down to play it off at his own piano. He played some dances from Purcell's *Fairy Queen,* and soon soothed himself into forgetfulness of the children's provoking behavior. Little did he know that three white faces, framed in long golden hair, were gazing through the window behind his back. When he had finished playing for the night the maidens from the forest turned and went regretfully back to the Castle.

"Well," asked the Wicked Countess, "and does he play as well as the village talk has it?"

"He plays till the ears come down off your head and go waltzing off along the road. Sure there's none is his equal in the whole wide world at all."

"I expect you are exaggerating," said the Countess sadly. "Still he would be a useful replacement for Bran the Harpist, ever since the fool went and had his head chopped off at the Debatable Ford."

She looked crossly over to a corner where a headless harpist was learning to knit, since being unable to read music he could no longer play.

"We must entice this schoolmaster up to the Castle," said the Wicked Countess. "'Twill cheer up our dull and lonely life to have a bit of music once again. Ah, that will be the grand day when they have the television broadcast throughout the length and breadth of the country for the entertainment and instruction of us poor sorcerers. I've heard they do be having lessons in ballet and basket-making and all sorts of wonderments."

"How will you entice him up?" asked one of the maidens.

"The usual way. I'll toss out my keys and let it be know that my hand and heart are in waiting for the lucky fellow who is after finding them. Then we'll give him a draught of fairy wine to lull him to sleep for seven years, and after that he's ours forever."

So the Countess arranged for the message about the keys to be relayed through the village and the keys were left lying in a conspicuous place in the middle of the schoolmaster's garden path, visible to him but invisible to everyone else. Quite a number of people became very excited at the thought of winning the Wicked Countess's heart and hand, and the forest was almost as crowded as Epping Forest at Bank Holiday, but the schoolmaster was very preoccupied just at that time with his search for the Scarlet Striped Orchis, which blooms only during the first week in May, and he hardly noticed the commotion.

He did observe the keys lying on his path, but he knew they did not belong to him, and they came into none of the categories of things that he collected, so he merely kicked them out of the way, and forgot them in the excitement of noticing a rare orange fritillary by his garden gate.

"The man's possessed," exclaimed the Countess in vexation. It was mortifying to have her message so completely ignored, but she did not give up.

"We'll try the snake trick—that'll be after fetching him in, and he interested in all manner of bugs and reptiles, the way it'd be a terrible life for his wife, poor woman."

The snake trick was a very old ruse for enticing mortals. One of the maidens of the forest changed herself into a beautiful many-colored snake with ruby eyes and lay in the path of the intended victim, who would be unable to resist picking it up and taking it home. Once inside his house, it would change back into the forest maiden's form, and the luckless man would be obliged to marry her. She would become more and more exacting, asking for a coat made from rose petals, or cherries in midwinter, until her husband had to go up to the Castle and ask them to supply one of these difficult requirements. Then of course he was in their power.

"Indeed, why didn't we try the snake trick before," said the Countess. "'Twould have fetched him better than any old bit of a bunch of keys."

Accordingly, when next Mr. Bond went into the forest, looking for green-glass snails and the salmon-spotted hellebore, he found this beautiful colored snake lying temptingly displayed in a wriggle of black, scarlet, white, and lemon-yellow across his path.

"Bless my soul," said Mr. Bond. "That is something unusual. Can it be *T. vulgaris peristalsis?* I must certainly take it home."

He picked up the snake, which dangled unresistingly in his hands, and rushed home with it. All the forest maidens and the ravens leaned out of the high branches, and the leprechauns pried between the stems of the branches to watch him go by. He ran up the garden path, shoved open the front door with his shoulder, and dropped the snake into a jar of brine which was standing ready for specimens on the kitchen table. He was unable to find a picture or description of the snake in any work of reference, and to his annoyance and disappointment the beautiful colors faded after a couple of hours. The Wicked Countess was also very annoyed. One of her forest maidens had been demolished, and she had been foiled again, which was galling to her pride.

"Maybe we could give him a potion?" suggested one of the maidens.

"He's a teetotaler, the creature," said the Wicked Countess in disgust. "Will you be after telling me how you can administer a potion to a man that will touch neither drop nor dram?"

"Well, but doesn't he take in each day the grandest bottle of milk you ever laid eyes on that would make any cow in Kerry sigh with envy at the cream there is on it?"

"Very well, you can try putting the potion in the milk but 'tis a poor way of instilling a magic draught into a man, I'm thinking, and little good will it do him."

Two enthusiastic maidens went to Mr. Bond's house at cock-crow the following morning and lay in wait for the milkman. As soon as he had left the bottle, they removed the cardboard bottle-top, tipped in the potion (which was a powder in a little envelope), put back the cap, and then hurried back to the Castle to report.

Unfortunately it was the schoolmaster's turn to be unwilling host to the village blue tits that morning. Shortly after the maidens had left, forty blue tits descended upon his doorstep, neatly removed the cap once more, and drank every drop of the milk. Mr. Bond was resigned to this happening every eleventh day, and swallowed his morning tea milkless, before setting off to open up the school, as the holiday was now over.

Up at the Castle the maidens had a difficult time explaining to the Wicked Countess the sudden appearance of forty blue tits who flew in through the window and absolutely refused to be turned out.

"How are we to get this miserable man up here, will you tell me that?" demanded the Countess. "I've lost patience with him entirely."

"You could write him a civil note of invitation, the way he'd be in no case to refuse without displaying terrible bad manners?"

"I never thought of that," admitted the Countess, and she sat down and penned a little note in her crabbed, runic handwriting, asking the schoolmaster for the pleasure of his company at a musical evening. She entrusted the note to Norah, who was now a kitchen-maid at the Castle, and asked her to give it into Mr. Bond's own hands. Norah skipped off, much pleased with the commission, and presented the note to Mr. Bond as he sat in morning school.

"Now isn't it herself has done you the great honor of requesting your worshipful presence at such a musical junketing and a singing and dancing you'd think it was King Solomon himself entertaining the Queen of Sheba."

Mr. Bond scrutinized the letter carefully.

"Now this is very interesting; the back of this document appears to be part of a version of the Cuchulainn legend written in a very early form of Gaelic. Dear me I must write to the Royal Society about this."

He became absorbed in the legend on the back, and clean forgot to read what was on the other side.

The Countess was very affronted at this, and scolded Norah severely.

"I've no patience with the lot of you at all. I can see I'll have to be after fetching him myself, the way otherwise we'll be having no music this side of winter."

It was now the middle of May, which is a very dangerous month of enchantment, the worst in the year apart from October.

The Wicked Countess set out her spies to inform her when Mr. Bond next took an evening walk in the forest. A few days later it was reported that he had set out with a tin of golden syrup and a paintbrush and was busy painting the trunks of the trees. The Countess hastily arrayed herself with all her enchantments and made her way to where he was working. The whole forest hummed with interest and excitement and the leprechauns were jumping up and down in their bushes to such an extent that showers of hawthorn blossoms kept falling down. Mr. Bond noticed nothing at all of this, but he was just able to discern the Wicked Countess with her streaming hair and her beauty. He thought she must be the District Nurse.

"The top of the evening to you," she greeted him, "and isn't it a grand and strange thing you do be doing there, anointing the bark of the trees with syrup as if they were horses and they with the knees broken on them? But perhaps 'tis a compliment you do be after paying me, and it meaning to say that the very trees in my forest are so sweet they deserve to be iced like cakes."

"Good evening," said Mr. Bond with reserve. "I'm after moths."

"And isn't it a wonderful thing to be pursuing those pitiful brown things when you could be stepping up to the Castle like a civilized creature and passing a musical evening with me and my maidens, the way our hearts and voices would be singing together like a flock of starlings?"

"Are you the Countess by any chance? I seem to have heard some vague tales about you, but I never thought that you were a real person. I hope you will forgive me if I have been guilty of any impoliteness."

"Sure our hearts are warmer than that in this part of the world, and what's a trifle of an insult between friends. Do you be after strolling up with me this minute for a drop of something to drink and a few notes of music, for they say music be a great healer when there's hurt feelings in the case, and it smoothing away the sore hearts and wounded spirits."

Mr. Bond gathered that he *had* in some way offended this talkative lady, and his mind went back guiltily to the note Norah had given him, which he had sent off to the Royal Society and forgotten to read.

He turned and walked with her, and was surprised to notice a gray and vine-wreathed tower standing in a part of the forest where, he would have been ready to swear, there had been nothing before.

"Walk in this way," said the Countess holding open a little private gate. "We won't stand on ceremony between friends."

They had to climb half a hundred steps of spiral staircase, but finally emerged in the Wicked Countess's bower, a dim, rush-strewn room full of maidens, leprechauns, and woodsmoke.

"Pray be taking a seat," said the Countess, "the while you do be getting your breath. Fetch a drink for the poor gentleman, one of you," she commanded the maidens, "he has no more breath in him than a washed sheet, and it clinging together on the line."

"Nothing stronger than tea for me, please," said the schoolmaster faintly.

"Tea, is it? We must be after brewing you a terrible strong potion of the stuff, for how can you make music worthy the name in a draught like that? Girls put the kettle on."

"It's all right, thank you. I'm better now. Please don't trouble."

"Do be after playing us a tune, then, for since you came here the village has hummed with your praise the way we've been after thinking 'twas a human nightingale had come to live among us."

"I will with pleasure," said Mr. Bond, "but I can't play without a piano, you know."

There was a disconcerted pause.

"Ah, sure, I'll send two of my leprechauns down to the little house for it," said the Countess rallying. "They'll be back in ten minutes, the creatures." Two of them scuttled off, in obedience to a ferocious look.

Mr. Bond gazed about him dreamily, lulled by the atmosphere of enchantment. The arrival of the tea roused him a little; he took one look at it and shuddered, for it was as black as the pit and looked as if it had been stewed for hours. The maidens were not very expert tea-makers. The Countess was delicately sipping at a tall flagon of mead.

Fortunately a diversion was created by the two leprechauns who came staggering back with the piano in an astonishingly short time. While they were getting it up the spiral staircase amid cries of encouragement from the maidens, Mr. Bond tipped his tea into the syrup can.

"What shall I play for you?" he asked the Countess.

She thought for a moment. Musicians were notoriously vain, and the best way to get him into a flattered and compliant mood would be to ask for one of his own compositions—he was sure to have written some himself.

"Best of all we'd be after liking a tune you've made up yourself," she told him.

Mr. Bond beamed. Here was a true music-lover without a doubt—a very rare thing in this wilderness.

"I'll play you my new fantasia and fugue in the whole-tone scale," he said happily, delighted at a chance to get away from the folk-songs and country dances which he was obliged to play for the children.

He brought his hands down on the keys in a prolonged, crashing, and discordant chord. The leprechauns shuddered from top to toe, the maidens clenched their teeth, and the Wicked Countess had to grip her hands on to the arms of her chair.

Then Mr. Bond really started to play, and the noise was so awful that the whole enchanted tower simply disintegrated, brick by brick. The Countess and her maidens vanished away moaning into the forest, the leprechauns retired grumbling into their bushes, and when the schoolmaster finished his piece and looked around, he was astonished to find himself seated at the piano in the middle of a forest glade. He had to ask the people from the village to help him back with the piano, and was at great pains to think up an explanation for its presence there.

They took no notice of what he said, however.

"Ah, sure, 'tis only some whimsy of the Countess's, the creature, bless her. What would the man expect, and he wandering about the forest on a May evening?"

After that, if by any chance Mr. Bond and the Wicked Countess met each other while walking in the forest, they said nothing at all, and each pretended that the other was not there.

# Sonata for Harp and Bicycle

"No one is allowed to remain in the building after five o'clock," Mr. Manaby told his new assistant, showing him into the little room that was like the inside of a parcel.

"Why not?"

"Directorial policy, said Mr. Manaby. But that was not the real reason.

Gaunt and sooty, Grimes Buildings lurched up the side of a hill toward Clerkenwell. Every little office within its dim and crumbling exterior owned one tiny crumb of light—such was the proud boast of the architect—but toward evening the crumbs were collected as by an immense vacuum cleaner, absorbed and demolished, yielding to an uncontrollable mass of dark that came tumbling in through windows and doors to take their place. Darkness infested the buildings like a flight of bats returning willingly to roost.

"Wash hands, please. Wash hands, please," the intercom began to bawl in the passages at a quarter to five. Without much need of prompting, the staff hustled like lemmings along the corridors to green-and-blue tiled washrooms that mocked with an illusion of cheerfulness the encroaching dusk.

"All papers into cases, please," the voice warned, five minutes later. "Look at your desks, ladies and gentlemen. Any documents left lying about? Kindly put them away. Desks must be left clear and tidy. Drawers must be shut."

A multitudinous shuffling, a rustling as of innumerable bluebottle flies might have been heard by the attentive ear after this injunction, as the employees of Moreton Wold and Company thrust their papers into cases, hurried letters and invoices into drawers, clipped statistical abstracts together and slammed them into filing cabinets, dropped discarded copy into wastepaper baskets. Two minutes later, and not a desk throughout Grimes Buildings bore more than its customary coating of dust.

"Hats and coats on, please. Hats and coats on, please. Did you bring an umbrella? Have you left any shopping on the floor?" At three minutes to five the homegoing throng was in the lifts and on the stairs; a clattering, staccato-voiced flood darkened momentarily the great double doors of the building, and then as the first faint notes of St. Paul's came echoing faintly on the frosty air, to be picked up near at hand by the louder chimes of St. Biddulph's-on-the-Wall, the entire premise of Moreton Wold stood empty.

"But why is it?" Jason Ashgrove, the new copywriter, asked his secretary one day. "Why are the staff herded out so fast? Not that I'm against it, mind you; I think it's an admirable idea in many ways, but there is the liberty of the individual to be considered, don't you think?"

"Hush!" Miss Golden, the secretary, gazed at him with large and terrified eyes. "You mustn't ask that sort of question. When you are taken onto the Established Staff you'll be told. Not before."

"But I want to know now," Jason said in discontent. "Do you know?"

"Yes, I do," Miss Golden answered tantalizingly. "Come on, or we shan't have finished the Oat Crisp layout by a quarter to." And she stared firmly down at the copy in front of her, lips folded, candyfloss hair falling over her face, lashes hiding eyes like peridots, a girl with a secret.

Jason was annoyed. He rapped out a couple of rude and witty rhymes which Miss Golden let pass in a withering silence.

"What do you want for your birthday, Miss Golden? Sherry? Fudge? Bubble bath?"

"I want to go away with a clear conscience about Oat Crisps," Miss Golden retorted. It was not true; what she had chiefly wanted was Mr. Jason Ashgrove, but he had not realized this yet.

"Come on, don't tease! I'm sure you haven't been on the Established Staff all that long," he coaxed her. "What happens when one is taken on, anyway? Does the Managing Director have us up for a confidential chat? Or are we given a little book called *The Awful Secret of Grimes Buildings?*"

Miss Golden wasn't telling. She opened her drawer and took out a white towel and a cake of rosy soap.

"Wash hands, please! Wash hands, please!"

Jason was frustrated. "You'll be sorry," he said. "I shall do something desperate."

"Oh no, you mustn't!" Her eyes were large with fright. She ran from the room and was back within a couple of moments, still drying her hands.

"If I took you out for a coffee, couldn't you give me just a tiny hint?"

Side by side Miss Golden and Mr. Ashgrove ran along the green-floored passages, battled down the white marble stairs among the hundred other employees from the tenth floor, the nine hundred from the floors below.

He saw her lips move as she said something, but in the clatter of two thousand feet the words were lost.

"—fire escape," he heard, as they came into the momentary hush of the carpeted entrance hall. And "—it's to do with a bicycle. A bicycle and a harp."

"I don't understand."

Now they were in the street, chilly with the winter dusk smells of celery on carts, of swept-up leaves heaped in faraway parks, and cold layers of dew sinking among the withered evening primroses in the bombed areas. London lay about them wreathed in twilit mystery and fading against the barred and smoky sky. Like a ninth wave the sound of traffic overtook and swallowed them.

"Please tell me!"

But, shaking her head, she stepped onto a scarlet homebound bus and was borne away from him.

Jason stood undecided on the pavement, with the crowds dividing around him as around the pier of a bridge. He scratched his head, looked about him for guidance.

An ambulance clanged, a taxi hooted, a drill stuttered, a siren wailed on the river, a door slammed, a brake squealed, and close beside his ear a bicycle bell tinkled its tiny warning.

A bicycle, she had said. A bicycle and a harp.

Jason turned and stared at Grimes Buildings.

Somewhere, he knew, there was a back way in, a service entrance. He walked slowly past the main doors, with their tubs of snowy chrysanthemums, and up Glass Street. A tiny furtive wedge of darkness beckoned him, a snicket, a hacket, an alley carved into the thickness of the building. It was so narrow that any moment, it seemed, the overtopping walls would come together and squeeze it out of existence.

Walking as softly as an Indian, Jason passed through it, slid by a file of dustbins, and found the foot of a fire escape. Iron treads rose into the mist, like an illustration to a Gothic fairy tale.

He began to climb.

When he had mounted to the ninth story he paused for breath. It was a lonely place. The lighting consisted of a dim bulb at the foot of every flight. A well of gloom sank beneath him. The cold fingers of the wind nagged and fluttered at the tails of his jacket, and he pulled the string of the fire door and edged inside.

Grimes Buildings were triangular, with the street forming the base of the triangle, and the fire escape the point. Jason could see two long passages coming toward him, meeting at an acute angle where he stood. He started down the left-hand one, tiptoeing in the cavelike silence. Nowhere was there any sound, except for the faraway drip of a tap. No night watchman would stay in the building; none was needed. Burglars gave the place a wide berth.

Jason opened a door at random; then another. Offices lay everywhere about him, empty and forbidding. Some held lipstick-stained tissues, spilled powder and orange peels; others were still foggy with cigarette smoke. Here was a Director's suite of rooms—a desk like half an acre of frozen lake, inch-thick carpet, roses, and the smell of cigars. Here was a conference room with scattered squares of doodled blotting paper. All equally empty.

He was not certain when he first begin to notice the bell. Telephone, he thought at first; and then he remembered that all the outside lines were disconnected at five. And this bell, anyway, had not the regularity of a telephone's double ring: there was a tinkle, and then silence; a long ring, and then silence; a whole volley of rings together, and then silence.

Jason stood listening, and fear knocked against his ribs and shortened his breath. He knew that he must move or be paralyzed by it. He ran up a flight of stairs and found himself with two more endless green corridors beckoning him like a pair of dividers.

Another sound now: a waft of ice-thin notes, riffling up an arpeggio like a flurry of snowflakes. Far away down the passage it echoed. Jason ran in pursuit, but as he ran the music receded. He circled the building, but it always outdistanced him, and when he came back to the stairs he heard it fading away to the story below.

He hesitated, and as he did so heard again the bell; the bicycle bell. It was approaching him fast, bearing down on him, urgent, menacing. He could hear the pedals, almost see the shimmer of an invisible wheel. Absurdly, he was reminded of the insistent clamor of an ice-cream vendor, summoning children on a sultry Sunday afternoon.

There was a little fireman's alcove beside him, with buckets and pumps. He hurled himself into it. The bell stopped beside him, and then there was a moment while his heart tried to shake itself loose in his chest. He was looking into two eyes carved out of expressionless air; he was held by two hands knotted together out of the width of the dark.

"Daisy, Daisy?" came the whisper. "Is that you, Daisy? Have you come to give me your answer?"

Jason tried to speak, but no words came.

"It's not Daisy! Who are you?" The sibilants were full of threat. "You can't stay here. This is private property."

He was thrust along the corridor. It was like being pushed by a whirlwind—the fire door opened ahead of him without a touch, and he was on the openwork platform, clutching the slender railing. Still the hands would not let him go.

"How about it?" the whisper mocked him. "How about jumping? It's an easy death compared with some."

Jason looked down into the smoky void. The darkness nodded to him like a familiar.

"You wouldn't be much loss, would you? What have you got to live for?"

Miss Golden, Jason thought. She would miss me. And the syllables Berenice Golden lingered in the air like a chime. Drawing on some unknown deposit of courage he shook himself loose from the holding hands and ran down the fire escape without looking back.

Next morning when Miss Golden, crisp, fragrant, and punctual, shut the door of Room 492 behind her, she stopped short of the hat-pegs with a horrified gasp.

"Mr. Ashgrove, your hair!"

"It makes me look more distinguished, don't you think?" he said.

It had indeed this effect, for his impeccable dark cut had turned to a stippled silver which might have been envied by many a diplomat.

"How did it happen? You've not—" her voice sank to a whisper—"*you've not been in Grimes Buildings after dark?*"

"Miss Golden—Berenice," he said earnestly. "Who was Daisy? Plainly you know. Tell me the story."

"Did you see him?" she asked faintly.

"Him?"

"William Heron—The Wailing Watchman. Oh," she exclaimed in terror, "I can see you did. Then you are doomed—doomed!"

"If I'm doomed," said Jason, "let's have coffee, and you tell me the story quickly."

"It all happened over fifty years ago," said Berenice, as she spooned out coffee powder with distracted extravagance. "Heron was the night watchman in this building, patrolling the corridors from dusk to dawn every night on his bicycle. He fell in love with a Miss Bell who taught the harp. She rented a room—this room—and gave lessons in it. She began to reciprocate his love, and they used to share a picnic supper every night at eleven, and she'd stay on a while to keep him company. It was an idyll among the fire buckets and the furnace pipes.

"On Halloween he had summoned up the courage to propose to her. The day before he had told her he was going to ask her a very important question, and he came to the Buildings with a huge bunch of roses and a bottle of wine. But Miss Bell never turned up.

"The explanation was simple. Miss Bell, of course, had been losing a lot of sleep through her nocturnal romance, and so she used to take a nap in her music room between seven and ten, to save going home. In order to make sure that she would wake up, she persuaded her father, a distant relative of Graham Bell, to attach an alarm-waking fixture to her telephone which called her every night at ten. She was too modest and shy to let Heron know that she spent those hours in the building, and to give him the pleasure of waking her himself.

"Alas! On this important evening the line failed, and she never woke up. The telephone was in its infancy at that time, you must remember.

"Heron waited and waited. At last, mad with grief and jealousy, having called her home and discovered that she was not there, he concluded that she had betrayed him; he ran to the fire escape, and cast himself off it, holding the roses and the bottle of wine.

"Daisy did not long survive him but pined away soon after. Since that day their ghosts have haunted Grimes Buildings, he vainly patrolling the corridors on his bicycle, she playing her harp in the room she rented. *But they never meet.* And anyone who meets the ghost of William Heron will himself, within five days, leap down from the same fatal fire escape."

She gazed at him with tragic eyes.

"In that case we must lose no time," said Jason, and he enveloped her in an embrace as prompt as it was ardent. Looking down at the gossamer hair sprayed across his pin-stripe, he added, "Just the same it is a preposterous situation. Firstly, I have no intention of jumping off the fire escape—" here, however, he repressed a shudder as he remembered the cold, clutching hands of the evening before—"and secondly, I find it quite nonsensical that those two inefficient ghosts have spent fifty years in this building without coming across each other. We must remedy the matter, Berenice. We must not begrudge our new-found happiness to others."

He gave her another kiss so impassioned that the electric typewriter against which they were leaning began chattering to itself in a frenzy of enthusiasm.

"This very evening," he went on, looking at his watch, "we will put matters right for that unhappy couple and then, if I really have only five more days to live, which I don't for one moment believe, we will proceed to spend them together, my bewitching Berenice, in the most advantageous manner possible."

She nodded, spellbound.

"Can you work a switchboard?" he added. She nodded again. "My love, you are perfection itself. Meet me in the switchboard room then, at ten this evening. I would say, have dinner with me, but I shall need to make one or two purchases and see an old R.A.F. friend. You will be safe from Heron's curse in the switchboard room if he always keeps to the corridors."

"I would rather meet him and die with you," she murmured.

"My angel, I hope that won't be necessary. Now," he said, sighing. "I suppose we should get down to our day's work."

Strangely, enough the copy they wrote that day, although engendered from such agitated minds, sold more packets of Oat Crisps than any other advertising matter before or since.

That evening when Jason entered Grimes Buildings he was carrying two bottles of wine, two bunches of red roses, and a large canvas-covered bundle. Miss Golden, who had concealed herself in the switchboard room before the offices closed for the night, eyed these things with surprise.

"Now," said Jason, after he had greeted her. "I want you first to ring our own extension."

"No one will reply, surely?"

"I think *she* will reply."

Sure enough, when Berenice rang Extension 170 a faint, sleepy voice, distant and yet clear, whispered, "Hullo?"

"Is that Miss Bell?"

"Yes."

Berenice went a little pale Her eyes sought Jason's and, prompted by him, she said formally, "Switchboard here, Miss Bell. Your ten o'clock call."

"Thank you," the faint voice said. There was a click and the line went blank.

"Excellent," Jason remarked. He unfastened his package and slipped its straps over his shoulders. "Now plug into the intercom."

Berenice did so, and then said, loudly and clearly, "Attention. Night watchman on duty, please. Night watchman on duty. You have an urgent summons to Room 492." The intercom echoed and reverberated through the empty corridors, then coughed itself to silence.

"Now we must run. You take the roses, sweetheart, and I'll carry the bottles."

Together they raced up eight flights of stairs and along the passages to Room 492. As they neared the door a burst of music met them—harp music swelling out, sweet and triumphant. Jason took a bunch of roses from Berenice, opened the door a little way, and gently deposited them, with a bottle, inside the door. As he closed it again Berenice said breathlessly, "Did you see anyone?"

"No," he said. "The room was too full of music." She saw that his eyes were shining.

They stood hand in hand, reluctant to move away, waiting for they hardly knew what. Suddenly the door opened again. Neither Berenice nor Jason, afterward, would speak of what they saw but each was left with a memory, bright as the picture on a Salvador Dali calendar, of a bicycle bearing on its saddle a harp, a bottle of wine, and a bouquet of red roses, sweeping improbably down the corridor and far, far away.

"We can go now," Jason said.

He led Berenice to the fire door, tucking the bottle of Médoc in his jacket pocket. A black wind from the north whistled beneath them as they stood on the openwork platform, looking down.

"We don't want our evening to be spoiled by the thought of a curse hanging over us," he said, "so this is the practical thing to do. Hang onto the roses." And holding his love firmly, Jason pulled the rip cord of his R.A.F. friend's parachute and leaped off the fire escape.

A bridal shower of rose petals adorned the descent of Miss Golden, who was possibly the only girl to be kissed in midair in the district of Clerkenwell at ten minutes to midnight on Halloween.

# The Cold Flame

I was asleep when Patrick rang up. The bell sliced through a dream about this extraordinary jampot factory, a kind of rose-red brick catacomb, much older than time, sunk deep on top of the Downs, and I was not pleased to be woken. I groped with a blind arm and worked the receiver in between my ear and the pillow.

"Ellis? Is that you?"

"Of course it is," I snarled. "Who else do you expect in my bed at three a.m.? Why in heaven's name ring up at this time?"

"I'm sorry," he said, sounding muffled and distant and apologetic. "Where I am it's only half-past something." A sort of oceanic roar separated us for a moment, and then I heard him say, ". . . rang you as soon as I could."

"Well, where are you?"

Then I woke up a bit more and interrupted as he began speaking again. "Hey, I thought you were supposed to be dead! There were headlines in the evening papers—a climbing accident. Was it a mistake then?"

"No, I'm dead right enough. I fell into the crater of a volcano."

"What were you doing on a *volcano,* for goodness' sake?"

"Lying on the lip writing a poem about what it looked like inside. The bit I was lying on broke off." Patrick sounded regretful. "It would have been a good poem too."

Patrick was a poet, perhaps I should explain. Had been a poet. Or said he was. No one had ever seen his poetry because he steadfastly refused to let anyone read his work, though he insisted, with a quiet self-confidence not otherwise habitual to him, that the poems were very good indeed. In no other respect was he remarkable, but most people quite liked Patrick; he was a lanky, amusing creature with guileless blue eyes and a passion for singing sad, randy songs when he had had a drink or two. For some time I had been a little in love with Patrick. I was sorry to hear he was dead.

"Look, Patrick," I began again. "Are you sure you're dead?"

"Of course I'm sure."

"Where are you then?"

"Lord knows. I've hardly had time to look round yet. There's something on my mind; that's why I contacted you."

The word contacted seemed inappropriate. I said, "Why ring up?"

"I could appear if you prefer it."

Remembering the cause of his death, I said hastily, "No, no, let's go on as we are. What's on your mind?"

"It's my poems, Ellis. Could you get them published, do you think?"

My heart sank a bit, as anybody's does at this sort of request from a friend, but I said, "Where are they?"

"At my flat. A big thick stack of quarto paper, all handwritten. In my desk."

"Okay. I'll see what I can do. But listen, love—I don't want to sound a gloomy note, but suppose no publisher will touch them—what then? Promise you won't hold me responsible? Keep hanging around, you know, haunting, that kind of thing?"

"No, of course not," he said quickly. "But you needn't worry. Those poems are good. There's a picture at the flat as well, though, behind the wardrobe, with its face to the wall. As a matter of fact, it's a portrait of my mother. It's by Chapdelaine—done before he made his name. About seven years ago I got him to paint her for her birthday present (this was before I quarreled with Mother, of course). But she didn't like it—said it was hideous—so I gave her a bottle of scent instead. Now, of course, it's worth a packet. You can get Sowerby's to auction it, and the proceeds would certainly pay for the publication of the poems, if necessary. But only in the last resort, mind you! I'm convinced those poems can stand on their own. I'm only sorry I didn't finish the volcano one—maybe I could dictate it—"

"I really must get some sleep," I broke in, thinking what a good thing it was they hadn't got direct dialing yet between this world and the next. "I'll go round to your flat first thing tomorrow. I've still got the key. Good-bye, Patrick."

And I clonked back the receiver on its rest and tried to return to my lovely deep-hidden jampot factory among the brooding Downs. Gone beyond recall.

Next day at Patrick's flat I found I had been forestalled. The caretaker told me that a lady, Mrs. O'Shea, had already called there and taken away all her son's effects.

I was wondering how to inform Patrick of this development—he hadn't left a number—when he got through to me again on his own phone. At the news I had to relate he let out a cry of anguish.

"Not Mother! God, what'll we do now? Ellis, that woman's a vulture. You'll have the devil's own job prising the poems out of her."

"Why not just get in touch with her direct—the way you did with me—and tell *her* to send the poems to a publisher" I said."Suggest trying Chatto first."

"You don't understand! For one thing, I couldn't get near her. For another, she has this grudge against me; when I gave up going home it really dealt her a mortal blow. It'd give her the most exquisite pleasure to thwart me. No, I'm afraid you'll have to use all your tact and diplomacy, Ellis; you'd better drive down to Clayhole tomorrow—"

"But look here! Suppose she won't—"

No answer. Patrick had disconnected.

So next afternoon found me driving down to Clayhole. I had never been to Patrick's home—nor had Patrick since the quarrel with his mother. I was quite curious to see her, as a matter of fact; Patrick's descriptions of her had been so conflicting. Before the breach she was the most wonderful mother in the world, fun, pretty, sympathetic, witty—while after it, no language had been too virulent to describe her, a sort of female Dracula, tyrannical, humourless, blood-sucking.

One thing I did notice as I approached the house—up a steep, stony, unmetalled lane—the weather had turned a bit colder. The leaves hung on the trees like torn rags, the ground was hard as iron, the sky leaden.

Mrs. O'Shea received me with the utmost graciousness. But in spite of this I retained a powerful impression that I had arrived at an awkward moment; perhaps she had been about to bathe the dog, or watch a favorite programme, or start preparing a meal. She was a small, pretty Irishwoman, her curling hair a beautiful white, her skin a lovely tea-rose pink, her eyes the curious opaque blue that goes with a real granite obstinacy. One odd feature of her face was that she appeared to have no lips; they were so pale they disappeared into her powdered cheeks. I could see why Patrick had never mentioned his father. Major O'Shea stood beside his wife, but he was a nonentity: a stooped, watery-eyed, dangling fellow, whose only function was to echo his wife's opinions.

The house was a pleasant Queen Anne manor, furnished in excellent taste with chintz and Chippendale, and achingly, freezingly cold. I had to clench my teeth to stop them chattering. Mrs. O'Shea, in her cashmere twinset and pearls, seemed impervious to the glacial temperature, but the Major's cheeks were blue; every now and then a drop formed at the tip of his nose which he carefully wiped away with a spotless silk handkerchief. I began to understand why Patrick had been keen on volcanoes.

They stood facing me like an interview board while I explained my errand. I began by saying how grieved I had been to hear of Patrick's death, and spoke of his lovable nature and unusual promise. The Major did look genuinely grieved, but Mrs. O'Shea was smiling, and there was something about her smile that irritated me profoundly.

I then went on to say that I had received a communication from Patrick since his death, and waited for reactions. They were sparse. Mrs. O'Shea's lips tightened fractionally, the Major's lids dropped over his lugubrious milky tea-coloured eyes; that was all.

"You don't seem surprised," I said cautiously. "You were expecting something of the kind perhaps?"

"No, not particularly," Mrs. O'Shea said. She sat down, placed her feet on a footstool, and picked up a circular embroidery frame. "My family is psychic, however; this kind of thing is not unusual. What did Patrick want to say?"

"It was about his poems."

"Oh, yes?" Her tone was as colourless as surgical spirit. She carefully chose a length of silk. Her glance flickered once to the object she was using as a footstoll: a solid pile of papers about a foot thick, wrapped up clumsily in an old grey cardigan which looked as if it had once lined a dog basket; it was matted with white terrier hairs.

My heart sank.

"I believe you have his poems now? Patrick is most anxious that they should be published."

"And I'm not at all anxious they should be published," Mrs. O'Shea said with her most irritating smile.

"Quite, quite," the Major assented.

We argued about it. Mrs. O'Shea had three lines of argument: first, that no one in her family had ever written poetry, therefore Patrick's poems were sure to be hopeless; second, that no one in her family had ever written poetry and, even in the totally unlikely event of the poems being any good, it was a most disreputable thing to do; third, that Patrick was conceited, ungrateful, and self-centered, and it would do him nothing but harm to see his poems in print. She spoke as if he were still alive.

"Besides," she added, "I'm sure no publisher would look at them."

"You have read them?"

"Heavens, no!" She laughed. "I've no time for such rubbish."

"But if a publisher did take them?"

"You'd never get one to risk his money on such a venture."

I explained Patrick's plans regarding the Chapdelaine portrait. The O'Sheas looked skeptical. "You perhaps have it here?" I asked.

"A hideous thing. Nobody in their senses would give enough money for that to get a book published."

"I'd very much like to see it, all the same."

"Roderick, take Miss Bell to look at the picture," Mrs. O'Shea said, withdrawing another strand of silk.

The picture was in the attic, face down. I saw at once why Mrs. O'Shea had not liked it. Chapdelaine had done a merciless job of work. It was brilliant—one of the best examples of his early Gold Period. I imagined it would fetch even more than Patrick hoped. When I explained this to the Major, an acquisitive gleam came into his eye.

"Surely that would more than pay for the publication of the poems."

"Oh, certainly," I assured him.

"I'll see what my wife has to say."

Mrs. O'Shea was not interested in cash. She had a new line of defence. "Of course you've no actual proof that you come from Patrick, have you? I don't really see why we should take your word in the matter."

Suddenly I was furious. My rage and the deadly cold were simultaneously too much for me. I said, as politely as I could, "Since I can see you are completely opposed to my performing this small service for your son, I won't waste any more of our time," and left them abruptly. The Major looked a little taken aback, but his wife calmly pursued her stitchery.

It was good to get out of that icy, lavender-scented morgue into the fresh, windy night.

My car limped down the lane pulling to the left, but I was so angry that I had reached the village before I realized I had a flat tyre. I got out and surveyed it. The car was slumped down on one haunch as if Mrs. O'Shea had put a curse on it.

I went into the pub for a hot toddy before changing the wheel, and while I was in there the landlord said, "Would you be Miss Bell? There's a phone call for you."

It was Patrick. I told him about my failure and he cursed, but he did not seem surprised.

"Why does your mother hate you so, Patrick?"

"Because I got away from her. That's why she can't stand my poetry—because it's nothing to do with her. Anyway she can hardly read. If my father so much as picks up a book, she gets it away from him as soon as she can and hides it. Well, you can see what he's like. Sucked dry. She likes to feel she knows the whole contents of a person's mind, and that it's entirely focused on *her*. She's afraid of being left alone; she's never slept by herself in a room in her life. If ever he had to go away, she'd have my bed put in her room.

I thought about that.

"But as for your authority to act for me," Patrick went on, "we can easily fix that. Have a double whisky and get a pen and paper. Shut your eyes."

Reluctantly I complied. It was an odd sensation. I felt Patrick's light, chill clutch on my wrist moving my hand. For a moment, the contrast with the last time I had held his hand made a strangling weight of tears rise in my throat; then I remembered Mrs. O'Shea's icy determination and realized that Patrick resembled her in this; suddenly I felt free of him, free of sorrow.

When I opened my eyes again, there was a message in Patrick's odd, angular script, to the effect that he authorized me to sell his Chapdelaine picture and use the proceeds to pay for the publication of his poems, if necessary.

The drinks had fortified me, so I got a garage to change my wheel and walked back up the lane to Clayhole. The O'Sheas had just finished their supper. They invited me civilly, but without enthusiasm, to drink coffee with them. The coffee was surprisingly good, but stone cold, served in little gold-rimmed cups the size of walnut shells. Over it Mrs. O'Shea scanned Patrick's message. I glanced round—we were in the arctic dining room—and noticed that

Chapdelaine's picture now hung on the wall. It smiled at me with Mrs. O'Shea's own bland hostility.

"I see; very well," she said at last. "I suppose you must take the picture then."

"And the poems too, I hope."

"Oh no. Not yet," she said. "*When* you've sold the picture, for this large sum you say it will fetch, *then* I'll see about letting you have the poems."

"But that's not—" I began, and then stopped. What was the use? She was not a logical woman, no good reasoning with her. One step at a time was fast as one could go.

The sale of an early Chapdelaine portrait made quite a stir, and the bidding at Sowerby's began briskly. The picture was exhibited on an easel on the auctioneer's dais. From my seat in the front row I was dismayed to notice, as the bids rose past the four-figure mark, that the portrait was beginning to fade. The background remained, but by the time twenty-five hundred had been reached, Mrs. O'Shea had vanished completely. The bidding faltered and came to a stop; there were complaints. The auctioneer inspected the portrait, directed an accusing stare at me, and declared the sale null. I had to take the canvas ignominiously back to my flat, and the evening papers had humorous headlines: WHERE DID THE COLOURS RUN TO? NO BID FOR CHAPDELAINE'S WHITE PERIOD.

When the telephone rang, I expected that it would be Patrick and picked up the receiver gloomily, but it was a French voice.

"Armand Chapdelaine here. Miss Bell?"

"Speaking."

"We met, I think, once, a few years ago, in the company of young Patrick O'Shea. I am ringing from Paris about this odd incident of his mother's portrait."

"Oh, yes?"

"May I come and inspect the canvas, Miss Bell?"

"Of course," I said, slightly startled. "Not that there's anything to see."

"That is so kind of you. Till tomorrow, then."

Chapedelaine was a French Canadian: stocky, dark, and full of *loup-garou* charm.

After carefully scrutinising the canvas, he listened with intense interest to the tale about Patrick and his mother.

"Aha! This is a genuine piece of necromancy," he said, rubbing his hands. "I always knew there was something unusually powerful about that woman's character. She had a most profound dislike for me; I recall it well."

"Because you were her son's friend."

"Of course." He inspected the canvas again and said, "I shall be delighted to buy this from you for two thousand five hundred pounds, Miss Bell. It is the only one of my pictures that has been subjected to black magic, up to now."

"Are you quite sure?"

"Entirely sure." He gave me his engagingly wolfish smile. "Then we will see what shot Madame Mére fetches out of her locker."

Mrs. O'Shea was plainly enjoying the combat over Patrick's poems. It had given her a new interest. When she heard the news that two thousand five hundred pounds were lodged in a trust account, ready to pay for the publication of the poems, if necessary, her reaction was almost predictable.

"But that wouldn't be honest!" she said. "I suppose Mr. Chapdelaine bought the canvas out of kindness, but it can't be counted as a proper sale. The money must be returned to him." Her face set like epoxy, and she rearranged her feet more firmly on the footstool.

"On no account will I have it back, madame," Chapdelaine riposted. He had come down with me to help persuade her; he said he was dying to see her again.

"If you won't, then it must be given to charity. I'm afraid it's out of the question that I should allow money which was obtained by what amounts to false pretences to be used to promote that poor silly boy's scribblings."

"Quite, quite," said the Major.

"But it may not be necessary—" I began in exasperation. An opaque blue gleam showed for an instant in Mrs. O'Shea's eye. Chapdelaine raised a hand soothingly and I subsided. I'd known, of course, that I too was an object of her dislike, but I had not realised how very deep it went; the absolute hatred in her glance was a slight shock. It struck me that, unreasonably enough, this hate had been augmented by the fact that Chapdelaine and I were getting on rather well together.

"Since madame does not approve of our plan, I have another proposition," said Chapdelaine, who seemed to be taking a pleasure in the duel almost equal to that of Mrs. O'Shea. I felt slightly excluded. "May I be allowed to do a second portrait, and two thousand five hundred shall be the sitter's fee?"

"Humph," said Mrs. O'Shea. "I'd no great opinion of the last one ye did."

"Hideous thing. Hideous," said the Major.

"Oh, but this one, madame, will be quite different!" Chapdelaine smiled, at his most persuasive. "In the course of seven years, after all, one's technique alters entirely."

She demurred for a long time, but in the end, I suppose, she could not resist this chance of further entertainment. Besides, he was extremely well known now.

"You'll have to come down here though, Mr. Chapdelaine; at my age I can't be gadding up to London for sittings."

"Of course," he agreed, shivering slightly; the sitting room was as cold as ever. "It will be a great pleasure."

"I think the pub in the village occasionally puts up visitors," Mrs. O'Shea added. "I'll speak to them." Chapdelaine shuddered again. "But they only have one bedroom, so I'm afraid there won't be room for *you*, Miss Bell." Her tone expressed volumes.

"Thank you, but I have my job in London," I said coldly. "Besides, I'd like to be getting on with offering Patrick's poems; may I take them now, Mrs. O'Shea?"

"The?—Oh, gracious, *no*—not till the picture's finished! After all," she said with a smile of pure, chill malice, "I may not like it when it's done, may I?"

"It's a hopeless affair, hopeless!" I raged as soon as we were away from the house. "She'll always find some way of slipping out of the bargain; she's utterly unscrupulous. The woman's a fiend! Really I can't think how Patrick could ever have been fond of her. Why do you bother to go on with this?"

"Oh, but I am looking forward to painting this portrait immensely!" Chapdelaine wore a broad grin. "I feel convinced this will be the best piece of work I ever did. I shall have to get that house warmed up though, even if it means myself paying for a truckload of logs; one cannot work inside of a deep freeze."

Somehow he achieved this; when I took down a photographer to get a story, with pictures, for the magazine on which I work, we found the sitting room transformed, littered with artists' equipment and heated to conservatory temperature by a huge roaring fire. Mrs. O'Shea, evidently making the most of such unaccustomed sybaritism, was seated close by the fire, her feet, as ever, firmly planted on the blanket-wrapped bundle. She seemed in high spirits. The Major was nowhere to be seen; he had apparently been banished to some distant part of the house. Chapdelaine, I thought, did not look well; he coughed from time to time, complained of damp sheets at the pub, and constantly piled more logs on the fire. We took several shots of them both, but Mrs. O'Shea would not allow us to see the uncompleted portrait.

"Not till it's quite done!" she said firmly. Meanwhile it stood on its easel in the corner, covered with a sheet, like some hesitant ghost.

During this time I had had numerous calls from Patrick, of course; he was wildly impatient about the slow progress of the painting.

"Do persuade Armand to go a bit faster, can't you, Ellis? He used to be able to dash off a portrait in about four sittings."

"Well, I'll pass on your message, Patrick, but people's methods change, you know."

When I rang Clayhole the next day, however, I was unable to get through; the line was out of order apparently, and remained so; when

I reported this to the local exchange, the girl said," Double four six three . . . wait a minute; yes, I thought so. We had a nine-nine-nine call from them not long ago. Fire brigade. No, that's all I can tell you, I'm afraid."

With my heart in my suede boots I got out the car and drove down to Clayhole. The lane was blocked by police trucks, fire engines, and appliances; I had to leave my car at the bottom and walk up.

Clayhole was a smoking ruin; as I arrived they were just carrying the third blackened body out to the ambulance.

"What began it?" I asked the fire chief.

"That'll be for the insurance assessors to decide, miss. But it's plain it started in the lounge; spark from the fire, most likely. Wood fires are always a bit risky, in my opinion. You get that green applewood—"

A spark, of course; I thought of the jersey-wrapped pile of poems hardly a foot distant from the crackling logs.

"You didn't find any papers in that room?"

"Not a scrap, miss; that being where the fire started, everything was reduced to powder."

When Patrick got through to me that evening, he was pretty distraught.

"She planned the whole thing!" he said furiously. "I bet you, Ellis, she had it all thought out from the start. There's absolutely nothing that woman won't do to get her own way. Haven't I always said she was utterly unscrupulous? But I shan't be beaten by her, I'm just as determined as she is—*Do* pay attention, Ellis!"

"Sorry, Patrick. What were you saying?" I was very low-spirited, and his next announcement did nothing to cheer me.

"I'll dictate you the poems; it shouldn't take more than a month or so if we keep at it. We can start right away. Have you a pen? And you'll want quite a lot of paper. I've finished the volcano poem, so we may as well start with that—ready?"

"I suppose so." I shut my eyes. The cold clutch on my wrist was like a fetter. But I felt that having gone so far, I owed this last service to Patrick.

"Right—here we go." There followed a long pause. Then he said, with a great deal less certainty:

> "*On each hand the flames*
> *Driven backward slope their pointing spires*—"

"That's from *Paradise Lost,* Patrick," I told him gently.

"I know. . . ." His voice was petulant. "That isn't what I meant to say. The thing is—it's starting to get so cold here. Oh, God, Ellis—it's so *cold*. . . ."

His voice petered out and died. The grasp on my wrist became freezing, became numbing, and then, like a melted icicle, was gone.

"Patrick?" I said. "Are you there, Patrick?"

But there was no reply, and, indeed, I hardly expected one. Patrick never got through to me again. His mother had caught up with him at last.

# The Dark Streets of Kimball's Green

"Em! You, Em! Where has that dratted child got to? Em! Wait till I lay hold of you, I won't half tan you!"

Mrs. Bella Vaughan looked furiously up and down the short street. She was a stocky woman, with short, thick, straight grey hair, parted on one side and clamped back by a grip; a cigarette always dangled from one corner of her mouth and, as soon as it dwindled down, another grew there. "Em! Where have you got to?" she yelled again.

"Here I am, Mrs. Vaughan!" Emmeline dashed anxiously round the corner.

"Took long enough about it! The Welfare Lady's here, wants to know how you're getting on. Here, let's tidy you up."

Mrs. Vaughan pulled a comb and handkerchief out of her tight-stretched apron pocket, dragged her comb sharply through Emmeline's hair, damped the handkerchief with spit and scrubbed it over Emmeline's flinching face.

"Hullo, Emmeline. Been out playing?" said the Welfare Lady, indoors. "That's right. Fresh air's the best thing for them, isn't it, Mrs. Vaughan?"

"She's always out," grunted Mrs. Vaughan. "Morning, noon and night. I don't hold with kids frowsting about indoors. Not much traffic round here."

"Well, Emmeline, how are you getting on? Settling down with Mrs. Vaughan, quite happy, are you?"

Emmeline looked at her feet and muttered something. She was thin and small for her age, dark-haired and pale-cheeked.

"She's a mopey kid," Mrs. Vaughan pronounced. "Always want to be reading, if I didn't tell her to run out of doors."

"Fond of reading, are you?" the Welfare Lady said kindly. "And what do you read, then?"

"Books," muttered Emmeline. The Welfare Lady's glance strayed to the huge, untidy pile of magazines on the telly.

"Kid'll read anything she could lay hands on, if I let her," Mrs. Vaughan said. "I don't though. What good does reading do you? None that I know of."

"Well, I'm glad you're getting on all right, Emmeline. Be a good girl and do what Mrs. Vaughan tells you. And I'll see you next month again." She got into her tiny car and drove off to the next of her endless list of calls.

"Right," said Mrs. Vaughan. "I'm off too, down to the town hall to play bingo. So you hop it, and mind you're here on the doorstep at eleven sharp or I'll skin you."

Emmeline murmured something.

"Stay indoors? Not on your nelly! And have them saying if the house burnt down, that I oughtn't to have left you on your own?"

"It's so cold out." A chilly September wind scuffled the bits of paper in the street. Emmeline shivered in her thin coat.

"Well, run about then, and keep warm! Fresh air's good for you, like that interfering old busybody said. Anyway she's come and gone for the month, that's something. Go on, hop it now."

So Emmeline hopped it.

Kimball's Green, where Mrs. Vaughan had her home, was a curious, desolate little corner of London. It lay round the top of a hill, which was crowned with a crumbling, blackened church, St. Chad's. The four or five streets of tiny, aged houses were also crumbling and blackened, all due for demolition, and most of them empty. The houses were so old that they seemed shrunk and wrinkled, like old apples or old faces, and they were immeasurably, unbelievably dirty, with the dirt of hundreds of years. Around the little hill was a flat, desolate tract of land, Wansea Marshes, which nobody had even tried to use until the nineteenth century; then it became covered with railway goods yards and brick-works and gas-works and an electric power station, all of which belched their black smoke over the little island of Kimball's Green on the hilltop.

You could hardly think anybody would *choose* to live in such a cut-off part; but Mrs. Vaughan had been born in Sylvan Street, near the top of the hill, and she declared she wasn't going to shift until they came after her with a bulldozer. She took in foster children when they grew too old for the Wansea Orphanage, and, though it wasn't a very healthy neighbourhood, what with the smoke and the damp from the marshes, there were so many orphans, and so few homes for them to go to, that Emmeline was the latest of a large number who had stayed with Mrs. Vaughan. But there were very few other children in the district now; very few inhabitants at all, except old and queer ones who camped secretly in the condemned houses. Most people found it too far to go to the shops: an eightpenny bus-ride, all the way past the goods yards and the gas-works, to Wansea High Street.

So far as anyone knew, Emmeline belonged in the neighbourhood; she had been found on the step of St. Chad's one windy March night; but in spite of this, or because of it, she was rather frightened by the nest of little dark empty streets. She was frightened by many things, among which were Mrs. Vaughan and her son Colin. And she particularly hated the nights, five out of seven, when Mrs. Vaughan went off to play bingo, leaving Emmeline outside in the street. Indeed, if it hadn't been for two friends, Emmeline really didn't know how she could have borne those evenings.

As Mrs. Vaughan's clumping steps died away down the hill, one of the friends appeared: his thin form twined out from between some old black railings and he rubbed encouragingly against Emmeline's ankles, sticking up his tail in welcome.

"Oh, Scrawny! There you are," she said with relief. "Here, I've saved you a piece of cheese-rind from tea."

Old Scrawny was a tattered, battered tabby, with ragged whiskers, crumpled ears, and much fur missing from his tail; he had no owner and lived on what he could find; he ate the cheese-rind with a lot of loud, vulgar, guzzling noise, and hardly washed at all afterwards; but Emmeline loved him dearly, and he loved her back. Every night she left her window open, and old Scrawny climbed in, by various gutters, drainpipes, and the wash-house roof. Mrs. Vaughan wouldn't have allowed such a thing for a minute if she had known, but Emmeline always took care that old Scrawny had left long before she was called in the morning.

When the rind was finished Scrawny jumped into Emmeline's arms and she tucked her hands for warmth under his scanty fur; they went up to the end of the street by the old church, where there was a telephone booth. Like the houses around it was old and dirty, and it had been out of order for so many years that now nobody even bothered to thump its box for coins. The only person who used it was Emmeline, and she used it almost every night, unless gangs were roaming the streets and throwing stones, in which case she hid behind a dustbin or under a flight of area steps. But when the gangs had gone elsewhere the call-box made a very convenient shelter; best of all, it was even light enough to read there, because although the bulb in the call-box had been broken long ago, a street lamp shone right overhead.

"No book tonight, Scrawny, unless Mr. Yakkymo comes and brings me another," said Emmeline, "so what shall we do? Shall we phone somebody, or shall I tell you a story?"

Scrawny purred, dangling round her neck like a striped scarf.

"We'll ring somebody up, shall we? All right."

She let the heavy door close behind her. Inside it was not exactly warm, but at least they were out of the wind. Scrawny climbed from Emmeline's shoulder into the compartment where the telephone books would have been if somebody hadn't made off with them; Emmeline picked up the broken receiver and dialled.

"Hullo, can I speak to King Cunobel? Hullo, King Cunobel, I am calling to warn you. A great army is approaching your fort—the

Tribe of the Children of Darkness. Under their wicked queen Belavaun they are coming to attack your stronghold with spears and chariots. You must tell your men to be extra brave; each man must arm himself with his bow and a sheaf of arrows, two spears and a sword. Each man must have his faithful wolfhound by his side." She stroked old Scrawny, who seemed to be listening intently. "Your men are far outnumbered by the Children of the Dark, King Cunobel, so you must tell your Chief Druid to prepare a magic drink, made from vetch and mallow and succory, to give them courage. The leaves must be steeped in mead and left to gather dew for two nights, until you have enough to wet each man's tongue. Then they will be brave enough to beat off the Children of the Dark and save your camp."

She listened for a moment or two with her ear pressed against the silent receiver, and then said to old Scrawny,

"King Cunobel wants to know what will happen if the Children of Dark get to the fort before the magic drink is prepared?"

"Morow," said Scrawny. He jumped down from the bookshelf and settled himself on Emmeline's feet, where there was more room to stretch out.

"My faithful wolfhound says you must order your men to make high barricades of brambles and thorns," Emmeline told King Cunobel. "Build them in three rings round the encampment, and place one-third of your men inside each ring. King Cunobel and the Druids will be in the middle ring. Each party must fight to the death in order to delay the Children of Dark until the magic drink is ready. Do you understand? Then good-bye and good luck."

She listened again.

"He wants to know who I am," she told Scrawny, and she said into the telephone, "I am a friend, the Lady Emmeline, advised by her faithful enchanted wolfhound Catuscraun. I wish you well."

Then she rang off and said to Scrawny, "Do you think I had better call the Chief Druid and tell him to hurry up with that magic drink?"

Old Scrawny shut his eyes.

"No," she agreed, "you're right, it would only distract him. I know, I'll ring up the wicked Queen of Dark."

She dialled again and said,

"Hullo, is that the wicked Queen Belavaun? This is your greatest enemy, ringing up to tell you that you will never, never capture the stronghold of King Cunobel. Not if you besiege it for three thousand years! King Cunobel has a strong magic that will defeat you. All your tribes, the Trinovans and the Votadins and the Damnons and the Bingonii will be eaten by wolves and wild boars. Not a man will remain! And you will lose your wealth and power and your purple robes and fur cloaks, you will have nothing left but a miserable old mud cabin outside King Cunobel's stronghold, and every day his men will look over the walls and laugh at you. Good-bye, and bad luck to you forever!"

She rang off and said to Scrawny, "That frightened her."

Scrawny was nine-tenths asleep, but at this moment footsteps coming along the street made him open his eyes warily. Emmeline was alert too. The call-box made a good look-out point, but it would be a dangerous place in which to be trapped.

"It's all right," she said to Scrawny, then. "It's only Mr. Yakkymo."

She opened the door and they went to meet their other friend.

Mr. Yakkymo (he spelt his name Iachimo, but Yakkymo was the way it sounded) came limping slightly up the street until he reached them; then he rubbed the head of old Scrawny (who stuck his tail up) and handed Emmeline a book. It was old and small, with a mottled binding and gilt-edged leaves; it was called *The Ancient History of Kimball's Green and Wansea Marshes,* and it came from Wansea Borough Library.

Emmeline's eyes opened wide with delight. She began reading the book at once, skipping from page to page.

"Why, this tells all about King Cunobel! It's even better than the one you brought about ancient London. Have you read this, Mr. Yakkymo?"

He nodded, smiling. He was a thin, bent old man with rather long white hair; as well as the book he carried a leather case, which contained a flute, and when he was not speaking he would often open this case and run his fingers absently up and down the instrument.

"I thought you would find it of interest," he said. "It's a pity Mrs. Vaughan won't let you go to the public library yourself."

"She says reading only puts useless stuck-up notions in people's heads," Emmeline said dreamily, her eyes darting up and down the pages of the book. "Listen! It tells what King Cunobel wore—a short kilt with a gold belt. His chest was painted blue with woad, and he had a gold collar round his neck and a white cloak with gold embroidery. He carried a shield of beaten brass and a short sword. On his head he wore a fillet of gold, and on his arm gold armlets. His house was built of mud and stone, with a thatched roof; the walls were hung with skins and the floor strewn with rushes."

They had turned and were walking slowly along the street; old Scrawny, after the manner of cats, sometimes loitered behind investigating doorsteps and dark crannies, sometimes darted ahead and then waited for them to come up with him.

"Do you think any of King Cunobel's descendants still live here?" Emmeline said.

"It is just possible."

"Tell me some more about what it was like to live here then."

"All the marshes—the part where the brick-works and the goods yards are now—would have been covered by forest and threaded by slow-flowing streams."

"Threaded by slow-flowing streams," Emmeline murmured to herself.

"All this part would be Cunobel's village. Little mud huts, each with a door and a chimney hole, thatched with reeds."

Emmeline looked at the pavements and rows of houses, trying to imagine them away, trying to imagine forest trees and little thatched huts.

"There would be a stockade of logs and thorns all round. A bigger hall for the King, and one for Druids near the sacred grove."

"Where was that?"

"Up at the top of the hill, probably. With a specially sacred oak in the middle. There is an oak tree, still, in St. Chad's churchyard; maybe it's sprung from an acorn of the Druid's oak."

"Maybe it's the same one? Oaks live a long time, don't they?"

"Hark!" he said checking. "What's that?"

The three of them were by the churchyard wall; they kept still and listened. Next moment they all acted independently, with the speed of long practice: Mr. Iachimo, murmuring, "Good night, my child," slipped away round a corner; Emmeline wrapped her precious book in a polythene bag and poked it into a hole in the wall behind a loose stone; then she and old Scrawny raced downhill, back to Mrs. Vaughan's house. She crouched, panting on the doorstep, old Scrawny leapt up on to a shed roof and out of reach, just as a group of half a dozen people came swaggering and singing along the street.

"What was that?" one of them called.

"A cat."

"Let's go after it!"

"No good. It's gone."

When they got to Mrs. Vaughan their chief left the others and came over to Emmeline.

"It's you, is it, Misery?" he said. "Where's Ma?"

"Out at bingo."

"She would be. I wanted to get a bit of the old girl's pension off her before she spent it all."

He gave Emmeline's hair a yank and flipped her nose, hard and painfully, with his thumbnail. She looked at him in stony silence, biting her lip.

"Who's *she*, Col?" a new gang-member asked. "Shall we chivvy her?"

"She's one of my Ma's orphanage brats—just a little drip. Ma won't let me tease her, so long as she's indoors, or on the step. But watch it, you, if we catch you in the street." Colin flipped Emmeline's nose again and they drifted off, kicking at anything that lay on the pavement.

At half-past eleven Mrs. Vaughan came home from her bingo and let in the shivering Emmeline, who went silently up to her bed in the attic. At eleven thirty-five old Scrawny jumped with equal silence on to her stomach, and the two friends curled round each other for warmth.

Colin was not at breakfast next morning. Often he spent nights on end away from home; his mother never bothered to ask where.

Emmeline had to run errands and do housework in the morning but in the afternoon Mrs. Vaughan, who wanted a nap, told her to clear off and not show her face a minute before six. That gave her five whole hours for reading; she dragged on her old coat and flew up to the churchyard.

The door in the high black wall was always kept locked, but someone had once left a lot of rusty old metal pipes stacked in an angle of the wall; Emmeline, who weighed very little more than old Scrawny, clambered carefully up them, and so over.

Inside, the churchyard was completely overgrown. Blackthorn, plane and sycamore trees were entangled with great clumps of bramble. Groves of mares'-tails, chin-high to Emmeline, covered every foot of the ground. It made a perfect place to come and hide by day, but was too dark at night and too full of pitfalls; pillars and stone slabs leaned every which way, hidden in the vegetation.

Emmeline flung herself down on the flat tomb of Admiral Sir Horace Tullesley Campbell and read her book; for three hours she never moved; then she closed it with a sigh, so as to leave some for the evening in case Mrs. Vaughan went out.

A woodpecker burst yammering from the tallest tree as Emmeline shut the book. Could that be the Druids' oak, she wondered, and started to push her way through to it. Brambles scratched her face and tore her clothes; Mrs. Vaughan would punish her but that couldn't be helped. And at last she was there. The tree stood in a little clear space of bare leaf-mould. It was an oak, a big one, with a gnarled, massive trunk and roots like knuckles thrusting out of the ground. This made an even better secret place for reading than the

Admiral's tomb, and Emmeline wished once again that it wasn't too dark to read in the churchyard at night.

St. Chad's big clock said a quarter to six, so she left *The Ancient History of Kimball's Green* in its plastic bag hidden in a hollow of the tree and went draggingly home; then realized, too late, that her book would be exceedingly hard to find once dark had fallen.

Mrs. Vaughan, who had not yet spent all her week's money, went out to bingo again that evening, so Emmeline returned to the telephone box and rang up King Cunobel.

"Is that the King? I have to tell you that your enemies are five miles nearer. Queen Belavaun is driving a chariot with scythes on its wheels, and her wicked son Coluon leads a band of savage followers; he carries a sling and a gold-handled javelin and is more cruel than any of the band. Has the Chief Druid prepared the magic drink yet?"

She listened and old Scrawny, who was as usual sitting at her feet, said "Prtnrow?""

"The Chief Druid says they have made the drink, Scrawny, and put it in a flagon of beaten bronze, which has been set beneath the sacred oak until it is needed. Meanwhile the warriors are feasting on wheat-cakes, boars' flesh and mead."

Next she rang up Queen Belavaun and hissed, "Oh, wicked queen, your enemies are massing against you! You think you will triumph, but you are wrong! Your son will be taken prisoner, and you will be turned out of your kingdom; you will be forced to take refuge with the Iceni or the Brigantes."

It was still only half-past nine and Mr. Iachimo probably would not come this evening, for two nights out of three he went to play his flute outside a theatre in the West End of London.

"Long ago I was a famous payer and people came from all over Europe to hear me," he had told Emmeline sadly, one wet evening when they were sheltering together in the church porch.

"What happened? Why aren't you famous now?"

"I took to drink," he said mournfully. "Drink give you hiccups. You can't play the flute with hiccups."

"You don't seem to have hiccups now."

"Now I can't afford to drink any longer."

"So you can play the flute again," Emmeline said triumphantly.

"True," he agreed; he pulled out his instrument and blew a sudden dazzling shower of notes into the rainy dark. "But now it is too late. Nobody listens; nobody remembers the name of Iachimo. And I have grown too old and tired to make them remember."

"Poor Mr. Yakkymo," Emmeline thought, recalling this conversation. "He could do with a drop of King Cunobel's magic drink; then he'd be able to make people listen to him."

She craned out of the telephone box to look at St. Chad's clock: quarter to ten. The streets were quiet tonight: Colin's gang had got money from somewhere and were down at the Wansea Palais.

"I'm going to get my book," Emmeline suddenly decided. "At least I'm going to try. There's a moon, it shouldn't be too dark to see. Coming, Scrawny?"

Scrawny, intimated, stretching, that he didn't mind.

The churchyard was even stranger under the moon than by daylight; the mares'-tails threw their zebra-striped shadows everywhere and an owl flew hooting across the path; old Scrawny yakkered after it indignantly to come back and fight fair, but the owl didn't take up his challenge.

"I don't suppose it's really an owl," Emmeline whispered. "Probably one of Queen Belavaun's spies. We must make haste."

Finding the oak tree was not so hard as she had feared, but finding the book was a good deal harder, because under the tree's thick leaves and massive branches no light could penetrate; Emmeline groped and fumbled among the roots until she was quite sure she must have been right round the tree at least three times. At last her right hand slipped into a deep crack; she rummaged about hopefully, her fingers closed on something, but what she pulled out was a small object tapered at one end. She stuck it in her coat pocket and went on searching. "The book must be here somewhere, Scrawny; unless Queen Belavaun's spy has stolen it."

At last she found it; tucked away where she could have sworn she had searched a dozen times already.

"Thank goodness! Now we'd better hurry, or there won't be any time for reading after all."

Emmeline was not sorry to leave the churchyard behind; it felt *crowded,* as if King Cunobel's warriors were hiding there, shoulder to shoulder among the bushes, keeping vigilant watch; Sylvan Street outside was empty and lonely in comparison. She scurried into the phone box, clutching Scrawny against her chest.

"Now listen while I read to you about the Druids, Scrawny; they wore long white robes and they liked mistletoe—there's some mistletoe growing on that oak tree, I'm positive!—and they used rings of sacred stones, too. Maybe some of the stones in the churchyard are left over from the Druids."

Scrawny purred agreeingly, and Emmeline looked up the hill, trying to move St. Chad's church out of the way and replace it by a grove of sacred trees with aged, white-robed men among them.

Soon it was eleven o'clock: time to hide the book behind the stone and wait for Mrs. Vaughan on the doorstep. Along with his mother came Colin, slouching and bad-tempered.

"Your face is all scratched," he told Emmeline. "You look a sight."

"What have you been up to?" Mrs. Vaughan said sharply.

Emmeline was silent but Colin said, "Reckon it's that mangy old cat she's always lugging about."

"Don't let me see you with a cat around *this* house," Mrs. Vaughan snapped. "Dirty, sneaking things, never know where they've been. If any cat comes in here, I tell you, I'll get Colin to wring its neck!"

Colin smiled; Emmeline's heart turned right over with horror. But she said nothing and crept off upstairs to bed; only, when Scrawny arrived later, rather wet because it had begun to rain, she clutched him convulsively tight; a few tears wouldn't make much difference to the dampness of his fur.

"Humph!" said Mrs. Vaughan, arriving early and unexpectedly in Emmeline's attic. "I thought as much!"

She leaned to slam the window but Scrawny, though startled out of sleep, could still move ten times faster than any human; he was out and over the roof in a flash.

"Look at that!" said Mrs. Vaughan. "Filthy, muddy cat's footprints all over my blankets! Well that's one job you'll do this morning my young madam—you'll wash those blankets. And you'll have to sleep without blankets till they've dried—I'm not giving you any other. Daresay they're all full of fleas' eggs too."

Emmeline, breakfastless, crouched over the tub in the back wash-house; she did not much mind the job, but her brain was giddy with worry about Scrawny; how could she protect him? Suppose he were to wait for her, as he sometimes did, outside the house. Mrs. Vaughan had declared that she would go after him with the chopper if she set eyes on him; Colin had sworn to hunt him down.

"All right, hop it now," Mrs. Vaughan said, when the blankets satisfied her. "Clear out, don't let me see you again before six. No dinner? Well, I can't help that, can I? You should have finished the washing by dinner-time. Oh, all right, here's a bit of bread and marge, now make yourself scarce. I can't abide kids about the house all day."

Emmeline spent most of the afternoon in a vain hunt for Scrawny. Perhaps he had retired to some hidey-hole for a nap, as he often did at that time of day; but perhaps Colin had caught him already?

"Scrawny, Scrawny," she called softly and despairingly at the mouths of alleys, outside gates, under trees and walls; there was no reply. She went up to the churchyard, but a needle in a hundred haystacks would be easier to find than Scrawny in that wilderness if he did not choose to wake and show himself.

Giving up for the moment Emmeline went in search of Mr. Iachimo, but he was not to be found either; he had never told Emmeline where he lived and was seldom seen by daylight; she thought he probably inhabited one of the condemned houses and was ashamed of it.

It was very cold; a grey, windy afternoon turning gloomily to dusk. Emmeline pushed cold hands deep in her pockets; her fingers met and explored a round, unusual object. Then she remembered the thing she had picked up in the dark under the oak tree. She pulled it out, and found she was holding a tiny flask, made of some dark lustreless metal tarnished with age and crusted with earth. It was not quite empty; when Emmeline shook it she could hear liquid splashing about inside, but very little, not more than a few drops.

"Why," she breathed, just for a moment forgetting her fear in the excitement of this discovery, "It is—it *must* be the Druids' magic drink! But why, why didn't the warriors drink it?"

She tried to get out the stopper; it was made of some hard blackish substance, wood, or leather that had become hard as wood in the course of years.

"Can I help you, my child?" said a gentle voice above her head.

Emmeline nearly jumped out of her skin—but it was only Mr. Iachimo, who had hobbled silently up the street.

"Look-look, Mr. Yakkymo! Look what I found under the big oak in the churchyard! It must be the Druids' magic drink—mustn't it? Made of mallow and vetch and succory, steeped in mead, to give warriors courage. It must be!"

He smiled at her; his face was very kind. "Yes, indeed it must!" he said.

But somehow, although he was agreeing with her, for a moment Emmeline had a twinge of queer dread, as if there were nothing—nothing at all—left in the world to hold on to; as if even Mr. Iachimo were not what he seemed but, perhaps, a spy sent by Queen Belavaun to steal the magic flagon.

Then she pushed down her fear, taking a deep breath, and said, "Can you get the stopper out, Mr. Yakkymo?"

"I can try," he said, and brought out a tiny foreign-looking penknife shaped like a fish with which he began prising at the fossil-hard black substance in the neck of the bottle. At last it began to crumble.

"Take care—do take care," Emmeline said. "There's only a very little left. Perhaps the defenders did drink most of it. But anyway there's enough left for you, Mr. Yakkymo."

"For me, my child? Why for me?"

"Because you meed to be made brave so that you can make people listen to you play your flute."

"Very true," he said thoughtfully. "But do not you need bravery too?"

Emmeline's face clouded. "What good would bravery do me?" she said. "*I'm* all right—it's old Scrawny I'm worried about. Oh, Mr. Yakkymo, Colin and Mrs. Vaughan say they are going to *kill* Scrawny. What can I do?"

"You must tell them they have no right to."

"*That* wouldn't do any good," Emmeline said miserably. "Oh!—You've got it out!"

The stopper had come out, but it had also crumbled away entirely.

"Never mind," Emmeline said. "You can put in a bit of the cotton-wool that you use to clean your flute. What does it smell of, Mr. Yakkymo?"

His face had changed as he sniffed; he looked at her oddly. "Honey and flowers," he said.

Emmeline sniffed too. There was a faint—very faint—aromatic, sweet fragrance.

"Wet your finger, Mr. Yakkymo, and lick it! Please do! It'll help you, I know it will!"

"Shall I?"

"Yes, do, do!"

He placed his finger across the opening, and quickly turned the bottle upside down and back, then looked at his fingertip. There was the faintest drop of moisture on it.

"Quick—don't waste it," Emmeline said, breathless with anxiety.

He licked his finger.

"Well? does it taste?"

"No taste." But he smiled, and bringing out a wad of cotton tissue, stuffed a piece of it into the mouth of the flask, which he handed to Emmeline.

"This is yours, my child. Guard it well! Now, as to your friend Scrawny—I will go and see Mrs. Vaughan tomorrow, if you can protect him until then."

"Thank you!" she said. "The drink *must* be making you brave!"

Above their heads the clock of St. Chad had tolled six.

"I must be off to the West End," Mr. Iachimo said. "And you had better run home to supper. Till tomorrow, then—and a thousand, thousand thanks for your help."

He gave her a deep, foreign bow and limped, much faster than usual, away down the hill.

"Oh, do let it work," Emmeline thought, looking after him.

Then she ran home to Mrs. Vaughan's.

Supper was over; Colin, thank goodness, did not come in, and Mrs. Vaughan wanted to get through and be off; Emmeline bolted down her food, washed the plate, and was dismissed to the streets again.

As she ran up to the churchyard wall, with her fingers tight clenched round the precious little flask, a worrying thought suddenly struck her.

The magic drink had mead in it. Suppose the mead were to give Mr. Iachimo hiccups? But there must be very little mead in such a tiny drop, she consoled herself; the risk could not be great.

When she pulled her book from the hole in the wall a sound met her ears that made her smile with relief: old Scrawny's mew of greeting, rather creaking and scratchy, as he dragged himself yawning, one leg at a time, from a clump of ivy on top of the wall.

"*There* you are, Scrawny! If you knew how I'd been worrying about you!"

She tucked him under one arm, put the book under the other, and made her way to the telephone box. Scrawny settled on her feet for another nap, and she opened *The Ancient History of Kimball's Green.* Only one chapter remained to be read; she turned to it and became absorbed. St. Chad's clock ticked solemnly round overhead.

When Emmeline finally closed the book, tears were running down her face.

"Oh, Scrawny!—they didn't win! They *lost!* King Cunobel's men were all killed—and the Druids too, defending the stronghold. Every one of them. Oh, how can I bear it? Why did it have to happen, Scrawny?"

Scrawny made no answer, but he laid his chin over her ankle. At that moment the telephone bell rang.

Emmeline stared at the instrument in utter consternation. Scrawny sprang up; the fur along his back slowly raised, and his ears flattened. The bell went on ringing.

"But," whispered Emmeline, staring at the broken black receiver, "it's out of order. It *can't* ring! It's never rung! What shall I do, Scrawny?"

By now, Scrawny had recovered. He sat himself down again and began to wash. Emmeline looked up and down the empty street. Nobody came. The bell went on ringing.

At the same time, down below the hill and some distance off, in Wansea High Street, ambulance attendants were carefully lifting an old man off the pavement and laying him on a stretcher.

"Young brutes," said a bystander to a policeman who was taking notes. "It was one of those gangs of young hooligans from up Kimball's Green way; I'd know several of them again if I saw them. They set on him—it's the old street musician who comes from up there too. Seems he was coming home early tonight, and the boys jumped on him—you wouldn't think they'd bother with a poor fellow like him, he can't have much worth stealing."

But the ambulance men were gathering up handlfuls of half-crowns and two-shilling pieces which had rolled from Mr. Iachimo's pockets; there were notes as well, ten shillings, a pound, even five-and ten-pound notes. And a broken flute.

"It was certainly worthy their while tonight," the policeman said. "He must have done a lot better than usual."

"He was a game old boy—fought back like a lion; marked some of them, I shouldn't wonder. They had to leave him and run for it. Will he be all right?"

"We'll see," said the ambulance man, closing the doors.

"I'd better answer it," Emmeline said at last. She picked up the receiver, trembling as if it might give her a shock.

"Hullo?" she whispered.

And a voice—a faint, hoarse, distant voice—said,

"This is King Cunobel. I cannot speak for long. I am calling to warn you. There is danger on the way—great danger coming towards you and your friend. Take care! Watch well!"

Emmeline's lips parted. She could not speak.

"There is danger—danger!" the voice repeated. Then the line went silent.

Emmeline stared from the silent telephone to the cat at her feet.

"Did you hear it too, Scrawny?"

Scrawny gazed at her impassively, and washed behind his ear.

Then Emmeline heard the sound of running feet. The warning had been real. She pushed the book into her pocket and was about to pick up Scrawny, but hesitated, with her fingers on the little flask.

"Maybe I ought to drink it, Scrawny? Better that than have it fall into the enemy's hands. Should I? Yes, I will! Here, you must have a drop too."

She laid a wet finger on Scrawny's nose; out came his pink tongue at once. Then she drained the bottle, picked up Scrawny, opened the door, and ran.

Turning back once more to look, she could see a group of dark figures coming after her down the street. She heard someone shout,

"That's her, and she's got the cat too! Come on!"

But beyond, behind and *through* her pursuers, Emmeline caught a glimpse of something else: a high, snow-covered hill, higher than the hill she knew, crowned with great bare trees. And on either side of her, among and in front of the dark houses, as if she were seeing two pictures, one printed on top of the other, were still more trees, and little thatched stone houses. Thin animals with red eyes slunk silently among the huts. Just a glimpse she had, of the two worlds, one behind the other, and then she had reached Mrs. Vaughan's doorstep and turned to face the attackers.

Colin Vaughan was in the lead; his face, bruised, cut, and furious, showed its ugly intention as plainly as a raised club.

"Give me that damn cat. I've had enough from you and your friends. I'm going to wring its neck."

But Emmeline stood at bay; her eyes blazed defiance and so did Scrawny's; he bared his fangs at Colin like a sabre-toothed tiger.

Emmeline said clearly, "Don't you dare lay a finger on me, Colin Vaughan. Just don't you dare touch me!"

He actually flinched, and stepped back half a pace; his gang shuffled back behind him.

At this moment Mrs. Vaughan came up the hill; not at her usual smart pace but slowly, plodding, as if she had no heart in her.

"Clear out, the lot of you," she said angrily. "Poor old Mr. Iachimo's in the Wansea Hospital, thanks to you. Beating up old men! That's all you're good for. Go along, scram, before I set the back of my hand to some of you. Beat it!"

"But we were going to wring the cat's neck. You wanted me to do that," Colin protested.

"Oh, what do I care about the blame cat?" she snapped, turning to climb the steps, and came face to face with Emmeline.

"Well, don't *you* stand there like a lump," Mrs. Vaughan said angrily. "Put the blasted animal down and get to bed!"

"I'm not going to bed," Emmeline said. "I'm not going to live with you any more."

"Oh, indeed? And where are you going, then?" said Mrs. Vaughan, completely astonished.

"I'm going to see poor Mr. Yakkymo. And then I'm going to find someone who'll take me and Scrawny, some place where I shall be happy. I'm never coming back to your miserable house again."

"Oh, well suit yourself," Mrs. Vaughan grunted. "You're not the only one. I've just heard: fifty years in this place and then fourteen days' notice to quit; in two weeks the bulldozers are coming."

She went indoors.

But Emmeline had not listened; clutching Scrawny, brushing past the gang as if they did exist, she ran for the last time down the dark streets of Kimball's Green.

# The Lame King

"Crumbling rainbows are useless as a diet," said Mrs. Logan. "I don't like 'em. Prefer something solid to bite on."

Under her breath in the front passenger's seat, Mrs. Logan's daughter-in-law Sandra muttered, "Shut up, you dotty old bore." And, above her breath, she added to her husband, "*Can't* you drive a bit faster, Philip? It will be terribly late by the time we get home. There's the sitter's fee, don't forget. And we've got all our packing to do."

"You have all tomorrow to do it in," mildly pointed out her father-in-law from the backseat.

She flashed him an angry diagonal glance, and snapped, "There's plenty of other things to do, as well as packing. Cancel the milk, take Buster to the dog's hotel, fill out all the notification forms—"

"I would have done that, if you had let me," said old Mr. Logan in his precise tones. He had been a headmaster. Sandra made no answer to this, merely pressed her lips tight together and clenched her gloved hands in her lap. "Do drive faster, Philip," she said again.

Philip frowned and slightly shook his head, without taking his eyes off the road. He was tall and pale, with a bony righteous face and eyes like faded olives. "Can't; you know that perfectly well; it's illegal to go over sixty with senior citizens in the car," he said in a low voice.

His remark was drowned, anyway, by the voice of his mother, old Mrs. Logan, who called from the back, "Oh, no, don't drive faster, Philip dear, please don't drive any faster! I am so *loving* this landscape—I don't want to lose a moment of it! Our heroine, speeding to who knows where or what destination, is reminded of childhood—those bare trees, the spring mornings passed paddling in brooks when the water went over the tops of your wellies—the empty fields—"

Old Mr. Logan gently took her hand in his, which had the effect of checking her.

"It *is* a pretty country," he said. "I like all the sheep. And the shapes of the hills around here."

"How much farther?" said Sandra to her husband.

"About another four hours' driving. We'd better stop for a snack at a Cook's Tower."

"Oh, why?" Sandra said crossly, in a low tone. "It's just a waste of money giving them a—"

"No wolves now. It must have been so exciting for shepherds in the old days," dreamily remarked old Mrs. Logan. "Virginia came down like a wolf on the . . . but then when you try and fold on the dotted line it *never* tears straight. That is one thing they should put right in the next world."

"And I'm sure they will," said her husband comfortingly.

"I hope my thoughts are not without sense."

"Never to me, my love. Look at that farm, tucked so snugly in the hollow."

"Will the place we are going to be like that?"

"Anyway the tank needs filling," said Philip to his wife.

"What this trip will have *cost*," she muttered.

"It had to be taken sometime. And we'll get the Termination Grants, don't forget," Philip reminded his wife in a murmur.

"Well, but then you have to deduct all the expenses—"

"Sometimes I think my daughter-in-law treads in the footsteps of Sycorax," absently remarked old Mrs. Logan, who sometimes caught Sandra's tone, though not the things she actually said.

"Oh, come, you would hardly call little Kevin a Caliban?" her husband remonstrated mildly.

"Parting from Kevin is the least of my regrets. He is all the chiefs and none of the Indians. And stubborn! Combs his hair five times and then says 'I don't want to go.'"

"Kevin will grow up by and by. If he were a character in one of your books, you would know how to make him grow up."

"Ah," she said with a sigh, "no story would grow in my hands now. It would fly apart in a cloud of feathers. You say a few words—and they come back and hit you like boomerangs. What did Western man do before he know about the boomerang? What did swallows do before they invented telegraph wires? Language is so inexact—I do not mean to assert that swallows themselves invented the wires—"

"For God's *sake,* shut up," muttered young Mrs. Logan in the front seat. Old Mr. Logan laid an arm protectively round his wife's shoulders. She, with an alert, happy face, white hair flying around in wisps, continually gazed out of the window as the car sped along. "Haven't seen so much grass in ten years," she whispered. Her elderly husband looked at her calmly and fondly. Sometimes a shadow of pain flitted across his face, like that of a high jet over a huge field, but it was gone the moment after.

"There's a place," said Philip. "We'll stop there."

A Cook's Tower had come in sight: square white pillar, castellated at the top, with red zigzags all the way down, and a wide parking lot glittering with massed vehicles.

"Park somewhere close in, we don't want to waste twenty minutes helping them hobble," muttered Sandra.

"I'll park as close as I can," replied Philip with a frown, and called to the pair in the back, "Fancy a snack, Mum and Dad? Cup o' tea? Sandwich?"

He tried to make his voice festive.

"Oh, there's no need for that, my boy," said his father. "We're all right, we're not hungry. Save your money." But his mother called, "Oh, yes! A nice cup of tea and a last rock cake. Rock of ages cleft for me. . . . A book called *The Last Rock Cake,* now . . . that would have been a certain seller, once; these days, I suppose, *The Last Croissant.* Take the queen *en croissant*; a husband in Bohemia would be a Czech mate. Oh, cries his poor silly wife, I am nothing but a blank Czeque; good for nothing but to be wheeled away to the Death House."

"*Will* you be quiet, Mother?" gritted Sandra, turning to the rear of the car a face of real ferocity.

"Never mind, my dear, you won't have us for much longer. It has been a stony row, I know, but tomorrow this time you will be en route for Ibiza—"

Philip, who had been weaving thoughtfully through the parking lot, eyes veering sharply this way and that, now whipped his Algonquin neatly into a just-vacated gap close to the main entrance.

Inside, at this time of day, the Quick-Snak cafeteria was half empty; most customers were up on the top floor having the Three Course Special.

"You sit here."

Philip edged his parents alongside a glass-topped table by the window.

"Sandra and I will forage at the counter. What's it to be? Buttered toast?"

"A rock cake," sighed Mrs. Logan. "Just a rock cake. To remind me of our honeymoon in Lynmouth."

Mr. Logan said he wanted nothing but a cup of tea. He placed a careful hand to his side. Mrs. Logan noticed this and sighed again, but said nothing.

Their table was littered with crumby plates, crumpled napkins, half-empty cups, and, on the windowsill, a grease-smeared, dog-eared paperback.

"Why, look, my dear," said old Mr. Logan, turning it over. "It's one of yours. *The Short Way Back.* Now, isn't that a remarkable coincidence. A good omen, wouldn't you say?"

They gazed at each other, delighted.

"I was only twenty-five when I wrote that one," sighed his wife. "Philip already on the way. . . . How could I *do* it? What came into my head? *Now,* I couldn't. . . ."

She handled the book gently, affectionately, smiling at the absurd picture on the front.

"Nothing to do with what's inside. But then, whatever is?"

A small old man, limping, passed by their table. His heavy metal tray held a glass of stout, black, froth-topped, and a shiny Bath bun.

"*That* looks good," said Mrs. Logan to him confidentially. "Now I'm sorry that I didn't ask for stout. And a Bath bun. . . . Do you know what? We found, we actually found a book I once wrote, lying here on a windowsill. Now isn't that a thing!"

"Well, I never!" The man with the stout beamed at her. "So you're a book writer, are you?" His voice held a slight regional burr. Welsh? Wondered Mrs. Logan. Or Scottish?

"Was once. In those *jeunesse dorée* days. Do re me, lackaday dee—" she sang softly.

"He sipped no sup and he craved no crumb," joined in the old man with the tray, "as he sighed for the love of a lady."

"Why!" exclaimed Mrs. Logan in astonished pleasure. "Now you remind me—you remind me of somebody I once knew—"

"I was just thinking the very same thing!" said her husband. "But who—?"

All three looked at one another in excitement and suspense.

"Now when was it, where was it?" murmured Mrs. Logan.

But at this moment Philip came back with a tray, followed by Sandra, with another.

"Excuse *me*," he said with brisk chill, and the old man with the stout moved quickly on his way.

"*Really*, Mother," snapped Sandra, "must you get into conversation with all and sundry?" and she thumped down in front of her mother-in-law a thick china plate on which lay a flat pale macaroon, ninety-percent gray pastry, with a flat wan dob of fawn-colored substance in the middle.

"Oh, but I asked for a rock cake. This isn't—"

"No rock cakes. Only jam tarts, buns, or macaroons."

Mrs. Logan drank her tea but declined the macaroon. "Too hard on my teeth. You have it, love." So Philip ate it, after his ham roll, with the harassed air of doing so only because it had been paid for and must not go to waste. Sandra nibbled a salad which was largely cress. She looked repeatedly at her watch.

"Philip, we should be getting on. Need the Ladies, Mother? You'd better, you don't know what there will be at—"

Rather reluctantly Mrs. Logan rose to her feet and followd her daughter-in-law to the pink boudoir, peppered over with hearts and cupids.

"Sandra," she said—and for the first time a slight tremor entered her voice—"Sandra, will it be *frightening*, do you think—where we're going?"

Sandra angrily banged at her nose with a makeup puff and skated a comb through her perm. "Frightening? Why should it? Everyone's got to go through it sometime, haven't they? Not just you. We'll have to, too, Philip and me, when our turn comes. There's nothing *frightening* about it. Come along—the others will be waiting. Hurry up!"

Philip and his father waited at the window table. Philip had impatiently piled together all the used cups, plates, napkins, and the paperback book, without observing its title.

"Women take so long, always," he muttered. "Can't think what they get up to."

The limping old man passed their table again and nodded in a friendly way at Mr. Logan.

"On the way to Last House, are you?"

"Why should you ask that?" said Philip sharply.

"Many who stop here are going that way. There's a bad greasy patch at the S-bend going over Endby Hill—you'll want to watch it there. Quite a few have come off at that corner."

"Thank you," said old Mr. Logan. "We'll remember."

Philip gave a curt nod, as if he needed no lame old strangers to teach him about careful driving, and Mr. Logan added cheerfully,

"It'd be a piece of irony, wouldn't it, if just when you were taking us—*there*—we all went off the road and ended up together!"

"Father! *Really!*"

"Little Kevin would have to go into an orphanage."

"Here come the girls," said Philip, with a jocularity he did not feel.

"What's that about an orphanage?" inquired his mother, who, her husband noticed, had a drawn and anxious look on her face. She plunged into the conversation as if trying to distract her own mind. "They say many a home is worse than an orphanage. Remember, some also agree that impatience is the worst sin. I suffered from it myself, to an extreme degree, when I was young. . . ."

"Come along, let's go," said Philip, showing signs of suffering from the worst sin himself.

A frail dusk had begun to fall as they resumed their journey. The landscape became ghostly, wreathed in layers of mist. Trees loomed, fringed by creepers, then swung past; the road wound uphill through forest.

"I wonder if there will be a view?" murmured old Mrs. Logan, more to herself than to her companions. Her husband took her hand, holding it close and firmly. She went on, still to herself, "He was always delighted with your comments on landscape, chaffinches, and so forth; I wonder if he would be still? That was a curious encounter, a curious coincidence. Candied apple, quince and plum and gourd . . . I wonder what candied *gourd* would be like? Not very nice, I'd think. But then the whole of that picnic sounded decidedly sickly—lucent syrups tinct with cinnamon; *not* what one would wish on one's bed in the middle of the night."

"Please be quiet, Mother," said Philip edgily. "There's a bad place along here, we were warned about it; I don't want any distraction, if you would be so kind."

"Of course, Philip, of course. I am so very sorry, I know I am a nuisance to you."

The bad place was negotiated, and passed, in complete silence. The elderly pair at the back drew close together in the darkness until they seemed like one person. The headlights in front converged to a sharp white V through the foggy murk.

At last the car rolled to a stop.

"Is this the place?" Mrs. Logan's voice quavered a very little.

"This is it."

Philip, relieved at having completed the outward trip, stamped to get the stiffness out of his knees; his voice was rather too cheerful. "Come along, Mother, Dad; we'll just get you registered, then we must be on our way; we're going to have to hurry to get home by the time the sitter wants to leave—"

The old people crept awkwardly out from the back of the car.

"One thing, there's no luggage to bother about," muttered Sandra. "But you would think they'd make these places more accessible—"

The small group of persons passed inside a building which was so closely surrounded by creeper-hung trees of large size that, in the foggy dark, no architectural detail was visible; it was like walking into a grove, Mrs. Logan thought.

The elderly people clung together, hand clasped tightly in hand, while forms were filled out at the desk.

Then—

"Well, we'll be leaving you now, then, Mum and Dad," said Philip, falsely hearty. "Cheerio! Take care! All the best. Bon voyage, and all that." He gave them each a peck on the cheek. Sandra muttered something inaudible, and the younger pair walked hastily out through the front entrance.

"Whooo!" Philip muttered, after a moment, slamming the car into gear. "Wouldn't want to go through *that* again in a hurry."

"Now," hissed his wife, "now will you *please* drive at a reasonable speed? No more dawdling, if you please. There's a whole *lot* to do when we get home."

"All right, all right—" and he accelerated so sharply that the engine let out a squawk of protest.

Old Mr. and Mrs. Logan were led in different directions.

"But can't we be together?" she protested.

"No. We are very sorry, but that is an absolute rule. There is nothing to worry about, though—"

They gave each other a cold, steady kiss, aged cheek against soft aged cheek.

"Now, then, where?"

Mrs. Logan was taken to a kind of garden room. One wall was totally lacking; darkness, trees, and mist lay beyond the area of dim illumination.

"If you wouldn't mind just waiting here. . . . He won't be long."

"Will it be Ted's turn first, or mine?"

No answer came back. Or had the guide perhaps said, "Both together?" as the door closed?

Mrs. Logan sat on a bench, looking out anxiously into the dark.

It isn't very cold, she thought. Not as cold as you'd expect. Not cold at all, really. Cold blows the wind tonight, true love. . . . Wasn't that queer, though, finding that book? Then tell to me, my own true love, when shall we meet again? When the autumn leaves that fall from the trees, are green and spring again. Yes, but *do* they spring again? Leaves, like the things of man you with your fresh thoughts care for, can you? Always dwell as if about to depart, they say in Yorkshire. Do they depart so easily, up there, in Yorkshire? Questions are better than answers, for they lead you on, like signposts, whereas answers pin you down, like javelins. Will Ted remember to tell them about his diet?

Somebody was approaching through the darkness, walking slowly and carefully; the sound of the footfalls came with an irregular beat, as if the person limped.

Vulcan, thought Mrs. Logan; Richard III. "Beware the lame king, for then shall Sparta fall. But the lame god is kind, he knows our frailties all . . ." that line does not scan as it should. One foot too many, like a three-legged stool. Or too few . . .

"There you are, then," said the old lame man. "I brought you a glass of stout; and a Bath bun."

"So it was you, all along?"

She gazed at him in amazement.

"All along."

"All along," she echoed happily, "down along, out along lee."

"That's it!"

And they began to sing together, their voices combining gently in old, remembered graceful cadences. Oh, I hope Ted is as happy as this! she thought.

Far away, from Endby Hill, the sound of a long-drawn-out crash came faintly through the foggy dark. But neither of the singers paid it any heed.

# The Last Specimen

The Reverend Matthew Pentecost, aged seventy, had a regular monthly habit. On his way to conduct Evensong in the tiny church of St.-Anthony-under-the-Downs, he invariably parked his aged Rover for ten minutes by the side of a small patch of woodland about ten minutes' drive from the church.

Services at St. Anthony's took place only once a month; for the rest of the time the isolated building with its Saxon stonework, Douai font, willful hand organ, and two massive yew trees, drowsed undisturbed, save by casual tourists who occasionally wandered in, looked around, dropped a ten-pence piece into the box that begged help for the fabric of the roof, and inspected the small overgrown churchyard with its nineteen graves.

At the monthly services the congregation seldom exceeded half a dozen, and in wet weather or snow Mr. Pentecost and Miss Sedom, who played the organ, had the place to themselves. St. Anthony's lay three quarters of a mile from any house; the mild slopes of the Berkshire Downs enfolded it as sometimes after a falling tide a cup of sand will hold a single pebble.

One of the rector's favorite views was that of the church's swaybacked stone roof, bracketed between its two majestic dark yew trees, with the leisurely gray-green of the hillsides beyond. This was one reason for his pre-Evensong period of meditation beside the little wood. The second reason was the tactful desire to allow his parishioners time to assemble, sit down, and rest from their cross-country walk for a few minutes before he appeared among them. Except for the trees on his left, the countryside thereabouts lay bare as an open hand, so that the members of the congregation could be seen from a great distance, making their way along the footpath that led to the church from Compton Druce, the nearest hamlet.

On this evening in mid-April Mr. Pentecost sat in his rusty Rover with an especially happy and benign expression on his face. After a rainy afternoon the sky had cleared: thrushes, larks, and blackbirds were singing in fervent appreciation of the sun's last rays, which turned the greenish-white pearls of the budding hawthorn to a silvery dazzle. In this light the Down grass and young wheat shone with an almost luminous intensity of color.

"Interesting," mused Mr. Pentecost, "how these early greens of the year, dog's mercury and elder leaves, and the green of bluebells, contain such a strong mixture of blue in their color."

Mr. Pentecost's hobby was painting delicate watercolor landscapes, and he was minutely observant of such niceties.

"Then, later in the spring, in May and June, the brighter, more yellowy greens appear: young beech and oak leaves with their buttery rich color; doubtless the extra degree of light from the sun has something to do with it."

Mr. Pentecost watched fondly as Ben Tracey, the farmer who owned the enormous pasture on his right, arrived in a Land-Rover with sacks of feed for the sheep. The spring had been an unusually cold one, and the grass remained unseasonably scanty. Sighting Ben, the sheep and lambs, well acquainted with the object of his daily visit, began purposefully making toward him from all corners of the vast field, lambs following their mothers like iron filings drawn to a magnet in regular converging lines, only broken at one point by the presence of a massive oak tree covered with reddish buds that grew toward the middle of the field. Mr. Pentecost eyed the tree thoughtfully. Was it not unusually advanced in its growth for such a cold season? And why had he not noticed it last month?

Farmer and rector waved to one another, then Mr. Pentecost, observing the last of his congregation pass through the churchyard and enter St. Anthony's porch, was about to start his motor again, when, in the rearview mirror, he noticed a girl, who had been slowly riding her pony along the road behind the car. At this moment she dismounted, tethered the pony to a tree, and vanished through a gate into the little wood.

Normally such a sight would have aroused no particular curiosity in Mr. Pentecost, but two unusual factors here caught his attention. First, neither girl nor mount were familiar to him; yet Mr. Pentecost was certain that he knew every girl and every pony within a ten-mile radius. So where had she come from? Second, the girl carried a trowel and a basket.

Without apparent haste, yet acting with remarkable calm and dispatch for a man of his age, Mr. Pentecost backed the Rover a hundred yards to the point where the pony stood tethered to a young ash tree. The rector got out of his car, studied the pony thoughtfully for a moment, then walked into the wood. The gate stood open: another factor worthy of note. Slightly compressing his lips, Mr. Pentecost closed it behind him and took the path that bisected the wood. The girl ahead of him was easily visible because of her bright-blue anorak; she was, in any case, walking slowly, glancing from side to side as if in search of something.

Mr. Pentecost could easily guess at the object of her quest. He caught up with her just as she had reached it: a patch of delicate spindly plants, each of them nine inches to a foot high, growing in a small sunny clearing. They had bell-shaped flowers the size of small, upside-down tulips—odd, elegant, mysterious flowers, white, with a pinkish-purple tracery over the fluted petals.

The girl knelt beside them and took her trowel from the basket.

"No, no. You mustn't," said Mr. Pentecost gently behind her. The girl gasped and spun around, gazing up at him with wide, frightened eyes. "My dear child, believe me, you mustn't," repeated the rector, the seriousness of his tone mitigated to some degree by the mild expression in his blue eyes. The girl gazed at him, nonplussed, embarrassed, temporarily speechless, it seemed.

She was, he noticed, a very pretty girl, about seventeen, perhaps, in the accustomed uniform of jeans and T-shirt and riding boots. On her head, though, she sported a slightly absurd and certainly unusual article of headgear—not a crash helmet, but a strapped furry hat with a cylindrical top, like the shakoes worn by cavalry in the Crimean War. Could she have inherited it from some great-great-grandfather? Or perhaps, thought the vicar indulgently, it was a prop borrowed from some local theatrical venture; the young loved to dress up in fancy dress. But, now that he saw her close to, he was certain that he did not know this girl; she was a total stranger. Her eyes were a clear beautiful greenish gold—like the color of the young oak leaves he had been thinking about earlier. Her hair, what could be seen of it under the shako, was the same color, with a decided greenish tint; punk, no doubt, thought Mr. Pentecost knowledgeably. The children nowadays dyed their hair extraordinary colors; green was nothing out of the common. He had seen pink, orange, and lilac.

The girl continued to gaze at him in silence, abashed and nervous, grasping her trowel.

"Wild fritillaries are so rare, so very rare," Mr. Pentecost mildly explained to her, "that it is wrong, it is most dreadfully wrong to dig them up; besides, of course, being against the law. Did you not know that? And why, do you suppose, are they so rare?" he went on, considerately giving her time to recover her composure. "Why, because of people like yourself, my dear, finding out about where they grow and coming to dig up specimens. I know the temptation—believe me, I know it!—but you really must *not*, you know."

"Oh dear," murmured the girl, finding her voice at last, it seemed. "I'm—I'm very sorry. I—I didn't know."

"No? You really didn't know? Where are you from?" he inquired, gently veiling his disbelief. "You are certainly not from anywhere around here, or I should have known you. And your steed," he added thoughtfully.

"No, I—I come from—from quite a long way away. I was sent"—she hesitated, looking sheepish and contrite—"sent to—to collect a specimen, as you say. It is the last, you see—we already have one of everything else."

Good gracious, thought Mr. Pentecost, in surprise and a certain amount of disapproval. *Everything* else? Aloud he said,

"It is for a school project, I conclude? Well, I am sorry to disappoint you, but you really must *not* remove the flowers from this precious patch. I will tell you what you can do, though—" as her face fell. "If you care to accompany me to Evensong in St. Anthony's—or, of course, wait outside the church if you prefer," he added kindly, "you may then come with me to my rectory in Chilton Parsley. I am fortunate enough to have quite a large number of fritillaries growing in my flower border, and I shall be happy to give you a specimen for your collection. How about that, my dear?"

"Why," said the girl slowly, "that—that is very kind of Your Reverence. I am indeed greatly obliged to you." She spoke with considerable formality; although English enough in appearance, she could, judging from her accent, have been a foreigner who had learned the language very correctly from some aristocratic old lady with nineteenth-century intonations. "I have instructions to be back though"—she glanced at the sky, then at the watch on her wrist—"by seven. Will that—?"

"Plenty of time," he assured her, smiling. "The evening service is never a long one. . . . Strict about that sort of thing, are they, at your school?"

She blushed.

Mr. Pentecost began walking back toward the gate, anxious, without making it too obvious that he was in a hurry, to join his patient parishioners, but also wishful to be certain that the girl accompanied him. She, however, showed no sign of intending to disobey his prohibition and came with him docilely enough. Once outside the copse gate—"You must *always* close gates, you know," Mr. Pentecost reminded her amiably but firmly—she remounted and he got into his car. "Just follow behind," he told her, poking his white-haired head out of the window. She nodded, kicking the shaggy pony into a walk; perhaps it was the late light filtered through the young hawthorns, but the pony, too, Mr. Pentecost thought, showed a decided touch of green in its rough coat. "Only a very short way to the church," he called, swerving his car erratically across the road as he put his head out again to impart this information.

The girl nodded and kicked her pony again. For its diminutive size—a Shetland cross, perhaps?—the pony certainly showed a remarkable turn of speed.

Mr. Pentecost had not expected that the girl would be prepared to attend his service, but she quietly tied her pony to the lych-gate, murmured some exhortation into its ear, and followed him through the churchyard, glancing about her with interest. Then a doubt seemed to overtake her: "Am I dressed suitably to come inside?" she asked in a low, worried tone, pausing at the church door.

"Perfectly," he assured her, smiling at the glossy shako. "Our congregation at St. Anthony is quite informal."

So she slipped in after him and demurely took her place in a pew at the back.

After the service—which, as he had promised, lasted no longer than twenty-five minutes—the rector exchanged a few friendly words with the six members of his congregation, stood waving good-bye to them as they set off on their return walk across the fields, and then said to the girl, who had remounted and was waiting by the gate:

"Now, if you will follow me again, my dear, I will drive slowly and I do not think the journey should take more than about fifteen minutes for that excellent little animal of yours."

She nodded, and they proceeded as before, the vicar driving at twenty miles an hour, not much less than his normal speed, while horse and rider followed with apparent ease.

As he drove, Mr. Pentecost reflected. During Evensong his mind, as always, had been entirely given over to the service, but he had, with some part of it, heard the girl's voice now and then, particularly in the hymn, Miss Sedom's favorite, "Glory to Thee My God This Night." So the girl was, at least, familiar with Christian ritual.

Or was a remarkably speedy learner. Or was it conceivable that she could be coached, as it were, continuously by—by whatever agency had sent her? There were so many things wrong with her—and yet, mused the rector, he could swear that there was no harm about her, not an atom.

When they reached the damp and crumbling laurel-girt rectory, Mr. Pentecost drove around, as was his habit, to the mossy yard at the rear, and parked there.

"You can tie your pony to the mounting block—" He gestured to the old stable. "Now, I will just leave my cassock inside the back door—so—and fetch a trowel—ah, no, of course there is no need for that, you already have one." It was a bricklayer's trowel, but no matter. "Follow me, then."

The rectory garden, beyond the overgrown laurel hedge, was a wonderful wilderness of old-fashioned flowers and shrubs that had grown, proliferated, and battled for mastery during the last hundred years. Smaller and more delicate plants had, on the whole, fared badly; but Mr. Pentecost adored his fritillaries and had cherished them as carefully as he was able: frail and beautiful, both speckled and white, they drooped their magic bells among a drift of pale blue anemones and a fringe of darker blue grape hyacinths.

"Aren't they extraordinary?" he said, fondly looking down at them. "It is so easy to believe in a benevolent Creator when one considers these and the anemones—which, I believe, are the lilies of the field referred to in St. Matthew. Now, this little clump, still in bud, would, I think, transfer without too much harm, my dear—er—what did you say your name was?"

She hesitated. Then: "My name is Anjla," she answered with a slight, uneasy tremor of her voice. And she knelt to dig up the clump of plants he had indicated. The rector fetched her a grimy plastic bag from the toolshed, but she shook her head.

"Thank you, but I can't take it. Only the flowers. This is—this is truly very kind of you."

A faint warning hum sounded in the air—like that of a clock before it strikes.

The vicar glanced across the wide meadow that lay alongside his garden. A large oak, leafless still, covered with reddish buds, grew in the middle of the grassy space. Mr. Pentecost eyed it thoughtfully. Beyond it, pale and clear, shone the evening star.

Mr. Pentecost said, "My dear—where do you really come from?"

The girl stood, tucking the plants into her basket. She followed the direction of his glance, but said defensively, "You would not know the name of the place."

It was, however, remarkably hard to evade Mr. Pentecost when he became as serious as he was now.

"Forgive my curiosity," he said, "but I do think it is important that I should know—precisely why are you collecting specimens?"

She was silent for a moment; for too long. Mr. Pentecost went on, "You see—I am an absentminded, vague old man, but even *I* could not help noticing that your pony has claws on its hooves. *Moropus!* A prehistoric horse not seen in these parts for a million years! And, well, there were various other things—"

She blushed furiously.

"That was the trouble!" she burst out. "For such a small errand—just one flower—they wouldn't allocate enough research staff. I *knew* there were details they had skimped on—"

"But why," he persisted mildly, "why are you collecting?"

Anjla looked at him sorrowfully. Then she said, "Well—as you seem to have spotted us, and it is so very late, in any case, I suppose it won't matter now if I tell you—"

"Yes, my dear?"

"This planet"—she glanced round at the stable yard—"is due to blow up—oh, very, very soon. Our scientists have calculated it to within the next three chronims—"

"Chronims?"

"Under one hundred of your hours, I think. Naturally, therefore, we were checking the contents of our own Terrestrial Museum—"

"Ah, I see." He stood thinking for a few minutes, then inquired with the liveliest interest, "And you really do have one of everything? Even—for instance—a rector of the Church of England?"

"I'm afraid so." Her tone was full of regret. "I *wish* I could take you with me. You have been so kind. But we have a vicar, a dean, a bishop, a canon—we have them all. Even an archbishop."

"My dear child! You mistake my meaning. I would not, not for one moment, consider leaving. My question was prompted by—by a simple wish to know."

The low hum was audible again. Anjla glanced at the sky.

"I'm afraid that now I really have to go."

"Of course you must, my dear. Of course."

They crossed the yard and found the shaggy Moropus demolishing, with apparent relish, the last of a bunch of carrots that had been laid on the mounting block for Mr. Pentecost's supper.

Anjla checked and stared, aghast. "*Sphim!* What have you *done?*"

She burst into a torrent of expostulations, couched in a language wholly unlike any earthly tongue; it appeared to have no consonants at all, to consist of pure sound like the breathy note of an ocarina.

The Moropus guiltily hung its head and shuffled its long-clawed feet.

Mr. Pentecost stood looking at the pair in sympathy and perplexity.

The warning hum sounded in the air again.

"Do I understand that your—um—companion has invalidated his chance of departure by the consumption of those carrots?"

"I don't know what *can* have come over him—we were briefed so carefully—told to touch nothing, to take in nothing except—over and over again they told us—"

"Perhaps it was a touch of Method," suggested Mr. Pentecost. "He was really getting into the skin of his part." And he added something about Dis and Persephone that the girl received with the blankness of noncomprehension. She had placed her hands on either side of the pony's hairy cheekbones; she bent forward until her forehead touched the other's. Thus she stood for a couple of moments in silence. Then she straightened and walked across the yard in the direction of the meadow. Her eyes swam with tears. Following her, interested and touched, Mr. Pentecost murmured,

"I will, of course, be glad to take care of your friend. During what little time remains."

"I am sure that you will. Thank you. I—I am glad to have met you."

"You could not—I suppose—show me what you both really look like?" he asked with a touch of wistfulness.

"I'm afraid that would be quite impossible. Your eyes simply aren't adapted, you see—"

He nodded, accepting this. Just the same, for a single instant he did receive an impression of hugeness, brightness, speed. Then the girl vaulted the fence and, carefully carrying her basket, crossed the meadow to the large oak tree in the center.

"Good-bye," called Mr. Pentecost. The Moropus lifted up its head and let out a soft groaning sound.

Beside the oak tree, Anjla turned and raised her hand with a grave, formal gesture. Then she stepped among the low-growing branches of the tree, which immediately folded like an umbrella, and, with a swift flash of no-colored brilliance, shot upward, disintegrating into light.

Mr. Pentecost remained for a few moments, leaning with his forearms on the wooden fence, gazing pensively at the star Hesperus, which, now that the tree was gone, could be seen gleaming in radiance above the horizon.

The rector murmured:

"Earth's joys grow dim, its glories pass away
Change and decay in all around I see;
O Thou, Who changest not, abide with me."

Then, pulling a juicy tussock of grass from beside one of the fence posts, he carried it back to the disconsolate Moropus.

"Here, my poor friend; if we are to wait for Armageddon together, we may as well do so in comfort. Just excuse me a moment while I fetch a deck chair and a steamer rug from the house. And do, pray, finish those carrots. I will be with you again directly."

He stepped inside the back door. The Moropus, with a carrot top and a hank of juicy grass dangling from its hairy lips, gazed after him sadly but trustfully.

# The Man Who Had Seen the Rope Trick

"Miss Drake," said Mrs. Minser. "When ye've finished with the salt and pepper, will ye please put them *together?*"

"Sorry, I'm sorry," mumbled Miss Drake. "I can't see very well as you know, I can't see very well." Her tremulous hands worked out like tendrils across the table and succeeded in knocking the mustard onto its side. An ochre blob defiled the snowy stiffness of the tablecloth. Mrs. Minser let a slight hiss escape her.

"That's the third tablecloth ye've dirtied in a week, Miss Drake. Do ye know I had to get up at four o'clock this morning to do all the washing? I shann't be able to keep ye if ye go on like this, ye know."

Without waiting for the whispered apologies she turned towards the dining-room door, pushing the trolley with the meat plates before her. Her straw-grey hair was swept to a knot on the top of her head, her grey eyes were as opaque as bottle tops, her mouth was screwed tight shut against the culpabilities of other people.

"Stoopid business, getting' up at four in the mornin'," muttered old Mr. Hill, but he muttered it quietly to himself. "Who cares about a blob of mustard on the tablecloth, anyway? Who cares about a tablecloth, or a separate table, if the food's good? If she's got to get up at four, why don't she make us some decent porridge instead of the slime she gives us?"

He bowed his head prayerfully over his bread plate as Mrs. Minser returned, weaving her way with the neatness of long practice between the white-covered tables, each with its silent, elderly, ruminating diner.

The food was not good. "Rice shape or banana, Mr. Hill?" Mrs. Minser asked, pausing beside him.

"Banana, thank'ee." He repressed a shudder as he looked at the colourless, glutinous pudding. The bananas were unripe, and bad for his indigestion, but at least they were palatable.

"Mr. Wakefield! Ye've spotted yer shirt with gravy! That means more washing, and I've got a new guest coming tomorrow. I cann't think how you old people can be so inconsiderate."

"I'll wash it, I'll wash it myself, Mrs. Minser." The old man put an anxious, protective hand over the spot.

"Ye'll do no such thing!"

"Who is the new guest, then, Mrs. Minser?" Mr. Hill asked, more to distract her attention from his neighbour's misfortune than because he wanted to know.

"A Mr. Ollendod. Retired from India. I only hope," said Mrs. Minser forebodingly, "that he won't have a great deal of luggage, else where we shall put it all I cann't imagine."

"India," murmured Mr. Hill to himself. "From India, eh? He'll certainly find it different here." And he looked round the dining room of the Balmoral Guest House. The name Balmoral, and Mrs. Minser's lowland accent, constituted the only Scottish elements in the guest house, which was otherwise pure Westcliff. The sea, half a mile away, invisible from the house, was implicit in the bracingness of the air and the presence of so many elderly residents pottering out twice a day to listen to the municipal orchestra. Nobody actually swam in the sea, or even looked at it much, but there it was anyway, a guarantee of ozone and fresh fish on the tables of the residential hotels.

Mr. Ollendod arrived punctually next day, and he did have a lot of luggage.

Mrs. Minser's expression became more and more ominous as trunks and cases—some of them very foreign-looking and made of straw—boxes and rolls and bundles were unloaded.

"Where does he think all that is going?" she said incautiously loudly to her husband, who was helping to carry in the cases.

Mr. Ollendod was an elderly, very brown, shriveled little man, but he evidently had all his faculties intact, for he looked up from paying the cab driver to say, "In my room, I trust, naturally. It is a double room, is it not? Did I not stipulate for a double room?"

Mrs. Minser's idea of a double room was one into which a double bed could be squeezed. She eyed Mr. Ollendod measuringly, her lips pursed together. Was he going to be the sort who gave trouble? If so, she'd soon find a reason for giving him his notice. Summer was coming, when prices and the demand for rooms went up; one could afford to be choosy. Still, ten guineas a week was ten guineas; it would do no harm to wait and see.

The Minser children, Martin and Jenny, came home from school and halted, fascinated, amonst Mr. Ollendod's possessions.

"Look, a screen, all covered with pictures!"

"He's got spears!"

"A tigerskin!"

"An elephant's foot!"

"What's this, a shield?"

"No, it's a fan, made of peacock's feathers." Mr. Ollendod smiled at them benevolently. Jenny thought that his face looked like the skin on top of cocoa, wrinkling when you stir it.

"Is he an Indian, Mother?" she asked when they were in the kitchen.

"No, of course he's not. He's just brown because he's lived in a hot climate," Mrs. Minser said sharply. "Run and do yer homework and stay out from under my feet."

The residents also were discussing Mr. Ollendod.

"Do you think he can be—*foreign?*" whispered Mrs. Pursey. "He is such an odd-looking man. His eyes are so bright—just like diamonds. What do you think, Miss Drake?"

"How should I know?" snapped Miss Drake. "You seem to forget I haven't been able to see across the room for the last five years."

The children soon found their way to Mr. Ollendod's room. They were strictly forbidden to speak to or mix with the guests in any way, but there was an irresistible attraction about the little bright-eyed man and his belongings.

"Tell us about India," Jenny said, stroking the snarling tiger's head with its great yellow glass eyes.

"India? The hills are blue and wooded, they look as innocent as Essex but they're full of tigers and snakes and swinging, chattering monkeys. In the villages you can smell dust and dung smoke and incense; there are no brown or grey clothes, but flashing pinks and blood reds, turquoises and saffrons; the cows have horns three yards wide."

"Shall you ever go back there?" Martin asked, wondering how anybody could bear to exchange such a place for the worn grey, black, and fawn carpeting, the veneer wardrobe and plate glass, the limp yellow sateen coverlid of a Balmoral bedroom.

"No," said Mr. Ollendod, sighing. "I fell ill. And no one wants me there now. Still," he added more cheerfully, "I have brought back plenty of reminders with me, enough to keep India alive in my mind. Look at this—and this—and this."

Everything was wonderful—the curved leather slippers, the richly patterned silk of Mr. Ollendod's dressing gown and scarves, the screen with its exotic pictures ("I'm not letting *that* stay there long," said Mrs. Minser), the huge pink shells with a sheen of pearl, the gnarled and grinning images, the hard, scented sweets covered with coloured sugar.

"You are *not* to go up there. And if he offers you anything to eat, you are to throw it straight away," Mrs. Minser said, but she might as well have spoken to the wind. The instant the children had done their homework they were up in Mr. Ollendod's room, demanding stories of snakes and werewolves, of crocodiles who lived for a hundred years, of mysterious ceremonies in temples, ghosts who walked with their feet swiveled backwards on their ankles, and women with the evil eye who could turn milk sour and rot the unripe fruit on a neighbour's vine.

"You've really seen it? You've seen them? You've seen a snake charmer and a snake standing on its tail? And a lizard break in half and each half run away separately? And an eagle fly away with a live sheep?"

"All those things," he said. "I'll play you a snake charmer's tune if you like."

He fished a little bamboo flageolet out of a cedarwood box and began to play a tune that consisted of no more than a few trickling, monotonous notes, repeated over and over agin. Tuffy, the aged, moth-eaten black cat who followed the children everywhere when they were at home and dozed in Mr. Ollendod's armchair when they were at school, woke up, and pricked up his ears; downstairs, Jip, the bad-tempered Airedale, growled gently in his throat; and Mrs. Minser, sprinkling water on her starched ironing, paused and angrily rubbed her ear as if a mosquito had tickled it.

"And I've seen another thing: a rope that stands on its tail when the man says a secret word to it, stands straight up on end! And a boy climbs up it, right up! Higher and higher, till he finally disappears out of sight."

"Where does he go to?" the children asked, huge-eyed.

"A country where the grass grows soft and patterned like a carpet, where the deer wear gold necklets and come to your hand for pieces of bread, where the plums are red and sweet and as big as oranges, and the girls have voices like singing birds."

"Does he never come back?"

"Sometimes he jumps down out of the sky with his hands full of wonderful grass and fruits. But sometimes he never comes back."

"Do *you* know the word they say to the rope?"

"I've heard it, yes."

"If I were the boy I wouldn't come back," said Jenny. "Tell us some more. About the witch woman who fans herself."

"She fans herself with a peacock-feather fan," Mr. Ollendod said. "And when she does that she becomes a snake and slips away into the forest. And when she is tired of being a snake and wants to turn into a woman again, she taps her husband's foot with her cold head till he waves the fan over her."

"Is the fan just like yours on the wall?"

"Just like it."

"Oh, may we fan ourselves with it, may we?"

"And turn yourselves into little snakes? What would your mother say?" asked Mr. Ollendod, laughing heartily.

Mrs. Minser had plenty to say as it was. When the children told her a garbled mixture of the snakes and the deer and the live rope and girls with birds' voices and plums as big as oranges, she pursed her lips together tight.

"A pack of moonshine and rubbish! I've a good mind to forbid him to speak to them."

"Oh, come, Hannah," her husband said mildly. "He keeps them out of mischief for hours on end. You know you can't stand it if they come into the kitchen or make a noise in the garden. And he's only telling them Indian fairy tales."

"Well anyway ye're not to believe a word he says," Mrs. Minser ordered the children. "Not a *single* word."

She might as well have spoken to the wind. . . .

Tuffy, the cat, fell ill and lay with faintly heaving sides in the middle of the hallway. Mrs. Minser exclaimed angrily when she found Mr. Ollendod bending over him.

"That dirty old cat! It's high time he was put away."

"It is a cold he has, nothing more," Mr. Ollendod said mildly. "If you will allow me, I shall take him to my room and treat him. I have some Indian gum which is very good for inhaling."

But Mrs. Minser refused to consider the idea. She rang up the vet, and when the children came home from school, Tuffy was gone.

They found their way up to Mr. Ollendod's room, speechless with grief.

He looked at them thoughtfully for a while and then said, "Shall I tell you a secret?"

"Yes, what? What?" Martin said, and Jenny cried, "You've got Tuffy hidden here, is that it?"

"Not exactly," said Mr. Ollendod, "but you see that mirror on the wall?"

"The big one covered with a fringy shawl, yes?"

"Once upon a time that mirror belonged to a queen in India. She was very beautiful, so beautiful that it was said sick people could be cured of their illnesses just by looking at her. In course of time she grew old and lost her beauty. But the mirror remembered how beautiful she had been and showed her still the lovely face she had lost. And one day she walked right into the mirror and was never seen again. So if you look into it, you do not see things as they are now, but beautiful as they were in their youth."

"May we look?"

"Just for a short time you may. Climb on the chair," Mr. Ollendod said, smiling, and they climbed up and peered into the mirror, while he steadied them with a hand on each of their necks.

"Oh!" cried Jenny, "I can see him; I can see Tuffy! He's a kitten again, chasing grasshoppers!"

"I can see him too!" shouted Martin, jumping up and down. The chair overbalanced and tipped them onto the floor.

"Let us look again, please let us!"

"Not today," said Mr. Ollendod. "If you look too long into that mirror, you, like the queen, might vanish into it for good. That is why I keep it covered with a shawl."

The children went away comforted, thiking of Tuffy young and frolicsome once more, chasing butterflies in the sun. Mr. Ollendod gave them a little ivory chess set, to distract them from missing their cat, but Mrs. Minser, saying it was too good for children and that they would only spoil it, sold it and put the money in the post office "for later on."

It was July now. The weather grew daily warmer and closer. Mrs. Minser told Mr. Ollendod that she was obliged to raise his rent by three guineas "for the summer prices." She rather hoped this would make him leave, but he paid up.

"I'm old and tired," he said. "I don't want to move again, for I may not be here very long. One of these days my heart will carry me off."

And, in fact, one oppressive, thundery day he had a bad heart attack and had to stay in bed for a week.

"I certainly don't want him if he's going to be ill all the time," Mrs. Minser said to her husband. "I shall tell him that we want his room as soon as he's better." In the meantime she put away as many as possible of the Indian things, saying that they were a dust-collecting nuisance in the sickroom. She left the swords and the fan and the mirror, because they hung on the wall, out of harm's way.

As she had promised, the minute Mr. Ollendod was up and walking around again, she told him his room was wanted and he must go.

"But where?" he said, standing so still, leaning on his stick, that Mrs. Minser had the uneasy notion for a moment that the clock on the wall had stopped ticking to listen for her answer.

"That's no concern of mine," she said coldly. "Go where you please, wherever anyone can be found who'll take you with all this rubbish."

"I must think this over," said Mr. Ollendod. He put on his Panama hat and walked slowly down to the beach. The tide was out, revealing a mile of flat, pallid mud studded with baked-bean tins. Jenny and Martin were there, listlessly trying to fly a homemade kite. Not a breath of wind stirred and the kite kept flopping down in the mud, but they knew that if they went home before six their mother would send them out again.

"There's Mr. Ollendod," said Jenny.

"Perhaps he could fly the kite," said Martin.

They ran to him, leaving two black parallel trails in the shining goo.

"Mr. Ollendod, can you fly our kite?"

"It needs someone to run with it *very* fast."

He smiled at them kindly. Even the slowest stroll now made his heart begin to race and stumble.

"Let's see," he said. He held the string for a moment in his hands and was silent; then he said, "I can't run with it, but perhaps I can persuade it to go up of its own accord."

The children watched, silent and attentive, while he murmured something to the rope in a low voice that they could not quite catch.

"Look, it's moving," whispered Martin.

The kite, which had been hanging limp, suddenly twitched and jerked like a fish at the end of a line, then, by slow degrees, drew itself up and, as if invisibly pulled from above, began to climb higher and higher into the warm grey sky. Mr. Ollendod kept his eyes fixed on it; Jenny noticed that his hands were clenched and the sweat was rolling off his forehead.

"It's like the story!" exclaimed Martin. "The man with the rope and the magic word and the boy who climbs it—may we climb it? We've learnt how to at school."

Mr. Ollendod couldn't speak, but they took his silence as consent. They flung themselves at the rope and swarmed up it. Mr. Ollendod still holding onto the end of the rope, gradually lowered himself to the ground and sat with his head bowed over his knees; then with a slow subsiding motion he fell over onto his side. His hands relaxed on the rope, which swung softly upwards and disappeared; after a while the tide came in and washed away three sets of footprints.

"Those children are very late," said Mrs. Minser at six o'clock. "Are they up in Mr. Ollendod's room?"

She went up to see. The room was empty.

"I shall let it to a couple, next time," reflected Mrs. Minser, picking up the peacock-feather fan and fanning herself, for the heat was oppressive. "A couple will pay twice the rent and they are more likely to eat meals out. I wonder where those children can have got to? . . ."

An hour later old Mr. Hill, on his way down to supper, looked through Mr. Ollendod's open door and saw a snake wriggling about on the carpet. He called out excitedly. By the time Mr. Minser had come up, the snake had slid under the bed and Mrs. Pursey was screaming vigorously. Mr. Minser rattled a stick and the snake shot out towards his foot, but he was ready with a sharp scimitar snatched from the wall, and cut off its head. The old people, clustering in a dithering group outside the door, applauded his quickness.

"Fancy Mr. Ollendod keeping a pet snake all this time and we never knew!" shuddered Mrs. Pursey. "I hope he hasn't anything else of the kind in here." Inquisitively she ventured in. "Why, what a beautiful mirror!" she cried. The others followed, pushing and chattering, looking about greedily.

Mr. Minser brushed through the group irritably and went downstairs with the decapitated snake. "I shall sound the gong for supper in five minutes," he called. "Hannah, Hannah! Where are you? Nothing's going on as it should in this house today."

But Hannah, needless to say, did not reply, and when he banged the gong in five minutes, nobody came down but blind old Miss Drake, who said rather peevishly that all the others had slipped away and left her behind in Mr. Ollendod's room.

"Slipped away! And left me! Amongst all his horrid things! Without saying a word, so inconsiderate! Anything might have happened to me."

And she started quickly eating up Mrs. Pursey's buttered toast.

# The Mysterious Barricades

The main thing about the mountains was their height. They were so high that they really did seem to join on to the sky; if you looked at them you had to tip your head back and back until your neck ached; then you were obliged to lie down so that your eyes might go travelling up to the final snow-crowned summits which were like needles among the clouds.

The people in the village never looked up at them. They had had enough gazing at mountains when they were babies and lay on their backs in prams. As soon as they could walk they turned away from white peaks and dark forests and staggered off in the other direction, towards the plains. If they had to walk towards the mountains they kept their eyes on their boots.

One day a man on a bicycle came to the village. He was a stranger, and consequently everyone stopped work and looked at him, but furtively. The blacksmith put down his hammer, but picked up a piece of string and pretended to be untying it, with his eyes fixed on the traveller. The postman stood gazing at a letter that he had been about to slip into a box as if he had suddenly forgotten how to read. The innkeeper came out on to his balcony and began busily polishing and repolishing a glass, though everyone knew that half the time he didn't trouble to wash them at all.

The traveller pedaled slowly along, glancing from side to side. He saw that every house had someone standing in its doorway or leaning from its window. Only one house seemed to take no interest in him; it was a small bungalow with the name 'Mountain View' painted on its gate. All its windows were lace-curtained and the door was tight shut. He put on his brakes and came to a stop outside it. All the heads craned out a little further to see what he was doing. He leaned his bicycle against the garden wall, unlatched the gate, walked up the path, and rapped at the door.

After a few moments it was opened, and a voice snapped:

"Well, come in, come in. Don't keep me waiting in the cold."

He hurriedly stepped into the dark interior. He could see hardly anything at first, except the glow of a fire. Both windows had ranks of dark, spreading pot-plants across them, as well as the lace curtains, and bird cages hung in front of the plants. It was very quiet inside; he could hear the clock tick, and the fire rustle, and the birds clearing their throats.

"Well," said the old woman who had let him in. "What have you come bothering me for? Aren't there enough busybodies in the village but you have to come and trouble someone who keeps herself to herself?"

"I thought I was more likely to hear the truth from someone who keeps herself to herself," said the traveller. "When was the last stranger seen in this village?"

"Ten years ago last Tuesday."

"And where did he go?"

"He went up the mountains."

"Did he have a canary and a roll of music with him?"

"As to a roll of music, I can't say; he had a big leather case. He certainly had a canary."

As she said this one of the birds in the cages began to hop up and down, twittering in a very excited manner.

"Is that the one?" asked the man, looking at it attentively.

"Yes, that's him. Pip, I call him. The man gave him to me for a cup of tea."

The traveller walked over to the cage, unlatched the door, and whistled a few bars of a tune. The canary continued the tune to its end, finishing with a triumphant trill, and then hopped out on to the man's shoulder.

"He seems to know you," said the old woman. "But he's mine for all that."

The man pulled a cup of tea out of his pocket and handed it to her.

"I'll buy him back off you," he said. "Can you tell me anything more? What did this man look like?"

"He had glasses. And a tie like yours. He went off to the mountains and that was the last we saw of him. Ten years is a long time."

She drank the tea, looking at him thoughtfully.

"I've been ten years tracing him," said the traveller. "He stole my canary and he stole my music. I'll go on now, and thank you kindly for the information."

He tucked the canary into a pocket so that only its head showed, and moved to the door.

"Wait a minute," said the old woman. "In return for the tea I'll give you a warning. Those mountains are dangerous. No one who goes up them comes back again. They say there are animals up there with huge feet who can fly faster than the wind."

"I can't help that. I have to go on," the traveller said.

"The other man said that too," the old woman muttered, shaking her head. "He talked about some mysterious barricades he wanted to find."

"Yes? In these mountains?" exclaimed the traveller, his face alight with interest and excitement.

"How should I know? It's only what he said. I've never heard of any mysterious barricades—nor do I know what they are, for that matter."

"They are where the Civil Servants go when they retire," he told her absently, and he thoughtfully fingered the black and red necktie he wore, which appeared to be made of typewriter ribbon. "Well, many thanks once more."

He walked down to the gate and threw one leg over his bicycle.

"You'll never get up the mountains on that," she called. "Better leave it here."

"This machine has a thirty-three speed," he called back. "It goes up any hill that isn't vertical," and he pedaled slowly off. The villagers watched him until he was past them, then they stopped looking in case they should catch a glimpse of the mountains, and went across to question the old woman about her visitor.

But—"He's been in the Civil Service," was all she would say, shortly.

"Civil Service!" They looked at their boots, spat, and went off to their own homes.

Meanwhile, the traveller had reached the foot of the great forest which cloaked the lower slopes of the mountains. He switched to the second of his thirty-three speeds, turned on his light, and pedaled boldly upwards. The road was good, although carpeted with pine needles as if it was rarely used. Far overhead the trees sighed to each other, and above them the out-thrust elbows of the mountain hung over his head.

Soon he came to snow, and the bicycle began to slip and stagger on the frozen crust. He took out chains from the saddlebag and painstakingly laced them round his wheels. This helped his progress, but he was now going more slowly and night was falling; in the pinewood it was already almost pitch dark. He decided to halt for the night, and leaned his bicycle against a tree. Taking out a groundsheet from the bag he hung it over the bicycle making a rude tent, into which he crawled. From his pocket he drew out another cup of tea and a biscuit. He drank the tea, shared the biscuit with the canary, and then settled himself to sleep.

He had been sleeping for perhaps two hours when he was woken by a terrible howling in the woods above him. It sounded almost like a human cry, but a thousand times louder and more mournful.

He started to his feet, upsetting the bicycle and groundsheet. He saw that it must have been snowing heavily while he slept, for all his footprints were gone and the groundsheet was covered several inches thick. All was silent again, and he moved cautiously a few feet from his encampment, turning his head this way and that to listen. Something caught his eye—a footprint—and he went over to look at it. It made him turn pale.

It was the print of an animal's paw, but what a size! He could have fitted his own foot into it four times over. When he looked for others he saw that they led in a single trail, fifteen feet apart, in a wide ring round his tent, and then away up the hill.

"Perhaps it has gone, whatever it is," he thought hopefully, but in the same instant he heard the terrible voice again, nearer than before. It seemed to lament, and also to threaten; it echoed among the trees until he could not tell from which quarter it came, and he fled back to his tree and cowered by the bicycle, looking haggardly in all directions. His canary had fallen into a terrified cheeping.

Then his pride began to stir.

"Come," he said to himself. "I am a Civil Servant. What would the lower grades think if they saw me now? What would my Administrator think?" And he recited to himself the little rhyme which the juniors in the lowest grades are set to learn when they first join the ranks of the Service.

"Always helpful, never hurried,
Always willing, never worried,
Serve the public, slow but surely,
Smile, however sad or poorly,
Duty done without a swerve is
Aimed at by the Civil Service."

This encouraged him, and as he saw no prospect of further sleep he packed up his groundsheet once more, shared a few biscuit crumbs with the canary and wheeled the bicycle back to the path. He changed down to his thirtieth gear and started to ride up the hill.

Once again he heard the voice reverberating through the trees and seeming to cry: "Woe! Oh, woe, woe."

He ducked his head over the handlebars and pedaled on, reciting to himself:

"Grade I, Step I, ten pounds a year. Step II, ten pounds twelve shillings. Step III, ten pounds fifteen shillings. Step IV, ten pounds nineteen shillings. Step V, ten pounds nineteen and six. Grade II, Step I, eleven pounds a year. What a very peculiar tree that is over there. I wonder why there is no snow on it? Annual ex gratia allowances for married men, wife, ten shillings. First child, five shillings. Every subsequent child, two and six. There's another tree on the other side, just the same shape."

He disliked the two trees which grew along the ground for some distance before turning upwards. They were so very black and so very symmetrical, on either side of the road. An unpleasant fancy came to him that they might be *legs*—but who ever heard of legs the size of pine trees? And if they were legs, where was the body that belonged to them?

He glanced up fearfully into the thickness of the branches above. The sky was beginning to pale with dawn around the edge of the forest, but overhead hung a dense mass of black, supported, it seemed, on those pillar-like trees. He put one foot on the ground and craned back, trying in vain to decide if it was merely the darkness of foliage or if there was something huge leaning over him? As he looked it seemed to move and draw downward, and all at once he saw two great pale eyes, mournful and menacing, descending on him.

With a frantic spasm of courage he flung the bicycle into twenty-second gear and pushed off. He felt a hot dry breath on his neck and struggled desperately up the hill, his heart almost bursting. The light grew ahead and in a few moments he was out of the trees, crashing across virgin snow with the rising sun striking warmly on the top of his head as he bent forward.

He could hear no sound behind, and finally ventured to stop and turn around. Nothing was visible except a distant agitation among the tree tops as if the creature was watching him from the cover of the forest but dared not come out. Encouraged by this he hurried on and was soon out of sight of the trees round a fold of the mountain.

All that day he climbed, and in the green light of evening he was nearing the top of a pass which seemed to cut right through the peak of the mountain. Huge rock walls, seamed with snow, reared up on either side of him.

The traveller was terribly tired. He had hardly halted all day and eaten nothing save a cup of tea and a biscuit when he paused to pump up his tyres. He had sweated under the fierce heat of noon, but now it was beginning to freeze again and he shivered and longed to lie down and cover himself with the friendly snow.

It seemed to be only a few hundred yards now to the top, and making a final effort he struggled up in ninth gear, to stop aghast at what he saw. The right-hand wall of the pass dropped away at the top, giving a fearful vista of snowy and cloud-wrapped peaks; but the left-hand cliff continued sheering up more and more steeply until it was vertical, with its top veiled in obscurity. Across the face of the cliff ran a narrow ledge—all that remained of the path.

For a moment the traveller was daunted and his heart sank. He had been sure that the top of the pass was the end of his journey and that there he would find the Mysterious Barricades. But his courage only faltered for a short space, and soon he began doggedly working his way along the little path. At first it was wide enough to ride on, but presently he came to a sharp corner in the cliff and he had to dismount. He tried to edge the bicycle round but it slipped from his grasp on the icy rock, and fell outwards. He leaned sideways, holding on to a projection in the cliff and saw the bicycle falling down and down. It became as small as a moth, then as small as a tea-leaf, and finally vanished without the faintest sound coming back to him from the gulf.

He turned, sick and shaken, to continue his journey on foot, but to his unutterable astonishment found the path ahead blocked by another traveller. A short man, wearing spectacles and carrying a leather case stood gazing at him seriously.

The traveller stood silent for a long time.

"Jones!" he said, at length. "I never expected to meet you here. I thought that you would have passed through the Mysterious Barricades many years ago, using my music as a passport."

Jones shook his head.

"For ten years I have been wandering in these mountains," he said sadly. "I am beginning to believe that the Mysterious Barricades do not exist. I thought that your music would open all gates, but though I have played it daily upon my flute there has been no sign. Perhaps that was the punishment for my theft."

"How have you lived?" asked the other, looking at him compassionately.

"Buns. They were all I was entitled to, as a Civil Servant Grade III. Would you care for one? I am sick of the sight of them."

"I'll give you a cup of tea for it."

"Tea!" Jones's eyes lit up. "I didn't know you had reached the higher grades." He drank it as if it was nectar, while the other man munched his bun, pleasantly filling after a prolonged diet of biscuit.

"Now what are we to do?" said Jones presently. "We cannot pass each other on this ledge and if one of us tries to turn round he will probably be dashed to destruction."

"Let us play my sonata for two flutes and continuo," said the traveller, who had been looking at the leather portfolio for some minutes past.

Jones cautiously drew out some sheets of manuscript music and passed them over. The traveller turned through them until he came to the piece he wanted, which was inscribed:

"Sonata in C major for two flutes and continuo by A. Smith."

The two men took out their flutes and Smith propped his manuscript on a ledge in the cliff face so that they could see it by looking sideways. They stood facing each other and played the sonata through, but when they came to the end nothing happened.

"It wants the continuo part," said Smith sadly. "Let us play it again and I will try to put it in."

They began again, though Jones looked doubtful.

This time the canary suddenly popped its head from Smith's pocket, where it had been sleeping, and began to sing with its eyes fixed on the distant peaks and its throat filling and emptying like the bellows of an organ. The two players gazed at each other over their flutes in astonishment but nothing would have made them stop playing, for the music produced by the two flutes and the bird was of more than mortal beauty. As they played the mountains trembled about them; great slabs of snow dislodged from their niches and slipped into the gulf, spires of rock trembled and tottered, and as the travellers came to the end of the sonata, the Mysterious Barricades opened to receive them.

Down below the villages felt the ground quiver as they trudged homewards with the sugar beet harvest, and their tractors snorted and belched blue smoke. But the men never lifted their eyes from the ground, and the woman turned their backs to the windows, so none of them saw the strange things that were happening in the mountains.

# The People in the Castle

The castle stood on a steep hill above the town. Round the bottom of the hill ran the outer castle wall with a massive gateway, and inside this gate was the doctor's house. People could approach the castle only by going in through his surgery door, out through his garden door, and up a hundred steps; but nobody bothered to do this, because the castle was supposed to be haunted, and in any case who wants to go and see an empty old place falling into ruins? Let the doctor prowl around it himself if he wanted to.

The doctor was thought to be rather odd by the townspeople. He was very young to be so well established, he was always at work writing something, and he was often quite rude to his patients if they took too long about describing their symptoms, and would abruptly tell them to get on and not beat about the bush.

He had arranged his surgery hours in a very businesslike way. The patients sat in rows in the large waiting room amusing themselves with the illustrated papers or with the view of the castle, which filled up the whole of one window in a quite oppressive manner. Each patient picked up a little numbered card from a box as he arrived and then waited until the doctor rang the bell and flashed his number on the indicator. Then the patient hurried to the office, breathlessly recited his symptoms before the doctor grew impatient, received his medicine, dropped his card into another little box, paid for his treatment (or not, after the National Health Service arrived), and hurried out by another door which led straight back to the main castle gateway.

By this means the incoming and outgoing patients were not allowed to become entangled in halls and passageways, creating confusion and holding up proceedings. The doctor was not very fond of people, and the sooner he could clear them all out of his house and get back to his writing, the better he was pleased.

One evening there were fewer patients than usual. It was late in October. The wind had been blowing in from the sea all day, but it dropped before sunset, and what leaves remained on the trees were hanging motionless in the clear dusk.

"Is there anyone after you?" the doctor asked old Mrs. Daggs, as he gave her some sardine ointment.

"Just one young lady, a stranger I reckon. Never seen her in the town."

"All right—good night," said the doctor quickly, and opened the door for the old woman, at the same time pressing the buzzer for the next number. Then he thought of a phrase for the paper he was writing on speech impediments and twiddled around in his revolving chair to put it down in the notebook on his desk. He was automatically listening for the sound of the waiting-room door, but as he heard nothing he impatiently pressed the buzzer again, and turning around, shouted:

"Come along there."

Then he stopped short, for his last patient had already arrived and was sitting in the upright chair with her hands composedly folded in her lap.

"Oh—sorry," he said. "You must have come in very quietly. I didn't know you were in here."

She inclined her head a little, as if acknowledging his apology. She was very white-faced, with the palest gold hair he had ever seen, hanging in a mass to her shoulders. Even in that dusky room it seemed to shine. Her dress was white, and over it she wore a gray plaid-like cloak, flung round her and fastening on her shoulder.

"What's your trouble?" asked the doctor, reaching for his prescription block.

She was silent.

"Come along, for goodness' sake—speak up," he said testily. "We haven't got all night." Then he saw, with surprise and some embarrassment, that she was holding out a slate to him. On it was written:

"I am dumb."

He gazed at her, momentarily as speechless as she, and she gently took the slate back again and wrote on it:

"Please cure me."

It seemed impolite to answer her in speech, almost like taking an unfair advantage. He felt inclined to write his message on the slate too, but he cleared his throat and said:

"I don't know if I can cure you, but come over to the light and I'll examine you." He switched on a cluster of bright lights by his desk, and she obediently opened her mouth and stood trustfully while he peered and probed with his instruments.

He gave an exclamation of astonishment, for at the back of her mouth he could see something white sticking up. He cautiously pulled it further forward with his forceps and discovered that it was the end of a long piece of cotton wool. He pulled again, and about a foot of it came out of her mouth, but that seemed to be nowhere near the end. He glanced at the girl in astonishment, but as she appeared quite calm he went on pulling, and the stuff kept reeling out of her throat until there was a tangle of it all over the floor.

At last the end came out.

"Can you speak now?" he asked, rather anxiously.

She seemed to be clearing her throat, and presently said with some difficulty:

"A little. My throat is sore."

"Here's something to suck. I'll give you a prescription for that condition—it's a result of pulling out the wool, I'm afraid. This will soon put it right. Get it made up as soon as you can."

He scribbled on a form and handed it to her. She looked at it in a puzzled manner.

"I do not understand."

"It's a prescription," he said impatiently.

"What is that?"

"Good heavens—where *do* you come from?"

She turned and pointed through the window to the castle, outlined on its hill against the green sky.

"From *there*? Who are you?"

"My name is Helen," she said, still speaking in the same husky, hesitant manner. "My father is King up there on the hill." For the first time the doctor noticed that round her pale, shining hair she wore a circlet of gold, hardly brighter than the hair beneath. She was then a princess?

"I had a curse laid on me at birth—I expect you know the sort of thing?" He nodded.

"A good fairy who was there said that I would be cured of my dumbness on my eighteenth birthday by a human doctor."

"Is it your birthday today?"

"Yes. Of course we all knew about you, so I thought I would come to you first." She coughed, and he jumped up and gave her a drink of a soothing syrup, which she took gratefully.

"Don't try to talk too much at first. There's plenty of time. Most people talk too much anyway. I'll have the prescription made up"—"and bring it round," he was going to say, but hesitated. Could one go and call at the castle with a bottle of medicine as if it was Mrs. Daggs?

"Will you bring it?" she said, solving his problem. "My father will be glad to see you."

"Of course, I'll bring it tomorrow evening."

Again she gravely inclined her head, and turning, was gone, though whether by the door or window he could not be sure.

He crossed to the window and stood for some time staring up at the black bulk of the castle on the thorn-covered hill, before returning to his desk and the unfinished sentence. He left the curtains open.

Next morning, if it had not been for the prescription lying on his desk, he would have thought that the incident had been a dream.

Even as he took the slip along to the pharmacist to have the medicine made up, he wondered if the white-coated woman there would suddenly tell him that he was mad.

That evening dusk was falling as the last of his patients departed. He went down and locked the large gates and then, with a beating heart, started the long climb up the steps to the castle. It was lighter up on the side of the knoll. The thorns and brambles grew so high that he could see nothing but the narrow stairway in front of him. When he reached the top he looked down and saw his own house below, and the town with its crooked roofs running to the foot of the hill, and the river wriggling away to the sea. Then he turned and walked under the arch into the great hall of the castle.

The first thing he noticed was the scent of lime. There was a big lime tree which, in the daytime, grew in the middle of the grass carpeting the great hall. He could not see the tree, but why was a lime tree blossoming in October?

It was dark inside, and he stood hesitating, afraid to step forward into the gloom, when he felt a hand slipped into his. It was a thin hand, very cool; it gave him a gentle tug and he moved forward, straining his eyes to try to make out who was leading him. Then, as if the pattern in a kaleidoscope had cleared, his eyes flickered and he began to see.

There were lights grouped around the walls in pale clusters, and below them, down the length of the hall, sat a large and shadowy assembly; he could see the glint of light here and there on armor, or on a gold buckle or the jewel in a headdress as somebody moved.

At the top of the hall, on a dais, sat a royal figure, cloaked and stately, but the shadows lay so thick in between that he could see no more. But his guide plucked him forward; he now saw that it was Helen, in her white dress with a gold belt and bracelets. She smiled at him gravely and indicated that he was to go up and salute the King.

With some vague recollection of taking his degree he made his way up to the dais and bowed.

"I have brought the Princess's cordial, Sire," he said, stammering a little.

"We are pleased to receive you and to welcome you to our court. Henceforth come and go freely in this castle whenever you wish."

The doctor reflected that he always *had* come and gone very freely in the castle; however, it hardly seemed the same place tonight, for the drifting smoke from the candles made the hall look far larger.

He lifted up his eyes and took a good look at the King, who had a long white beard and a pair of piercing eyes. Helen had seated herself on a stool at his feet.

"I see you are a seeker after knowledge," said the King suddenly. "You will find a rich treasure-house to explore here—only beware that your knowledge does not bring you grief."

The doctor jumped slightly. He had indeed been thinking that the King looked like some Eastern sage and might have information which the doctor could use in his study on occult medicine.

"I suppose all doctors are seekers after knowledge," he said cautiously, and handed Helen her bottle of medicine. "Take a teaspoon after meals—or—or three times a day." He was not sure if the people in the castle had meals in the ordinary way, though some kind of feast seemed to be in progress at the moment.

From that time on the doctor often made his way up to the castle after evening had fallen, and sat talking to the King, or to some of the wise and reverend knights who formed his court, or to Helen. During the daytime the castle brooded, solitary and crumbling as always, save for some occasional archaeologist taking pictures for a learned monthly.

On Christmas Eve the doctor climbed up with a box of throat tablets for Helen, who still had to be careful of her voice, and a jar of ointment for the King who had unfortunately developed chilblains as a result of sitting in the chill and draughty hall.

"You really should get him away from here, though I'd miss him," he told Helen. "I don't know how old he is—"

"A thousand—"she interjected.

"—Oh," he said, momentarily taken aback. "Well in any case it really is too damp and cold for him here. And you should take care of your throat too; it's important not to strain it these first months. The castle really is no place for either of you."

She obediently flung a fold of her gray cloak around her neck.

"But we are going away tomorrow," she said. "Didn't you know? From Christmas to Midsummer Day my father holds his court at Avignon."

The doctor felt as if the ground had been cut from under his feet.

"You're going away? You mean you'll none of you be here?"

"No," she answered, looking at him gravely.

"Helen! Marry me and stay with me here. My house is very warm—I'll take care of you, I swear it—" He caught hold of her thin, cold hand.

"Of course I'll marry you," she said at once. "You earned the right to my hand and heart when you cured me—didn't you know that either?"

She led him to her father and he formally asked for her hand in marriage.

"She's yours," said the King, "I can't prevent it though I don't say I approve of these mixed marriages. But mind you cherish her—the first unkind word, and she'll vanish like a puff of smoke. That's one thing we *don't* have to put up with from mortal man."

As soon as Helen married the doctor and settled in his house she became a changed creature. The people in the town were surprised and charmed to find what a cheerful, pretty wife their hermit-like doctor had found himself. She left off her magic robes and put on checked aprons; she learned to cook and flitted around dusting and tidying; moreover as her newly won voice gathered strength she chattered like a bird and hummed the whole day long over her work.

She abolished the buzzer in the office because she said it frightened people. She used to look through the door herself and say:

"The doctor will see you now, Mrs. Jones, and will you try not to keep him waiting please—though I know it's hard for you with your leg. It is any better, do you think? And how's your husband's chest?"

"She's like a ray of sunshine, bless her," people said.

The doctor was not sure about all this. What he had chiefly loved in her was the sense of magic and mystery; she had been so silent and moved with such stately grace. Still it was very pleasant to have this happy creature in his house attending to his comfort—only she did talk so. In the daytime it was not so bad, but in the evenings when he wanted to get on with his writing it *was* trying.

By and by he suggested that she might like to go to the cinema, and took her to a Disney. She was enchanted, and after that he was ensured peace and quiet on at least two evenings a week, for she was quite happy to go off by herself and leave him, only begging him not to work too hard.

One night he had nearly finished the chapter on Magic and Its Relation to Homeopathic Medicine, and was wishing that he could go up and discuss it with the King. He heard her come in and go to the kitchen to heat the soup for their late supper.

Soon she appeared with a tray.

"It was a Western," she said, her eyes sparkling. "The hero comes riding into this little town, you see, and he pretends he's a horse-dealer but really he's the D.A. in disguise. So he finds that the rustling is being run by the saloon keeper—"

"Oh, for goodness' sake, *must* you talk all the time," snapped the doctor. Then he stopped short and looked at her aghast.

A dreadful change had come over her. The gay print apron and hair ribbon dropped off her and instead he saw her clad in her white and gray robes and wreathed about with all her magic. Even as she held out her hands to him despairingly she seemed to be drawn away and vanished through the thick curtains.

"Helen!" he cried. There was no answer. He flung open the door and ran frantically up the steps to the castle. It was vacant and dark. The grass in the great hall was stiff with frost and the night sky showed pale above him in the roofless tower.

"Helen, Helen," he called, until the empty walls re-echoed, but no one replied. He made his way slowly down the steps again and back to his warm study where the steam was still rising from the two bowls of soup.

From that day the townspeople noticed a change in their doctor. He had been hermit-like before; now he was morose. He kept the castle gates locked except for the office hours and disconnected his telephone. No longer was there a pretty wife to tell them that the doctor would see them now; instead they were confronted by a closed door with a little grille, through which they were expected to recite their symptoms. When they had done so, they were told to go around by an outside path to another door, and by the time they reached it they found the necessary pill or powder and written instructions lying outside on the step. So clever was the doctor that even with this unsatisfactory system he still cured all his patients, and indeed it seemed as if he could tell more about a sick person through a closed door than other doctors could face to face; so that although people thought his treatment strange, they went on coming to him.

There were many queer tales about him, and everyone agreed that night after night he was heard wandering in the ruined castle calling "Helen! Helen!" but that no one ever answered him.

Twenty years went by. The doctor became famous for his books, which had earned him honorary degrees in all the universities of the world. But he steadfastly refused to leave his house, and spoke to no one, communicating with the tradespeople by means of notes.

One day as he sat writing he heard a knock on the outer gate, and something prompted him to go down and open it. Outside stood a curious looking little woman in black academic robes and hood, who nodded to him.

"I am Dr. Margaret Spruchsprecher, Rector of the University of Freiherrburg," she said, walking composedly up the path before him and in at his front door. "I have come to give you the degree of Master of Philosophy at our University, as you would not come to us or answer our letters."

He bowed awkwardly and took the illuminated parchment she offered him.

"Would you like a cup of coffee?" he said, finding his voice with difficulty. "I am most honored that you should come all this way to call on me."

"Perhaps now that I have come so far I can help you," she said. "You are seeking something, are you not? Something besides knowledge? Something that you think is in the castle, up there on the hill?"

He nodded, without removing his gaze from her. The keen, piercing look in her old eyes reminded him vividly of the King.

"Well! Supposing that all this time what you seek is not *inside*, but has gone *outside*; supposing that you have been sitting at the mouth of an empty mousehole; what then?" There was something brisk, but not unkindly, in her laugh as she turned and made off down the path again, clutching the voluminous black robes around herself as the wind blew them about. The gate slammed behind her.

"Wait—" the doctor called and ran after her, but it was too late. She was lost in the crowded High Street.

He went out into the town and wandered distractedly about the streets staring into face after face, in search of he hardly knew what.

"Why, it's the doctor, isn't it?" a woman asked. "My Teddy's been a different boy since that medicine you gave him, Doctor."

Someone else came up and told him how thankful they were for his advice on boils.

"My husband's never forgotten how you cured his earache when he thought he'd have to throw himself out of the window, the pain was so bad."

"I've always wanted to thank you, Doctor, for what you did when I was so ill with the jaundice—"

"You saved my Jennifer that time when she swallowed the poison—"

The doctor felt quite ashamed and bewildered at the chorus of thanks and greeting which seemed to rise on every side. He finally dived into a large doorway which seemed to beckon him, and sank relieved into a dark and sound-proof interior—the cinema.

For a long time he took no notice of the film which was in progress on the screen, but when he finally looked up his attention was attracted by the sight of galloping horses; it was a Western. All of a sudden the memory of Helen came so suddenly and bitterly into his mind that he nearly cried aloud.

"Excuse me, sir, that's the one and nine's you're sitting in. You should be in the two and three's."

He had no recollection of having bought any ticket, but obediently rose and followed his guide with her darting torch. His eyes were full of tears and he stumbled; she waited until he had caught up with her and then gave him a hand.

It was a thin hand, very cool; it gave him a gentle tug. He stood still, put his other hand over it and muttered:

"Helen."

"Hush, you'll disturb people."

"Is it you?"

"Yes. Come up to the back and we can talk."

The cinema was pitch dark and full of people. As he followed her up to the rampart at the back he could feel them all about him.

"Have you been here all these years?"

"All these years?" she whispered, mocking him. "It was only yesterday."

"But I'm an old man, Helen. What are you? I can't see you. Your hand feels as young as ever."

"Don't worry," she said soothingly. "We must wait until this film ends—this is the last reel—and then we'll go up to the castle. My father will be glad to see you again. He likes your books very much."

He was too ashamed to ask her to come back to him, but she went on:

"And you had better come up and live with us in the castle now."

A feeling of inexpressible happiness came over him as he stood patiently watching the galloping horses and feeling her small, cool hand in his.

Next day the castle gates were found standing ajar, and the wind blew through the open doors and windows of the doctor's house. He was never seen again.

# Watkyn, Comma

When Miss Harriet Sibley, not in her first youth, received an unexpected legacy from a great-uncle she had never met, there was not a single moment's hesitation in her mind. I shall give up my job at the bank, she thought, and live by making cakes.

Miss Sibley had never baked a cake in her life, nor was she even a great cake eater; once in a while, perhaps, she might nibble a thin slice of Madeira, or a plain rice bun; but rice buns were becoming exceedingly hard to find.

All the more reason why I should start up a little baking business, thought Miss Sibley triumphantly. I need not have a shop. I can do it from home. Word about good cakes very soon gets passed around.

And she began hunting for suitable premises.

Due to soaring house prices, she encountered difficulty in finding anything that lay within her means. For months every Saturday and Sunday was passed in the search. From cottages she turned to warehouses, from warehouses to barns. Even a ruined barn, these days, fetched hundreds of thousands.

But at last she came across exactly what she wanted, and the price, amazingly, was not unreasonable. Miss Sibley did not waste any time investigating possible disagreeable reasons for this; if there are drawbacks, I will deal with them as they come up, she decided in her usual swift and forthright way, and she made an offer for the ruins of Hasworth Mill. Her offer was instantly accepted, and she engaged a firm of local builders to render the ruins habitable.

The building stood on a small island, with the river Neap on one side, describing a semicircle, and the millrace on the other, spanned by a three-arched bridge.

What better place to bake cakes than a mill? thought Miss Sibley.

When she inquired why the place had remained uninhabited for so long, she received a variety of answers. The mill itself had ceased to grind corn after the closure of Hasworth Station and its branch railway line, which had made the transport of corn and flour so much more costly. Then there had been legal disputes between the heirs of the last owner. One had been in Canada, one in Australia; the affair had dragged on for years. Meanwhile the damp rotted the woodwork as the mill stood empty. Purchasers don't like damp, Miss Sibley was told. But damp is, after all, to be expected if you live on an island, she replied sensibly. Then there were the trees, very large: a huge cedar, twice the height of the mill, guarded the approach bridge; some willows grew on the island; a row of Lombardy poplars screened the meadow beyond. Trees make a place dark; some people dislike it.

Miss Sibley had lived all her life on a brick street; to her the prospect of owning twelve Lombardy poplars, five willows, and a giant cedar was intoxicating.

The word *haunted* never passed anyone's lips.

The island itself was small; not much bigger than a tennis court. During the years that the mill had stood empty, brambles had proliferated and the place was a wilderness; Miss Sibley looked forward to turning it into a garden by and by. Meanwhile the builders used it as a dumping place for their loads of brick and stacks of new timber The brambles were cut and trampled down, and some of them dug up as new drains had to be laid and damp-proof foundations inserted; in the process of this digging a male skeleton was unearthed.

It had been buried with care, and quite deep, handsomely coffined and wrapped in some half-rotted piece of brocade material, which Dr. Adams, the coroner, who was also a keen local historian, inspected carefully and pronounced to be the remains of an altar cloth or consecrated banner.

"In fact, my dear Miss Sibley, the body is probably that of a Catholic priest who died here while on an undercover mission during Queen Elizabeth's reign and was secretly buried. The age of the remains make that the most likely hypothesis."

"But why should he be buried on my island?" crossly demanded Miss Sibley.

"Why, Jeffrey Howard, the miller at that period, had been suspected of being an undeclared papist. This seems to confirm it. Perhaps he was giving hospitality to one of the traveling priests who rode about in disguise, saying a secret Mass here and there. I suppose there was some fatality. That would account—" began Dr. Adams, and stopped short.

"So what happens now?" inquired Miss Sibley, not noticing this.

"Oh, we'll have him reburied properly in the graveyard, poor fellow," said Dr. Adams cheerfully. "The vicar won't mind a bit. He'll enjoy an excuse for some research into the background of it all."

Once the coffin and its melancholy contents had been removed, Miss Sibley put the matter out of her mind. She was much too busy, buying curtain material and discussing fitments with the builders to trouble her head about old unhappy far-off things. Her new kitchen was taking shape, a fine, spacious room with a view through dangling willow fronds over the white, frothy, and turbulent millpond. The sun blazed through the wide new south window, her large modern oven would soon keep the kitchen warm and airy.

Miss Sibley had a deep trunk full of cake recipes which, all her life, she had been cutting out of newspapers. She could hardly wait to get started. Waffles, Aberdeen butteries, orange and walnut cake, tipsy cake, scruggin cake, apricot-caramel cake, mocha layer cake, Tivoli cake, orange tea bread, date shorties, fat rascals, cut-and-come-again cake, honey and walnut scone ring, Lancashire wakes cakes, nut crescent, currant roll-ups, rum baba—these names sang themselves through her head like a glorious invocation.

Just wait till I can get the builders out of here, she thought. And shelves put up in the little room and my cookery books on them.

She had collected cookbooks with the enthusiasm of an autograph hunter. Not a recipe had yet been tried.

To encourage them, Miss Sibley pampered her builders in every way possible. She brewed them cups of tea five or six times daily, accompanied by store bought biscuits. She mailed letters, took messages, phoned their wives, and ran errands for them. But none of this disguised her extreme impatience to see them leave. As soon as it was at all possible, she planned to move from her rented room over the post office into the mill; meanwhile she visited the site daily and dug up brambles on the island. She was therefore on hand when Mr. Hoskins, the foreman, came to say, "Beg your pardon, mum, but we found something you should see."

"And what is that?" asked Miss Sibley. The seriousness of his tone made her heart tip over most anxiously. What could the wretches have found *now?* A plague pit? A cavern under the foundation, requiring ninety tons of concrete? Some terrible gaping crack that would entail construction of five expensive buttresses?

"It's a room," said Mr. Hoskins.

"A room? A *room?* Surely there are plenty of those?"

"One we didn't know of," replied Mr. Hoskins, who had lived in the village all his life. "Halfway up a wall. Come and see, mum."

Her curiosity kindled, Miss Sibley came and saw.

The room was approached by a paneled door, neatly concealed at one side over the mantel in a small upstairs bedroom. The panel door was operated by a hidden spring, which one of the workmen had accidentally released. Inside, a flight of narrow dark stairs led up to a small, low, irregularly shaped chamber with a sloped ceiling and several oak beams passing through the floor at odd angles. The place was not much larger than a coat closet and was dimly lit by a tiny window, made of thick greenish glass tiles, which also admitted a little fresh air.

"Why has no one ever noticed the window?" demanded Miss Sibley.

"'Tis hid by the ivy, you see, mum, and also 'tis tucked in under the overhang of the eaves, like, where you'd never notice it," Mr. Hoskins pointed out.

Later, going outside, Miss Sibley verified this, and the fact that a projecting lower gable concealed the window from anyone standing on the ground.

Disappointingly the room held no furniture.

"But we did find this," said Mr. Hoskins, and handed Miss Sibley a small grimed leather-bound book. "'Twas tucked on the joist."

Opening the book, Miss Sibley found that the pages were handwritten. It seemed to be a diary.

"Thank you, Mr. Hoskins," she said.

"Would you want the room decorated, miss?"

"On the whole, no, thank you, Mr. Hoskins. I don't imagine I shall be using it a great deal. If you could just clear away the dust. . . ."

Miss Sibley's mind was already floating back to Sicilian chocolate cheesecake.

But she did take a cursory glance at the diary, which was written in faded brown ink and a decidedly crabbed and difficult handwriting.

"I, Gabriel Jerome Campion, S.J., leave this journal as a memorial in case it should happen that I do not quit this place a living man. And I ask whomsoever shall find it to pray for the repose of my soul. . . ."

Well, of course I will do that for the poor man, thought Miss Sibley, and she methodically tied a knot in her handkerchief to remind herself.

I wonder if he was in here for very long, and what did happen to him?

"Thank you, Mr. Hoskins," she repeated absently and withdrew down the narrow approach stair to the builder's stepladder, which stood below the panel opening.

"Woud you wish me to put a different fastening on the door, mum?"

"Why, no, thank you, I think the existing one will do well enough."

"Or build a flight of steps so's to reach the door?"

"No," said Miss Sibley, "as you may recall, I plan to turn this little bedroom into my cookery library, so I shall want shelves built across those two facing walls for my cookbooks. And then, you see, I'll buy one of those little library stepladders, so if I ever should wish to enter the secret room (which is not very likely), I can use the stepladder. Thank you, Mr. Hoskins. Gracious me—it is teatime already; I'll just run and put on the kettle."

Dr. Adams and Mr. Wakehurst the vicar were greatly excited by the discovery of the diary, news of which reached them that evening by village grapevine; and the next day Mr. Wakehurst came around to ask if he might borrow the document?

"This, you know, clears up a four-hundred-year-old mystery," said he, happily. "There is a local legend about a black-coated stranger who was heard asking the way to Hasworth Mill and was then never seen again. But that was the winter of the great flood, when the Neap overran its banks and covered all the land as far as the foot of Tripp Hill (where the deserted station now stands). Various people from the village were drowned in the floods, including Howard the miller. It was supposed that the stranger must have been drowned, too, and his body washed downstream to Shoreby. Now we can guess that he had been billeted in the secret room by Howard, who no doubt proposed to see him off the premises when the coast was clear; but because of his death in the flood he never did return. So the poor priest probably starved to death. Howard's son, a sailor who returned from the sea to claim his inheritance, no doubt found and secretly interred the body. Poor fellow, what a miserable, lonely end."

"Oh, he wasn't lonely," said Miss Sibley. "Somebody called Mr. Watkyn kept him company. He wrote, several times, in his diary,

'I don't know how I should have managed to remain tranquil and composed without the company of my dear and charming Watkyn.'"

"Indeed?" exclaimed the vicar, with the liveliest curiosity. "Now I *do* wonder who Watkyn can have been?"

"Another priest, I daresay," remarked Miss Sibley without a great deal of interest, and she handed Mr. Wakehurst the fragile and grimy little volume. "Please do keep it, Vicar, it is of no great interest to me."

"May I really? I shall write a paper on it for the Wessex Archaeological Society," cried the vicar joyfully, and hastened away with his treasure before she could change her mind.

At the door he turned, remembering his manners, to ask, "When do you plan to move in, Miss Sibley?"

"Why, tonight," said she. "There are still quite a few things to be done, but the kitchen stove works now, and the hot water is on, and one of the bedrooms is finished, so there is no reason why I can't sleep here. That way I shall be even more on the spot if there are any problems—not that I anticipate any."

Mr. Wakehurst's face wore a slightly doubtful, frowning look as he crossed the three-arched bridge and looked down at the careering millrace and swirling millpond. But what, after all, are ghosts? he thought. Some people never see them at all. And, as the century nears its end, they seem to be losing their power. And Miss Sibley is such a sensible, practical person, it would be a most unpardonable piece of folly to confuse her mind with ideas about things that may never happen.

Poor Father Gabriel! As good a man as ever stepped, I daresay, even if he did hold erroneous, wrongheaded religious opinions. In any case, we are all so much more ecumenical and broad-minded now.

I do wonder who Watkyn can have been? And why no other body was found? Dear me, how very, very interested Adams will be in this discovery.

Besides, nobody has actually seen anything in the mill. Or not that I have been told of. It is only some exaggerated stories about what people felt, or fancied they felt, or heard, or fancied they heard.

He hurried on, under a threatening and plum-colored sky, absorbed by the diary, which he read as he walked.

"Conducted a long dialogue on transubstantiation with Watkyn, which served to distract me from the pangs of hunger. His is a surpassingly sympathetic and comprehending nature. And his expression is so captivatingly cordial! If he chose, I know that he would confide in me all his innermost thoughts."

Can Watkyn have been a mute? wondered Mr. Wakehurst. Or a foreigner, speaking no English?

"I have confessed to Watkyn not only my major transgressions but the most minor peccadilloes, the kind of small sins that, in the presence of a confessor, one is often almost ashamed to mention. Watkyn, now, knows more of my faults than any other living being. He does not behave any less kindly. And I feel a wondrous easement of soul. Sick enfeebled, confused as I begin to grow, I do not at all fear to meet my Maker. And it is all thanks to my good Watkyn. If only I could bestow a like grace on him!"

"Another discussion with W. on the subject of miracles," recorded Father Gabriel a day later, in a hand that was perceptibly weaker.

Now, what in the world can have become of Watkyn? wondered the vicar.

"Talked to W. on the subject of Redemption . . ." The text trailed away.

Miss Sibley celebrated her first night of residence in Hasworth Mill by making a Swiss roll. Not surprisingly, it was a total disaster. What she had thought to be one of the most simple, basic, and boring of cakes is, on the contrary, the most tricky and delicate, on no account to be attempted by a beginner. The flour must be of a special kind, the eggs carefully chosen, the oven well trained, familiar to the cook, and under perfect control. Not one of these factors obtained at the mill. It was the first time Miss Sibley had used her new oven, which was not yet correctly adjusted; the flour was damp and in any case not a good brand. The eggs were a mixed lot. The cake turned out sodden, leathery, and had to be scraped from the bottom of the pan, like badly laid cement. Not surprisingly, after eating a mouthful or two, Miss Sibley went to bed very quenched and dejected and then found it almost impossible to fall asleep in her bare and paint-scented bedroom.

A gusty and fidgety wind had blown up. As Miss Sibley sat after supper in her warm kitchen, she could see, through the great pane of clear glass, long, dangling fronds of the willows in wild and eldritch motion, blown and wrung and swung like witches' locks. And after she retired to bed, her high window, facing out over the water-meadow, showed the row of Lombardy poplars like a maniac keep-fit class, violently bowing and bending their slender shafts in each and every direction.

Miss Sibley could not hear the wind, for, to anybody inside the mill house, the roar of water drowned out any external sound. But as the gale increased, she *could* hear that, somewhere within the house a door had begun to bang; and after ten minutes or so of increasing irritation she left her bed to find the source of the annoyance and put a stop to it.

The offending door proved to be the one opening into her little library room.

Queer, thought Miss Sibley; the window in here is shut; why should there be a draft? Why should the door bang?

And then she noticed the high black square in the wall, the cavity where the panel door stood open. That's very peculiar, she reflected. I'm sure Mr. Hoskins had left it closed when the men went off work, and I certainly haven't opened it, so how in the world could it have come open all by itself? But perhaps this wild and drafty wind somehow undid the catch. At any rate I may as well close it up again; it is letting a nasty lot of cold air into the upper story.

Since the panel door and its catch were too high for her to reach, she pushed a table, which she proposed to use as a writing desk, across the small room, perched a chair on the table, and then climbed up onto the chair.

She was in the act of closing the door when she thought she heard, from inside the little upper room, a faint and piteous moan. She paused, listened harder, but there was no repetition of the sound.

I was mistaken, decided Miss Sibley. She closed the panel, climbed down from the table, and was about to return to bed, when, from inside the panel, came three, loud, measured knocks.

Bang. Bang. Bang.

Then a moment's silence. Then the three knocks again.

Bang. Bang. Bang.

Can that be the wind? Miss Sibley wondered and, after a moment's hesitation and just a little nervous this time, she climbed up onto the table once more, reopened the door, and peered inside. There was nothing to be seen.

But again, after the door was shut, before she had left the room, she heard the three knocks: Bang. Bang. Bang.

"This is perfectly ridiculous," said Miss Sibley angrily. "However, I certainly can't lie all night listening to those thumps, so I suppose I shall have to investigate further. But I'm not going dressed like this."

Accordingly she returned to her bedroom, pulled on a pair of trousers and thick cardigan, and equipped herself with a powerful flashlight, which she had bought in case of any trouble with the newly installed electrical system. Once again she climbed onto the table, and this time scrambled right up into the panel entrance.

No sooner was she well inside the entrance than the door swung violently closed behind her and latched itself. She hard the spring click into place.

Miss Sibley was a calm and level-headed person. But even so, well aware that there was no means of opening the panel from the inside, she felt an acute lowering of the spirits. For she recalled also that tomorrow was Saturday, when the builders did not come to the house, and that was inevitably followed by Sunday, so that it might be at least fifty hours before anybody became aware of her plight and set her free.

What was she to do in the meantime?

I may as well survey my assets, she thought sensibly, and climbed the stair into the odd-shaped little room above.

The beam of her flashlight, exploring it, showed that the builders had cleared away the dust and left it clean, at least, and bare.

There was no indication of anything that might have caused the bangs. Furnishings there were none; Miss Sibley could sit either on the floor or, rather uncomfortably, on one of the cross-beams or joists about a foot above floor level, which meant that she would not be able to raise her head without banging it on the roof behind her.

Oh, well, she thought, at least it is a seat, and she chose the beam, reflecting, with some irony, that she had felt sorry for herself earlier, lying in a comfortable bed, because indigestion prevented her from sleeping; how luxurious, in retrospect, that bed now seemed!

Something scuttled in the corner, and she flinched uncontrollably, catching her breath in what was almost, but not quite, a scream; if there was one thing in the world that filled Miss Sibley with disgust and terror, it was a rat.

"You don't like rats, and yet you're going to live in a mill which must be full of them?" a surprised acquaintance at the bank had inquired, and Miss Sibley had pointed out that the mill had not been working as a mill for at least forty years and had been uninhabited for a further twenty; such rats as there might once have been must surely long since have migrated to more inviting premises and choicer pickings. "I suppose there might be water rats," she said doubtfully, "but they are not nearly so disagreeable, and besides I presume they will stay in the water."

But here, now, was something moving and rustling in that speedy, furtive, stealthy, and, above all, uncontrollable and unpredictable manner so horridly characteristic of rodents; Miss Sibley gave a jump of fright and, doing so, banged her head violently on the roof tiles above.

The pain was severe; she saw stars, and tears flooded her eyes, tears of pain and shock. She gasped out her very worst expletive: "*Oh, blast*"—and then, somehow, an entirely different deluge of feeling swept over her, different from anything she had ever experienced in her life before, a drenching, mountainous weight of intolerable woe. Like a rock dislodged in a landslip, Miss Sibley toppled to the floor and lay on the boards, with her head pillowed on her arms, drowned in a tidal wave of tears, weeping her heart out.

What for? If asked, she could not possibly have said: for wasted life, for love lost, young years misspent in dusty, unproductive work, for chances mislaid, lapsed friendships, the irretrievable past.

How long she wept she had no notion; hours may have gone by.

But at last, at very long last, like a tiny spark at the end of an immeasurably long tunnel, came into her head a faint thought: *Yet, after all, here you are, in a mill, as you have always wanted to be, and about to begin making cakes, just as you have always planned?*

That is true, she answered, surprised, and the voice, the thought, which seemed to exist outside, rather than inside her, added, *Perhaps this oddly shaped little room where you find yourself shut up at the moment is like a comma in your life?*

A comma?

*A comma, a pause, a break between two thoughts, when you take breath, reconsider, look about, wait for something new to strike you.*

Something new.

What in the world am I doing here on the floor, all quenched and draggled, Miss Sibley asked herself, and she raised her head. Unconsciously she had laid her right arm over the joist, and she now noticed, with a frown of surprise, that there was a patch of light on her right wrist, which looked like a luminous watch.

Then, blinking the tears from her eyes, she saw that it was no such thing.

Luminous it *was,* thought not very; a faint phosphorescent radiance glimmered from it, similar to that on stale fish, fish that is not all it should be. And two very bright sparks were set close together at one end; and the thing, which was about the size of a bantam's egg, suddenly moved, turning on her wrist, so that the sparks went out and reappeared in a different place.

Miss Sibley's first violent impulse was to shake her arm, jerk her wrist, rid herself of the thing, whatever it was—bat, vampire, death's-head moth? were some of the wilder notions that flashed into her head.

The second impulse, even more powerful, born of the thought that just a moment before had come to her, was to remain quite still, hold her breath, watch, wait, listen.

She kept still. She waited. She watched the faint luminosity on her wrist.

And she was rewarded.

After a long, quiet, breathing pause, it grew brighter and became recognizable.

*Not* a rat; definitely not big enough for a rat. But perhaps too large for a common house mouse?

A field mouse?

The thought slipped gently into her head, as had the suggestion about the comma. Wee, sleekit, cowering, something beastie, she thought. Field mice, I've heard, move indoors when autumn winds turn cold; perhaps this one had done that once. It must have been long, long ago, for the mouse was now completely transparent; it had started climbing gently up her arm and the stripes of the cardigan sleeve, red and blue, showed clearly through it.

Of course! Miss Sibley thought. I know who you are! You must be Mr. Watkyn. Dear and charming Watkyn.

A thought like a smile passed across the space between them.

*That was Gabriel, yes. He named me. And I, in turn, was able to help him. So we can open doors for one another. When he left—*

Yes? When he left?

*He left me changed; brought forward, you might say. In this attic here, now, there is still some residue of Gabriel: the pain, the fear; as well as the hope, comfort, friendship that we two built between us. Gabriel is buried by now in the churchyard, Watkyn is a pinch of bones and fur long since swallowed by some barn owl; but the product of them lives on and will live on as long as hope lives, and hearts to feel hope.*

Thank you, Watkyn, said Miss Sibley then; thank you for helping me, and I hope I, too, can help somebody, someday, in the same degree.

*Oh, never doubt it,* said the voice, closer now, and Miss Sibley lay down to sleep, comfortably, on the flat boards, with Watkyn a faint glimmer of light by her right shoulder.

On Saturday morning Mr. Hoskins visited the mill to pick up a tool he had left there; Mr. Wakehurst, the vicar, had come too, calling, at the same time, to thank Miss Sibley again for the immeasurably valuable gift of the diary; together, with concern, not finding the lady in her kitchen, they searched the house, and she, hearing voices, ran down the little stair and banged on the inside of the panel door until, aghast, they let her out.

"*Miss Sibley! What happened?*"

"Oh, the door blew closed, in the gale, and shut me in," she said gaily. "You were quite right, Mr. Hoskins; we must change the catch so that can't happen again."

"But you—you are all right? You have been there all night? You were not frightened?" asked the vicar, looking at her searchingly. "Nothing—nothing of an unfortunate nature—occurred?"

"Unfortunate? *No!* Nothing so fortunate has ever happened to me in my whole life!" she told him joyfully, thinking of her future here, decided on, it seemed, so carelessly, in such random haste. And yet what could be more appropriate than to make cakes, to bake beautiful cakes in Hasworth Mill? She would learn the necessary skill, her cakes would grow better and better; and if, at first, a few turned out badly—well, after all, who are more appreciative of cake crumbs than mice?

# Publication History

"Introduction" copyright © 2016 Kelly Link.
"The Power of Storytelling: Joan Aiken's Strange Stories" copyright © 2016 Elizabeth Delano Charlaff

Stories previously published in Joan Aiken collections as follows: "The People in the Castle," "A Room Full of Leaves," "Some Music for the Wicked Countess," "The Mysterious Barricades," in *More Than You Bargained For,* Cape 1955 © Joan Aiken.
"A Leg Full of Rubies," in *A Small Pinch of Weather,* Cape 1969 © Joan Aiken.
"Sonata for Harp and Bicycle," in *The Green Flash,* Holt, Rinehart & Winston, 1971 © Joan Aiken.
"The Dark Streets of Kimball's Green," "Hope," "Humblepuppy," in *A Harp of Fishbones,* Cape, 1972, © Joan Aiken.
"The Man Who Had Seen the Rope Trick," "The Cold Flame," "Furry Night," in *A Bundle of Nerves,* Gollancz, 1976 © Joan Aiken.
"Listening," in *A Touch of Chill,* Gollancz, 1979 © Joan Aiken Enterprises.
"She Was Afraid of Upstairs," in *A Touch of Chill,*

Delacorte, 1980 © Joan Aiken Enterprises.
"Old Fillikin," in *A Whisper in the Night,* Gollancz, 1982, © Joan Aiken Enterprises.
"The Last Specimen," "Lob's Girl," in *A Whisper in the Night,* Delacorte 1984, © Joan Aiken Enterprises.
"A Portable Elephant," in *Up the Chimney Down,* Cape, 1984 © Joan Aiken Enterprises.
"The Lame King," in *A Goose on Your Grave,* Gollancz, 1987 © Joan Aiken Enterprises.
"Watkyn, Comma," in *A Fit of Shivers,* Gollancz, 1990, © Joan Aiken Enterprises.

# About the Author

Best known for *The Wolves of Willoughby Chase,* Joan Aiken (1924-2004) wrote over a hundred books, including *The Monkey's Wedding and Other Stories* and *The Serial Garden: The Complete Armitage Family Stories* and won the Guardian and Edgar Allan Poe awards. After her first husband's death, she supported her family by copyediting at *Argosy* magazine and an advertising agency before turning to fiction. She went on to write for *Vogue, Good Housekeeping, Vanity Fair, Argosy, Women's Own,* and many others. Visit her online at: www.joanaiken.com.